Words
and Their
meanings

To Justin,
for redefining all the most important
words in our story.

Words and Their Meanings

Kate Bassett

flux
®

Woodbury, Minnesota

First Edition
First Printing, 2014

Cover design by Ellen Lawson
Back cover image © iStockphoto.com/15492447/@akiyoko

Flux, an imprint of Llewellyn Worldwide Ltd.

Library of Congress Cataloging-in-Publication Data
Bassett, Kate, 1978–
    Words and their meanings / Kate Bassett. — First edition.
        pages cm
    Summary: Seventeen-year-old Anna O'Mally is a gifted writer but for the past year, since her beloved uncle Joe died, she has been wrapped in grief that seems impenetrable until a strange email suggests she did not know Joe as well as she thought—and he was not the saint she believed he was.
    ISBN 978-0-7387-4029-4
[1. Grief—Fiction. 2. Family problems—Fiction. 3. Secret—Fiction. 4. Best friends—Fiction. 5. Friendship—Fiction. 6. Dating (Social customs)—Fiction. 7. Authorship—Fiction.] I. Title.

PZ7.1.B375Wor 2014
[Fic]—dc23

                                                        2014018777

Flux
Llewellyn Worldwide Ltd.
2143 Wooddale Drive
Woodbury, MN 55125-2989
www.fluxnow.com

1

I can't hold my breath for the full nineteen minutes. I made it to three minutes once, but then I passed out. Instead, I have to settle for statue stillness and bulging my eyes wide enough to hurt. Coffin yoga has a lot of rules, but I think the no-blinking part is most important. Pupils should show during the open casket experience.

Case in point: my Uncle Joe—who was more like my brother, right down to sleeping in the room across the hall until he went to college—died last year. He was nineteen. He got laid out in a pine box about the size of my twin bed. His eyes were closed and his smile was fake. My last image of him is dominated by powdered eyelids and a bad smirk.

And that sucks.

"Anna?" My grandfather's voice echoes up the stairs.

It's a mix of sandpaper and gravel. I listen until he reaches my bedroom door, knocks once, and repeats, "Anna?"

I can't answer. Corpses don't talk and I've only been at this for 2.5 minutes. That means I've got 16.5 to go, so Gramps will just have to keep standing there, thinking whatever it is he thinks about the immature, irrational shell of his once-brilliant granddaughter.

Damn it. I've lost concentration.

Now my nose itches.

"Anna? Are you doing that thing again? That thing your mother asked you to please stop doing?"

He could just walk in and see for himself. The first time Mom caught my mid-morning ritual, she thought I was dead for real. Took the door right off the hinges for a few weeks. When I finally got my door back, it was sans lock.

Crap. I blinked.

"Your mom had to go out and she didn't want you guys alone, so I came over early. I'm going to make breakfast for Bea. When I come back, you need to be up. And ready for the day."

Gramps doesn't elaborate, but I know Mom went to Joe's grave. And she went early because she's afraid of running into my dad. Right before he moved out, he said the one thing he can never take back: "The loss is less yours. Joe didn't share your blood." As if he could cut the strings of attachment from raising a child as her own for seventeen years.

I've still got one minute to go when Gramps returns. This time, he doesn't bother knocking.

His skin is Silly Putty and his walk is a little lopsided. But he's still a strong force and I feel him here, without looking. I wonder if his expression is sad. I wonder if he recognizes the blankness in my face.

Gramps has a dog named Morte, who happens to be a very dead stuffed German shepherd my grandmother bought at one of the garage sales she was famous for raiding. The dog has glass-black eyes and stares into the abyss and at people with the exact same intensity. It's the look I'm aiming to recreate. It's real. Morticians could take a lesson from taxidermists.

Thirty seconds to go.

The shrinks all want to talk about coffin yoga. They can't fathom the way some people have no rhyme or reason to their mourning. How maybe there are more ways to grieve than the stupid five steps outlined in their colorful pamphlets. Next time I see my new doc, I'll probably tell her I'm adding a no-thinking rule into coffin yoga. She'll ask what it might symbolize. And I'll glare at her ridiculous red-rimmed glasses and flowing tunic. I'll speak slow and clear, so she might understand there's nothing representative about this. My mind just needs the break.

Because:

That crack in the ceiling looks like a vein.
Maybe I should freak Mom out and paint the crack red.

3

It would almost look like a giant river of blood.

She'd have to call my dad and they'd fight when he showed up.

Maybe I'd let a real river of blood flow down the stairs while waiting.

What would Joe think of my imagination moonlighting as a total psychopath?

He'd laugh and remind me about my six-year obsession with Care Bears.

Love-a-Lot Bear. Good Luck Bear. Funshine Bear.

Wonder if those stuffed fluff-balls are buried in a box in the basement.

Bet they're all mildewed and moldy.

Gramps is starting to smell like mold.

I don't like it. Makes me think of why people get put in coffins in the first place.

Dead people.

Joe is a dead person.

Joe is a dead person because of me.

365 days later, those words still don't seem real.

Time's up.

I curl into myself for a second before swinging my legs over the side of the bed. Gramps sighs and sits down beside me.

"Good morning, sunshine. Seems like a good day to…"

He lets his voice trail off, willing me to finish the sentence.

I don't. Instead I wipe my eyes with the back of my hand and walk over to my white wicker desk. I got it at age eleven, back when things like pastel flowers and T-shirts with rainbows were all the rage. It's where I do part two of my morning ritual: write my daily verse.

"Look—the yoga…" I pause, motioning back to my bed/coffin. "I get how Mom thinks it's crazy. I know the therapists think I'm trying to 'bury my emotions.' But this is me. This is the way I deal with it."

Gramps looks at me. The weight of the day, of what I'm supposed to do now, it makes me itchy and reckless. I know what I'm risking. Right now, I don't care. I keep talking.

"Why is it such a big deal anyway? I've done some form of yoga since ninth grade. I've only changed how I practice. I mean, maybe this will catch on as a whole new style. Maybe I'll actually achieve Medusa-like stone stillness and I'll make DVDs and get super rich. Wonder what the therapists would say then."

He looks at the ceiling, shakes his head.

I open my laptop. I slam it shut. I stare at my mother's father, daring him.

"I love you," he says.

There's no judgment. No disappointment. No accusation. I wait for more, but Gramps stands up and pats my hand. His fingers shake a little. I hold them tight, but I'm also the first to let go.

"Come downstairs in a minute."

I nod.

Stepping toward the hall, his back already to me, Gramps pauses.

"Did you know I've started working on a project?" he asks. "It's a surprise. I hope you'll see it as a gift. I've been working on it downstairs all morning. And if that doesn't spark any interest, how about bribing you out of your room with a new origami design? Maybe I can teach you to fold a Yoda? You could tape him to the top of your laptop and get the lowdown on secrets of the universe. 'Better it will get, when trust the force, you do.'"

There's no way I can oblige him with a giggle or a smile, so I just nod again while reopening my laptop. I don't want his hope. I don't want to see myself the way he may still picture me. And I don't need his gentle reminders.

Joe's one-year deadaversary is supposed to mark the end of my period of mourning, as promised to shrink number nine, my parents, and my best friend, Nat.

But what are promises, really? Nothing but words.

We're all made up of opposites, and they often crucify us.

2

I used to have a matching oval wicker mirror above my desk. It's been replaced by a grid of photos, ripped out of magazines or printed off websites. The images are all the same girl. In the pictures, she'll be frozen forever at age twenty. Three years older than me. One year older than Joe. She's got stringy, wild black hair. Mostly, she's wearing white tank tops or dirty T-shirts and ripped-up jeans. Her chest is draped with handmade talismans or skinny suspenders. A girl who never smiles but stares at the camera with eyes like dark pools, like a nighttime lake waiting to pull you in, under.

Patti Smith in 1973. Go ahead. Google it. I'm a carbon copy.

Like practically everyone else in my generation who's grown up on shitty boy bands and reality shows, I'd never even heard of Patti Smith until 364 days ago. It took me exactly two weeks, one day, and six or so hours to slip into her skin. Not sleeping made it easy to match her sunken sockets and dark circles. My muddy brown hair, hacked chunky to my shoulders (or forehead or neck, depending on where you're looking), is now the color of spilled ink. It's fried from constant use of a straightening iron. My wardrobe imitates those feral images of a girl on the edge.

Beyond looks, here's a crash course in Patti Smith: she's an indisputable rock-and-roll legend. A captor of light and dark. People call her the Godmother of Punk, but she's so much more. She's the embodiment of a creative soul.

I can't sing. I pull in tons of dark but zilcho light, and I'm not exactly a legend or a godmother of any variety. Also, whatever soul I might have possessed flew out the window a year ago.

But Patti Smith was a poet before anything else. That's all I needed. A poet whose words could replace my own.

I discovered her in an old *Esquire* clip tucked in a hospital room drawer. Her attitude and stories and philosophies were magnets, drawing my fragmented pieces together again. I begged until a nurse gave in and snuck me my phone for supervised downloading of a bunch of Patti's music. Which led to dancing on a table as soon as the prefix "un" attached itself to "supervised." Which, of course, led to a four-point lockdown.

But that's another story.

My daily verse comes from Patti, always. Every morning, after exactly nineteen minutes of coffin yoga, I come over to my desk and wipe away the shadow of yesterday's verse with a baby oil-soaked cotton ball (today that was *"I have my dead and I live with them"*).

I find a lot of daily verses on Twitter, which seems to be the Internet's most formidable source of Patti's braindumps. Her thoughts are puncture wounds when jabbed into 140 characters or less.

Sometimes I scroll through a thousand duds before finding the right phrase, the right tone to set for my day. Those mornings are the worst. I lose focus on her words, instead remembering a time when my own thoughts got scribbled across my arms, legs, hands.

Joe used to tease my mother, his sister-in-law turned mom after his own parents died. He claimed I'd end up with a thousand real tattoos someday, because I like to write on myself so much. Mom responded with Oscar-worthy grimaces, even though everybody knew my scribbles only stayed on skin until I could transfer them to paper. I always kept a marker in my pocket in case I saw a sunset yolk break just so across the river, or overheard a conversation I knew had to be reinvented inside one of my stories.

"You could carry a little notebook, like normal people," Joe would say with his lopsided grin.

"But then I'd be normal," I'd reply, jaw dropping in mock horror.

Every so often, just when my ink started to run dry, a new Sharpie would appear on my desk.

Markers last a lot longer now. And the words on my skin are stolen from someone stronger. Today's only took six seconds to find. The first sentence I read reached into my gut. A renegade sob clawed up my throat. I swallowed again and again before pushing the black tip into my skin.

"We're all made up of opposites, and they often crucify us."

Joe loved human psychology. His favorite course freshman year, he'd come home from Ann Arbor and sit in my room explaining all hierarchies of need and personal myths and contradictions between ego and self. But he never told me how I could love and hate writing. Or how dependency can lead to so much loss.

And then he died.

And I lost my words.

And everything, everything fell apart.

Today's verse is war paint. I etch each letter inside my arm, between wrist and elbow, with bold marker strokes.

I trace the word CRUCIFY so many times, the letters don't move, even when I clench my fist.

3

Gramps doesn't give up as easily as Mom. If I don't go downstairs, he'll be back. So I put one foot in front of the other. Move toward the kitchen, even if the smell of bacon is turning my stomach. Even if the jazz music echoing up from our made-to-look-old radio stings my eyes. Dad's the early riser in our family. When he lived here, those jazz CDs went on before coffee each morning. A soundtrack for a different life.

In the front hall, the closet is ajar just a crack. My seven-year-old sister's toes are sticking out. Her attempt at a self-given pedicure looks like Smurfs puked on the tips of her feet.

"Shouldn't you be tucked into someplace a little more advanced?" I ask, pushing the doors shut. Her little toes are still visible. "Pretty lame hiding spot, Bea."

"You'd find me no matter what," she chimes before bursting out and wrapping herself around my waist.

"Coffee first, Buzzy," I groan as I shuffle to the kitchen. She grabs the bottom of my tank top until I lean over and kiss her freckled cheek.

Bea became our family's version of the Invisible Man a few days before Joe died. Vanishing act numero uno happened when Mom came home to get stuff to take to the hospital. As she walked back out the door, she called to us. I answered. Bea didn't. Mom paused. Tried again. Nothing.

An hour of frantic searching, begging, screaming "BEATRICE" at the tops of our lungs, put Mom into full freak-out mode. We'd checked her room, behind couches, in the playhouse, the backseat of the car, attic, under a pile of cardboard boxes waiting to be recycled. Every empty space caused Mom's breath to grow more jagged, quick.

I don't know what made me think to look in the oven. Maybe I was going from cupboard to cupboard, pantry to drawer, and opened the stainless steel Viking Range by mistake. Because I had to look twice before the sight registered in my brain: my sister, contorted like a pretzel, wiry red curls matted with sweat and eyes closed as if sound asleep. How she shut the door behind her is still a mystery.

Since then, Bea's been on the perpetual disappearance plan. I can't seem to provide the proper grief role model for her, but I've become a bloodhound of the baby-sister bounty-hunting variety. I make sure she knows I'll always find her. I'll see her, no matter how many times she tries to be erased.

4.

Three huge cranes are lined up in front of my grandfather. Their angles are precise. Each fold is crisp. There are no mistakes. No ghost edges smoothed and realigned. Gramps is hunched over a piece of pale cream paper, writing something in scratchy cursive. He puts a number four in the place I know will be a wing, and covers the page.

"What are you making?" I ask, a little louder than I'd intended.

"Your surprise. Eat while it's hot, girls. Anna, will you make Bea up a plate, please?"

"I have lost all interest in surprises, Gramps. Will you please just tell me what you're making?"

Gramps has perfect hearing, but he shuffles the squares of paper and tucks the extra-large birds into a bag beside him, as if I'd never spoken. "How about I teach you two some new designs when you're done? Maybe a butterfly or a box?"

"Or a rocket ship?" Bea asks, eyes wide.

"Sure. We can do a rocket ship. Maybe even one with a secret room inside the wing."

I slap a few pieces of bacon and a pancake on Bea's plate. Drown it all with syrup. "Whatever you're doing, if you can't tell me about it…I don't want it, okay?" I feel the familiar thump of blood in my neck.

"Don't sound so angry. I told you, I'm making you something. Explaining it now would be like handing one of my customers a typewriter with only half the keys fixed," Gramps shrugs.

"Did you used to use typewriters a lot, Gramps?" Bea asks, her mouth full of pancake.

"I used to fix them a lot," he says.

"And super heavy computers as big as me?"

"Those too." As my sister stretches herself tall and wide to mimic an old school computer machine, he smiles.

"And you also fixed radios, and clocks, and record turners, and—"

"It's record players, Bea. Duh."

She winces at my tone. Before Gramps can reprimand me, I head back to my room and gather a stack of papers buried in the bottom of my closet. Some are ripped in the corners. Some pieces still have tape flapping along the edges, sticky enough to catch against a few loose strands of my hair.

"I have a great idea for a project," I say when I come back down to the kitchen. "How about making little paper trash cans out of these?"

Gramps flips through the mess of writing awards and certificates I shoved in his lap. His frown runs the length of his chin. I answer with a yawn, long and loud, to punctuate my point.

"It's actually called a turntable, not a record player," is all he says.

The garage door rumbles opens. Bea ducks out of the room.

"Ah lovely," I say, really looking my grandfather in the eyes for the first time today. "She's already home. And so it begins."

5

When Sameera, Joe's girlfriend since eighth grade, called last week, I never should've given Mom the message. Maybe then we wouldn't be seeing her today. Maybe then her bright idea about spending the afternoon together, telling stories, looking at pictures, "celebrating" Joe wouldn't have reached my mother's ears, wouldn't have appeared like the missing piece in a puzzle she and the latest shrink have been putting together to create the perfect time-to-move-on moment for me.

But hearing Sameera's voice is like finding a time machine. A way to get back to before. We walk a little lighter after talking to her. I couldn't rob Mom of that.

"Did you get out the family albums? The ones from under the stairs? I left you a note," my mom says, arms full of groceries, as she kicks the door to the garage shut. Her face is blotchy. She isn't wearing mascara. I cross my arms and stare at the wall.

She bristles past and opens the fridge, rooting around for one of her stupid meal replacement shakes. I hid it behind a carton of expired eggs and half a chocolate cake last night.

"Anna," she starts, then stops. I watch her pace from fridge to counter, pulling Sameera-approved foods out of the grocery bags, like rice crackers, almonds, hot pink beet hummus, stuff to make kale salad (disgusting).

"Mom," I mimic.

"Okay, well, fine," she says, hands landing on her bony hips. "You aren't excited to see Sameera. Even though she took the day off from her biology lab internship and is driving up from Ann Arbor just to see us. I believe it's what he'd want—"

"Don't."

But she's just revving up now.

"He would want us talking and laughing and being together. He loved Sameera and you *love* Sameera." I can tell she's impressed with what she thinks emphasizing the present tense can convey. "You can try to fight this, but you will participate. And if you hate me for it, fine. You can do that too."

I glare. She sighs. Gramps chimes in something about my first night of work, which conveniently coincides with the deadaversary.

"Are you at all excited about this new job?" Mom asks.

She tilts her head and nods, as if she can answer yes for me. "It will be fun, getting to work alongside Nat all summer."

"Oh, yeah. I'm totally pumped," I say. My sarcasm drips thick as the leftover syrup on Bea's plate. "There's nothing I wanted more for my summer before senior year than to spend my nights kissing people's asses—"

"Watch your mouth, please," Gramps warns.

"Oh, sorry. I meant to say I'm *psyched* to be a waitress and I'm *grateful* Nat was able to get me a job, and I'm *thrilled* Sameera is coming over this afternoon."

Mom doesn't seem so impressed when I turn the italics back on her.

She straightens, tucks long blonde hairs behind her ear, and lifts up her chin a little. A triangle of silence bounces between us. Gramps chews a slice of pancake. I stare at my arm, still red from how hard I pressed ink against skin.

"Natalie seems to like the job well enough," Mom says finally, wiping the corners of her mouth with a napkin. "I think it's great she managed to get you in too. There aren't a lot of places hiring, you know."

She pauses, blows out a puff of air, and adds, "That being said, there's always Mrs. Risson's offer to participate in the Roethke Residency."

"No."

"I'm sure if we called her and explained you feel up to it now—"

"No."

"I'm only saying if you wanted to try writing again…a job doesn't have to be about the money."

"Mom." My voice is strained, the syllable measured. I know we've crossed into dangerous territory.

The Roethke Residency is my favorite English teacher's annual summer poetry study. It doesn't actually involve residing anywhere, but she calls it the Roethke Residency because the group meets at this dead, famous-for-our-town poet's house turned museum. Mrs. Risson invited me to participate last summer, when the plan everyone assumed I'd be following "fell through." I guess no one wanted to admit my star potential took a beating when I didn't get into the London Young Writers Intensive.

Only a handful of high school writers are even invited to apply to that uber-competitive wordsmith version of the ultimate summer camp. The five who get selected stay in a London loft with a rotating staff of today's best authors for two whole months. Finalists were given a writing prompt to determine the winners, and I thought I had it in the bag. It was a first line from a Shakespeare sonnet.

"Wherefore with infection should he live…" I turned the line into the title of a series of abstracts a painter created while dying. He gave them to his daughter as a way to explain the infinite nature of art. Each scene carried the perfect amount of weight. It's probably the best thing I've ever written.

I didn't make the cut.

The selection committee sent me a eight-line rejection. As if they couldn't fathom how I'd made it so far in the first place.

Thank you for submitting your writing sample to the pool of finalists for the London Young Writers Intensive. While your previous samples were astounding, we were disappointed with the caliber of writing and connection in your last piece. Please understand, this program is highly selective, and though your work was not for us, we hope you keep writing.

This should have broken me, but I just felt numb. The only real pain came from knowing I had to face Mom and Dad and Mrs. Risson and everyone else who believed in such big plans for my words.

Standing here in the kitchen with Mom and Gramps, I try not to let the hollow inside bleed into my voice.

"I am not a writer anymore. As of this evening, I will be a waitress. It's fine. I'm fine. Today is day one of me *loving* my life."

"Damn it, Anna. Enough."

Gramps is standing beside Mom now, drawn up to his full height and staring down at me with his bushy white brows furrowed.

"I'm merely telling her I am going to hold up my end of the bargain. That I'll pretend to be normal and happy from here on out," I say, lifting my hands in surrender.

Here's why I need to lock up the snark: fifteen days

ago, sitting in my ninth shrink's office, my parents both slipped into the room. Considering their affection for each other is now akin to cancer and chemotherapy—this tag-team drop-in indicated a serious change in psychological tactics.

I tried to avoid watching my parents' awkward attempt to sit separately but together. I still ended up seeing my father pull his yellow-and-white-striped tie as he nerve-cleared his throat. My mother's hand ticked once. I thought she'd have to physically restrain herself from straightening the tie to match back up with the buttons on his shirt. Instead, she closed her eyes.

On one side of my ~~psychologist~~ "healer" Liza's room there's a Technicolor comic-strip mural depicting Dr. Seuss's *Oh, the Places You'll Go!* Which is fitting, considering my folks were about to drop the as-of-next-week-you'll-be-going-to-hell-bomb. That's a literal statement, by the way.

Hell, Michigan (go ahead, look it up—on the map, not in the Bible) has this place called BrightLight, a year-round Christian boarding school for the afflicted, suicidal, and otherwise broken tween and teenage souls. Whatever brainiac founded the joint must be a marketing genius. The brochure reads, "From the depths of Hell comes a beacon of hope, love, and BrightLight." It's framed by a filmstrip of photos: beautiful boys and girls playing flag football, raising their hands in class, giggling inside what looks like a local shopping center.

Funny, I hadn't thought of offing myself once until that moment.

A blur of swearing (in ways even Dad found vulgar) filled the remainder of our hour, with my psycho-tamer applauding because I was SHOWING AN INTEREST IN MY LIFE. End result? A hold on crazy camp if I agreed to mark the end of my self-inflicted period of mourning on Joe's one-year deadaversary.

Our contractual bargain, drawn up by the three adults in the room, was pretty straightforward. Easy, even. It stated I must get a summer job and try at least once a week to wear something from the boxes in my closet containing the pre-Patti wardrobe. I agreed to all of it.

Liza started shifting in her seat, the universal sign for a shrink session timing out. I stood to go. But then Mom said, "What about her opening up with the...with the Joe stuff?"

"Ah, yes. Your parents are hoping, Anna, you'll consider spending some of our sessions talking directly about why your uncle's untimely death—" She paused here, looking to Mom and Dad for approval. "Why his death is tied to this personality you've adopted, as well as how it plays into your insistence on giving up your writing. I understand you are a very talented girl, and sometimes, locking away our passions only makes way for depression to sink its teeth deep into us. Do you understand what I'm saying?"

The air in the room turned to glue. My lungs heaved a little. Hell started to sound more appealing.

"Anna?" Hippie Dippie asked, pulling her multi-colored silk scarf over her shoulders. "I need to clarify here. This is the last part of the deal. You need to be willing to start talking about the tough stuff. We'll need to dig deep, set free your pain, be honest with each other."

Maybe not telling the truth is like trying to carry a boulder three times your size up a steep hill. Eventually, it'll tip backward and steamroll you.

Mom and Dad, they think I'm broken because I miss Joe. And I do miss him, so much. But they don't know the rest, and I'll never tell Liza the whole story. Still, the lie slipped out easy as Patti's poems slipped like songs from typewriter to page. I said I'd start talking. Whether my parents' reaction was disappointment or relief, I can't say.

6

The doorbell rings for the second time. Mom hesitates and then rushes into the front hall. Gramps follows. Sameera's early. Of course she's early. I can hear the laughing/crying happening in the next room. I don't want to see her. Not yet. But suddenly she's in front of me, throwing her arms around my shoulders before I can run or turn on my Bea radar and hide.

"Ohmygodthishairofyourshasgottogo," she blubbers into my neck, her tears mixed with fresh laughter.

It's one thing to talk to Sameera on the phone. It's another thing entirely to have her standing in our kitchen. There are certain people who trigger all the pain that comes with losing someone you love.

She must feel it too, because she weeps openly for a

minute, apologizing while wiping the flood from her wide, dark eyes.

"It's just…I haven't been here since Christmas…I always think it will be easier…"

Mom hugs her tight, pale white arms stark against Sameera's eternally bronzed skin. Her body racks up and down. I open the box of rice crackers and dump them into a bowl.

If this is their idea of "celebrating," we're in big trouble.

Bea slinks over and crawls into Sameera's arms like it's the most natural thing in the world. Her legs dangle past Sameera's knees now.

"Buzz! You've grown since Christmas. You'll be taller than me soon," Sameera says, rocking her back and forth.

"That's not saying much, Sammy," Bea replies with a giggle.

Laura, Sameera's best friend, is standing in the doorway, watching the whole scene unfold. I don't remember seeing her walk in, and no one else has noticed yet. She's almost invisible. Laura goes to school with Sameera at the University of Michigan. Her family lives down the street.

"Hi, Laura," I say.

Everyone turns and stares at her for a second too long. Mom rushes over and gives her a you-were-one-of-Joe's-favorite-friends squeeze.

"I didn't realize you were coming," Mom exclaims.

Laura's blonde hair is cropped into a pageboy bob.

The last time I saw her, it was down to her waist. She keeps tucking it behind her ears.

"Well, Sameera said she was coming home, and I figured I'd come too and visit my folks…and all of you."

We're standing here like actors waiting for direction. Gramps clears his throat again. Mom snaps out of it and pulls Sameera and Laura into the living room. I stay behind. Open the freezer and stick my head in for a second. Gulp down cold air. I grab my phone and sneak into the bathroom to text Nat.

> ME: I love Sameera. So why do I hate her so much right now?
> NAT: Duh.
> ME: This is such a stupid idea. Like sitting around holding hands is worthy of Joe. It's so…
> NAT: cliche.
> ME: exactly.
> NAT: Go out there and punch her in the face.
> ME: wtf? punch who? My mom? Sameera?
> NAT: nevermind. bad idea. just sit there. 1 or 2 hours of suck is better than Hell.
> NAT: ps- u ok?
> ME: …

I stand with my forehead against the door for what seems like one or two hours, trying to decide if I'm ever coming back out. When Joe died, Sameera spent the week at our house. She curled up with Mom and wept and wept and wept. At the funeral, she wore a little black hat with a tiny black veil but stayed in the back until I took her hand and led her to our row. She sent me emails every week when she first went back to college. *Just checking in…thinking of you…are you writing?*

But here's the awful truth: Sameera—the girl who throws her head back every single time she laughs, the one who once made my junk-food-loving dad go on a thirty-day vegan cleanse with her, who showed me how to use a freaking tampon the day I got my period—has become just another person I attach to the phrase "When Joe died."

"Anna?"

Sameera is leaning against the other side of the door. I can tell by how close her voice is to my ear. I bite my lip and think about pretending I'm not an inch away.

"So I wanted to, um, talk to you alone at some point. Can we go up to your room? Please?"

"Can we skip the circle jerk?" I ask as I crack open the door.

"Your mom is downstairs looking for some more videos, Bea is showing Laura a card trick, and your Gramps has the old DVD player half torn apart because it keeps spitting the discs out before they are done playing."

"What have you watched so far?"

"Joe learning to ride a bike. His fifth birthday—you had like, a million baby fat rolls when you were two"— she reaches in and pinches my skeleton arm—"and about three minutes of a talent show you guys put on when Joe was probably seven or eight."

I can picture him, floppy mop of black hair that Mom refused to cut short until he turned ten. It framed his face and neck and shoulders, like a Muppet. His round, pale-green eyes that lit up with mischief and flecks of gold, especially when whoopee cushions or those little handshake zappers were involved. I can picture every one of our videos without needing a screen. Images flicker, an old movie stuck on repeat in my brain.

"Yeah. Video is worse than pictures," Sameera says. "All it does is remind me he's frozen in time. Like all these moments still exist, but he'll never make more."

She isn't facing me, but I know her eyes are filling. She rubs the back of her neck.

"Come on," I say. "My door doesn't have a lock these days, but Mom probably won't come try to rescue you right away."

When we get to my room, Sameera walks around. She runs her hands along my bookcase. It used to be so full, standing within a foot radius would cause a paperback to slip to the floor. Now only three books sit on one shelf: *Slaughterhouse Five*, *Twenty Love Poems and a Song of Despair*, and *Great Expectations*. I gave the rest to our local library. The noise of so many stories distracted me during coffin yoga. The words had to go away.

Sameera picks up a porcelain unicorn, one Dad gave me for a birthday when I asked for a real one, I think.

She holds it and smiles before exchanging it with the tiny fabric lizard on my nightstand. She turns it over and over in her hand, remembering. During my entire eighth grade year, I sewed pockets onto my shirts and dresses and skirts so I could carry that stupid lizard with me everywhere. I don't know why.

"So how's Tess handling the whole Jack sitch?"

Great. We skip the dead-kid sob-fest, but go right into the your-dad-is-about-to-have-a-baby-with-someone-who-is-not-your-mom conversation?

"Mom's doing as well as anyone would, I guess, given the shocker of being told about a double pink line on a stick she didn't pee on, which amounted to a now-impending divorce. I mean all things considered, she's holding her own. After all, we went from a loving family of five to a family of three fractured fuckups in, uh, 365 days."

Sameera winces at my language, but nods in fervent agreement.

"It's so rough. It's like, I mean, it's like Jack's totally lost it. Your dad was the first person to teach Joe and me about 'attitudes of gratitude.' He gave us copies of David Foster Wallace's "This Is Water" graduation speech. He went on and on about the importance of 'getting it'— awareness and really living and existing and fighting our own selfish nature…and then he knocked up some temp law clerk in his new office six months after…It's a load of…shit. That's what it is."

I can't help a little smile, because Sameera is totally not a swearer. It's reason 578 Joe loved her.

"And not even a young, hot clerk either," I agree.

Sameera exhales with amusement. Then we both look at the floor, ceiling, anywhere but each other. Neither of us knows how to kickstart the conversation again.

Instead of more questions or rants, Sameera leans against the wall and just looks at me. That's another thing Joe loved about her, by the way. When she looks at you, with her honest, soft brown eyes crinkling in the corners, it's a real connection. I used to make up a lot of first lines about this sort of thing, like, "Truth is, most people spend their days in empty conversations. So when someone holds your eyes with theirs, when they say 'I see you' without words, it's like waking up and remembering you're alive."

It's not the kind of thing I feel like dealing with today.

When I break her gaze, Sameera plops down at my desk and leans so the chair balances on its two back legs. I watch her take in my collage of Patti Smith, waiting for some snarky comment about my choice of identity mimicry. But she sucks in and says something else altogether.

"I have a new boyfriend."

The chair falls back into place. She opens and shuts my laptop. Drums her fingers against it.

"Anna?"

"I—I heard you."

"He's...we started hanging out in January, just like studying together or going to the Union to get a late lunch, or whatever. He—Amar—he's a biology student too. You know what he wants to do with his life? He wants to be a microbiologist—a germ guy. Weird, huh? Anyway, he lived on my dorm floor last year but I was always at—"

"At Joe's?" I can't help the bitterness.

"Yes," she says, wavering a little. "Yes. At Joe's dorm. Because I loved him. I love him. But I don't know. Sometimes, Anna, sometimes I feel like we were slipping away from each other before it happened. Like we'd become so comfortable after seven years together—he was my best friend."

"Actually, he was my best friend."

"He was your bruncle," she says, referencing the joke term Joe made up for our weird familial situation. "And I know you miss him so—"

"He loved you, Sameera. Right to the very end."

My eyes burn. Energy pulses through me, and even though Sameera's face is streaked with tears, I can't stop.

"I mean, really? Is that why you came here? Do you need absolution?"

My comforter is clenched in my fists. Sameera slumps against the chair. She turns to face me.

"How could you say that?" she asks. Her eyes are bullets of sad shock.

"How could you use today to tell me this, Sameera? That's the real question," I hiss, acutely aware anything louder may carry down the stairs.

"I wanted it to be in person."

I roll my eyes.

"What is it you'd rather me do? I'm twenty years old. I have no clue if Joe and I would have gotten married or if we'd be apart right now. The only thing I know for certain is the first boy I ever loved is dead. He's dead and he's never coming back and I have two choices. I can die a little more every single second of the day, or I can try and live. Because I am still here. You are still here. We can still love him, Anna, and be happy. You don't have to do this to yourself. I mean, for God's sake, he was your uncle. You think he'd want you to act like your world ended when his did?"

I don't know I'm throwing the porcelain unicorn until it breaks against the wall behind Sameera's head. We freeze. My fingers buzz. I want to say I'm sorry, but if I open my mouth a sob will escape. So I swallow. And swallow. And stay silent as she gets up and walks out the door without looking back. Downstairs, I hear Mom ask if everything is okay.

"I think it's probably best if we leave her alone. Really, I don't mind," Sameera says, voice shaking. "Did you find those videos?"

I crawl into bed and stare at the crack in the ceiling. My breath is coming too fast to even try for coffin yoga, but I freeze up my muscles anyway. Try to imagine myself in a too-small pine box. Try to understand what it would be like to stop thinking and feeling and maybe, probably, existing at all.

When I open my eyes, the crack above me sways. I

picture it like a sky earthquake, tectonic clouds breaking apart, sending me floating up into black nothingness, into the space between here and gone.

I know I sound manic.

I know it isn't just Joe who is dead.

I am too.

I'm a ghost. Just a ghost that's still breathing.

7

"Can I come in?" Laura asks a few minutes later, walking through my still-open door.

"Was that a rhetorical question?"

Laura flops down on the bed.

"You don't do tough guy very well, Anna. I've known you your whole life, and I gotta say, you lack the necessary ingredients for being a smartass or a badass. You can dress Tinkerbell up in goth clothes, but she's still a wee little pixie with wings."

I squeeze my eyes shut and hope she goes away. Laura was the only girl in the neighborhood who still built forts down by the creek or came to the door for snowball fights when she was in high school. She wears combat boots and used to weave Mom's backyard daisies in her long braid. Our dads have been friends for eternity, and she and Joe were tight from, like, the crib all the way through high school. He introduced Sameera to Laura in eighth grade. And he made Laura and me hang out, because we were both "cool weirdos."

"Hey, listen," Laura says. I still won't look at her, so she pinches my arm. "Next time you talk, try to go easy on Sameera. She's had a hard time, you know. And she wanted to be honest with you because she still loves Joe, and your family, and wants to stay connected."

My eyelids hurt from how hard I'm squeezing them. Little bursts of stars float through the dark.

"Anyway," Laura continues, "I'm sorry you are sad and mad. I wish it was easier on you, like it was for Joe when his parents died. I always thought it was beautiful, the way he explained it. How he only had to do grief through the lens of memory, since he was so young when it happened."

I open my eyes.

Joe used to tell me the same exact thing. He said he'd never admitted it to anyone else—his guilt for the huge sense of loss my dad carried. Joe was his parents' "happy accident" and turned two not long before their car flipped off the road. My dad, on the other hand, had just turned twenty-one. Within six months of the accident, Dad graduated from college, started law school, married my mom. All Joe's memories were of my parents, me, Bea. He asked me once how he was supposed to grieve what he never knew.

"What did you just say?" I ask Laura.

"Nothing important." She stands up, her back to me. "I need to get downstairs. Just think about all this stuff with Sameera, okay? Oh, and Anna? The haircut sucks."

She leaves in a hurry. I pull the covers over my head.

———

At some point, Gramps shakes me awake, telling me Sameera and Laura are gone. Outside, the lawn mower sputters to a start. I know it's ours, because we're the only people on the block who don't have the tractor kind for our half-acre yard. Mom was "morally opposed" to such a thing, because she loved pushing the ancient beast up and down in neat rows. Gramps used to have to fix it for her at least three times a summer.

Last year, though, it never got hauled out of the garage after mid-June. When grass grew up past our shins, neighbors stepped in, taking turns driving their riding mowers across our lawn.

"Is that Mom?" I rub sleep from my tear ducts.

Gramps glances toward the window and taps a finger against his mouth thoughtfully.

"It is," he says. "Maybe change is in the air."

"If change smells like fresh-cut grass and gasoline, Gramps, you might be onto something."

"We all have to start somewhere."

"Why?" I ask. "Why do we have to start at all? We are born and there's some middle stuff and then we cease to exist. It's not like it matters."

Yanking the covers back up, I shut my eyes again. The next time I open them, Bea's nose is touching mine. Her breath smells like stale chocolate cake.

"Sarah Handy called. She said she was thinking of you today and had some stuff to tell you. That's what she said. Stuff. So I said, 'What stuff,' and she said, 'Just tell her I called. And I'm thinking of you all.'"

I throw my arm over my head and groan. Sarah Handy trailed Joe like a police dog on the drug trail for years. I can't believe she thinks she can call me today. She belongs to the Facebook crowd, the people who will grasp at a tiny moment with Joe, typing on and on about their loss, acting like they can stake a claim in his memory.

"But Nat called your phone too," Bea adds, sounding like Mom as she pulls me up with both hands. "She's gonna be here in like, twenty minutes. You need to get ready."

My work outfit, a hideous white button-down shirt with black button covers and a black to-the-knees polyester skirt, is already out of the closet and draped across the foot of my bed.

"You're the most capable seven-year-old I've ever met, Bea. You could go live in New York City or something right now and be totally fine."

Instead of laughing, her bottom lip quivers.

"But I want to live with you."

"Hey, hey. It's all right," I say, squeezing her hand. "I'm not going anywhere and neither are you. Everything's cool."

She closes her eyes and balls up her fists, letting each finger pop free in a silent ten count. Bea's had the same therapist for almost a year, so I know this trick. It's a coping mechanism for when she wants to hide, but can't.

I wait for her to open her eyes, and then I shake my head really fast, tossing my hair around like I'm shampooing.

"What am I going to do with this mess?"

Bea can't help grinning.

"You've got lightning strike hair. It's gonna take a miracle," she says, and rushes to the bathroom, emerging a minute later with a comb, two barrettes, a ponytail holder, and a box of bobby pins.

We're still jamming slivers of metal all over my head when Nat's car stalls out and roars back to life just before reaching our driveway. My best friend is a lot of things, but a good stick shift driver isn't one of them. She's burned through two clutches already, and didn't even turn sixteen until December of our junior year. Dolores (her car) heaves in exasperation, and a moment later, I hear Nat burst through the door.

"Annnnnnaaaa Baaannnnnnnaaaa—"

She's trying too hard. I know her acting voice. She's pretending my front door is actually part of a set. That she's only playing the role of sanity saver/grief sponge/ friend of a complete fun sucker.

"Let's go! We're going to be—oh. Hi Mrs. O."

I can't hear what my mom's saying, but Nat's voice gets louder with each response.

"No, I don't plan to bring it up on the way to work…
Well, of course I know it's today. I'm sure it is hard on all of
you…I don't think I can do that…Aaaannnnna! We really
need to hurry!"

She's caught between trying to be polite and a strong
urge to run back to Dolores.

"Tell me you look like a half-habited nun," I holler as
Bea adjusts my makeshift ponytail and I tuck my twine
necklace, with its single gold key, under my collar. There's
a rule against wearing jewelry on the job, but I'll get fired
before I cut this dirty string from my neck. I rush out of
my room, taking the stairs two at a time.

Despite matching right down to the button covers,
my bestie since age three looks entirely different in our
work ensemble. Probably because Natalie Alkandros was
born to wear an Oxford—or anything else—well.

"You look mah-vel-ous, darling," she says with false
enthusiasm, tugging out my folded-up collar and yanking
my skirt down over my knees. "No time to waste. This
isn't the kind of job you want to be late for, especially
since it's your first day."

She hustles to her car, waving for me to follow even
though Mom's calling both of us back inside. I glance up
at Bea peering out my bedroom window, and I blow her a
quick kiss before slipping into the passenger seat.

"Hey," Nat says as soon as we turn the corner out of
my neighborhood. She pats my arm a little but doesn't say
anything else.

Some relationships might crumble under the weight of tragedy, but Nat and I, we keep going through the motions. She cried for me when it all first happened. And then we buried—no pun intended—most of it. Nat is my keeper of secrets, and she just gets it. We pass the minutes, days, months without ever stopping to ask why.

"I think I threw a unicorn at Sameera's head this morning," I say.

Nat jerks toward me. Spits out a laugh.

"Seriously! It isn't funny," I say. I'm trying to cough away my own sudden fit of laughter, which makes me snort, which launches Nat into full-fledged hysterics.

We are still trying to regain composure when we pull up to the Fala house, where we're waitressing tonight. It's one of the biggest houses in town, shaped like three cement block steps. Everything inside and out is either glass or white. I've heard there used to be colorful art all over the place. Not anymore. Sterile white walls without so much as the ghost of a nail hole now.

We're ushered into the kitchen in time to catch the end of the servers' meeting. It goes something like this: blah, blah, don't touch anything, blah, blah, make sure you wait until they give you back the shrimp tails, blah, blah. I stop paying attention after the third round of *blahs* because I notice every girl in our little penguin colony is looking toward my left. So I turn to see if there's a ghost in the pantry but instead discover a real-time movie otherwise known as "beautiful boy in kitchen making magic with his hands."

Crab cake-covered fingers aren't the typical image I'd find myself swooning over, but still. This guy is moving to music that's not playing. His hands cradle scoops of goop like it is gold, making perfect, squished circles. He adds each to the pan without so much as a flinch when oil spits back in protest. Confidence radiates from him. It's like I can actually taste it. The other, much older chefs keep catching each other's eyes and smiling in his direction. As if they are all keepers and he is the secret.

And that's as hot as it gets.

Full-fledged zombie staring ensues. I've never paid attention to guys without a full head of hair. His is shaved. But it makes his face, I don't know...vulnerable? I tick off a grocery list of features: one dimple; two worry lines; almond eyes framed by long, black lashes; a scar on the left side of his jaw big enough to make me wince. It's light against his skin.

"Earth to Anna," Nat says, pulling my mess of a half-ponytail. Bea's right. Too many angled scissor cuts equals impossible-to-contain hair. "What are you staring—oh, yes. I know. Per-fec-tion."

Bless that girl and her inability to be quiet. It makes the boy glance from his pan orchestration long enough to give the gaggle of now-giggling waitresses an amused grin. He looks back down, and then snaps his eyes up. To meet mine.

He half-smiles and there's this pull, like we're opposite poles inside a magnetic field. Like we're sharing a story in a two-second glance. I almost walk toward him.

"Everybody wants him, but he's like, not interes—" Nat stops, mouth open, eyebrows up. Yanking me outside by my elbow, she grins wide. "Did you see that?"

"What?" I look around, pretending to be confused. It takes everything in my power not to look back, to see if our eyes would lock again.

"He was totally checking you out."

"Pfft. Right."

"Anna, come on. He was staring. And he flashed that adorable dimple. There was a spark."

Her voice catches for a quarter of a second. I know she's thinking about how today is supposed to be a mix of sad and hopeful. Nat's empathy goes beyond measure, which is why she's plugging her tear ducts with her pinkie fingers.

"A spark?" I fan my face. "Oh my stars, I'm burning so bright."

"Your Southern accent sucks," she says, rolling her eyes and walking across short green grass toward the long line of white linen-covered tables. "We're on buffet duty. I promise I'll find a reason for you to head back into the kitchen soon, though."

I mutter, "Whatever," and walk toward the chafing dishes, trying to forget the eyes that just clicked with mine.

"Don't 'whatever' me. It's time to start, like, experiencing the good things in life again, Anna."

Gone is the phony pretend-everything-is-fine routine.

Nat's invading a place reserved for my parents and shrinks. She does not get to do this. Not today.

"Why," I ask between clenched teeth, "are you pushing this?"

A man comes up to the buffet table, lifts one of the pan lids, sniffs, makes a face, and walks away.

Nat stirs some saucy junk around and tugs out a mascara-heavy eyelash. She wipes her hands on a napkin before answering.

"We're about to be seniors." She says "seniors" like it is the greatest novelty on earth. "Today is supposed to mark the end of this. I don't care if you want to keep channeling Patti Smith. I don't even care if you continue to turn your bed into a coffin at least once a day. We still need to move forward."

She blinks at me, adjusting her acting mask until it's once again snug against her olive skin.

"Anyway, I'm just saying, that boy in there is, like, the hottest ticket of the summer and he was completely checking you out."

"Getting sick of dealing with me, are you? You picked a perfect day to let me know it. Sorry, I don't think dating is on the five stages of grief pamphlet. I'm not like you. I can't fall for a boy just because he played Danny in *Grease the Musical* freshman year. So I apologize, for being screwed up and for not believing I'll find my 'life's co-star' in high school."

I stick my finger in the back of my throat.

"Alex has nothing to do with this," Nat says of her

on-again, off-again boyfriend. She moves down the buffet table. "And I'm not sick of you. I just—"

"Forget it."

"You always interrupt people," she says, flicking her hand up. "'Forget it' is right. I'm going to see if I can switch with someone doing app rounds. Stay here and be miserable."

When she stomps across the lawn, I don't try to follow. A year ago, this never would have happened. I can almost remember how it felt, to be the one full of patience, charm, faith in the universe. I can almost taste that girl inside me. But I can't make her come back, and Nat, of all people, knows it.

So I guess it makes sense. Today is a remembering kind of day and Nat's only memories of me from the past year are a mess of chains and anchors dragging her down.

We've always been seen as one entity—"Annat" was our shared nickname in middle school—but Nat is the one with social status. Joe once asked why I wasn't more popular, or why I never got asked to dances or on dates or whatever. I shrugged my shoulders and said I didn't try to fit in, or more accurately, didn't even know how to be normal enough to know what fitting in means.

"You know what? Don't change," he'd said. "Don't ever change one bit. If you weren't different, you wouldn't be able to write like you do."

I bear-hugged Joe. My biggest supporter. My other best friend. My bruncle. What a stupid term.

———

"Hello?" A guy in a pastel pink polo shirt and aviator sunglasses is waving his arm in front of my face. I jump a little, hitting a serving spoon resting inside a pan full of scallops and other fishy-smelling stuff. Some sauce goes flying, and after an all-too-brief moment of airtime suspension, lands Jackson Pollock-style onto the white silk dress Mrs. Fala is wearing.

Mrs. Fala, who is hosting this party as a fundraiser for the Kristin Fala Fund, a charity set up in memory of her daughter. It pays for a drug counselor at our high school.

I'm stuck to my spot next to the table. Mrs. Fala's face is melting a little, her layers of makeup beading with sweat, her mascara clumping with blinked-away tears. Nat must have seen it happen. She's rushing over with a bottle of club soda and a white cloth. When Mrs. Fala swats her away, Nat hesitates only a second before leading our now-humiliated hostess into the house. Squaring my shoulders, I walk slow and steady toward the kitchen's sliding glass door.

The second I enter the house, though, I start shaking. I rake my fingers through my hair, pulling out what's left of my shoddy ponytail. Thirty minutes into the job and my future is bleaker than ever. Either I have to face that crowd and Mrs. Fala again, take my chances finding another job in the next three hours, or go home and pack my bags to spend the rest of my summer repeating phrases like "I am worthy" in Hell. Every scenario is full of gag-worthy, monumental suck.

"Step out here. No one will see you."

The boy with a deep dimple and arched eyebrow leans in from a side screen door. The boy who makes sparks. He flicks his shaved head for me to join him.

I slide out to the nook where the Falas hide their garbage cans, partitioned off the side lawn by a wall of white lattice.

"You okay?"

"Fine. I'm fine."

His voice flushes my whole body pink. His brown eyes are like a doe's. His slow blinks untwist and re-knot my stomach. I start to crack my knuckles, then stop, folding my hands together to keep from fidgeting. Patti Smith cool. Patti Smith strong. Patti Smith, Patti Smith, Patti Smith.

"Fine seems to be the *palabra* of the day around here." He pulls a green-and-white pack of Kool cigarettes from his back pocket.

I reply something stupid like, "I take French not Spanish," and he shakes his head a little, unlit cigarette dangling between his lips.

"It means 'word,'" he laughs, flipping open his lighter and taking a puff. His eyes never leave mine. "I'm Mateo."

Mateo. I turn the name over in my mind, deciding it's poetry against the tongue.

"Anna," I say. My eyes burn. "Thanks for the momentary hiding spot. I just splattered your scallop sauce all over Mrs. Fala's dress."

"Bouillabaisse. Probably won't come out." He shrugs,

taking a long drag. The tip of his cigarette turns orange and shoots close to the filter. "Want a hit for nerves?"

"Not exactly the party to sound like a pusher, you know."

In an interview, Patti once said she liked to smoke but not inhale, because she didn't want to hurt her lungs. She did it for the show of it. I take the Kool from Mateo. My body hums as his fingertip grooves scrape against mine. I can't do anything but let ash grow between my lips.

When I give it back, Mateo's hand reaches up and catches my wrist, light and strong all at once. He holds us together for a second.

"It's sad, what happened to that girl," he says. "Too much money might be worse than not enough of it."

His words call for a somber gesture, a straight-faced nod. But I offer up a shy smile instead. The cigarette drops. I step on it. Twist my black ballet flat to grind its little fire between the pavement and thin sole of my shoe. He steps closer, his expression reminding me of Patti's one-time lover and forever best friend, the photographer Robert Mapplethorpe, in one of the pictures that always pops up first on Patti Smith Internet searches. In it, she's staring at the camera, one finger in her mouth. Robert stares at her, drinking up every feature of her face. Putting every sensor of their bodies on high alert.

Behind us, the kitchen is coming to life again. The head chef yells for Mateo. Once. Twice. We are still here. When she hollers next, it's with a threat of being a job without second chances, and how he knows there's a line of wannabes waiting to take his place. He starts to move, but stops again, kind of rocking back on his feet.

"You've got a nice smile," he says. "I gotta go. See you later, Anna." It's a statement, not a question.

The space we're standing in is small, and we have to shuffle around each other. The screen door opens, snaps shut again. He disappears inside and I slump against the concrete step, unable to shake the warmth spreading in my face, stomach, hands.

He said my name. Match struck. Spark. Explosion. I can't help the thought burning inside that flame: maybe the year mark does matter. Maybe there's a way to shift and change again.

I hold this idea, cup it in my hands like river water, then spread my fingers and let it fall through. Because believing I deserve to feel anything good or true or real ever again is like saying it isn't my fault—like I don't care Joe will never get to feel anything ever again. Like I can heal.

It's a thought far scarier than going to Hell.

8

It's way past Bea's bedtime when I walk in the front door, but she's sitting on Mom's lap, wide awake and glued to whatever is playing without sound on TV. I cringe, knowing I need to walk in there. Mom looks beyond exhausted. The crazy Botox binge she went on does little to hide the weariness in her face.

My mother used to be one of those *au naturel* women, a rare gem in a sea of perfectly coifed and manicured suburban wives. She owned a horticulture business, and her gardens were known all over the city. She sold—or "gave away" if you ask my dad—the business to her favorite employee three months ago. About the time she started getting needles filled with the same toxin found in botulism shoved into her forehead.

"What's going on?" I whisper, motioning toward the

giant painting leaning against the wall. It normally hangs in our front hall. My Gran painted it, and no matter how many times I've stood in front of the canvas, I can't quite get what she was saying when she swept her brush across again and again in rough red and orange strokes.

"Hi, Anna," Bea says without looking away from the television.

"Hi, Bea. Mom? What happened?"

"Your sister got it off the wall. Hid behind it like a lean-to, and I looked for her for almost two hours—two hours—before I noticed. Bea was curled up there. She'd fallen asleep. So when bedtime rolled around…"

I sit down on the couch and lean my head against Mom's shoulder, just for a moment. There's a huge vase of white roses and two cheap-looking bouquets sitting next to the TV. The room smells sickly sweet.

"Where'd those come from?"

Mom sighs.

"The Sarahs," Bea pipes up. "Sarah H. delivered the roses today. She said she was hoping to see you. And the other two Sarahs came together with those flowers. They're like the ones they sell at 7-Eleven."

The "Sarahs" are a trio of pathetic puppies who despised Sameera and loved Joe. They showed up at the house, together, when he died, making a shrine at the end of the driveway: pictures, candles, horrible—I mean horrible—poems.

"The Sarahs," Mom repeats with a sad laugh. "And of course one had to pick Madame Legras de St. Germain roses. The whole house smells like bad floral perfume. But let's not talk about that. How was work?"

"I didn't get fired," I shrug. She tips her head back a little but doesn't push the issue. Instead, she holds out her hand. I take it.

We sit together, the three of us, watching some show about stupid pet tricks. The volume stays off, but for some reason, the silence isn't so loud tonight.

You can't let emotions consume you.

9

More than anyone else, Joe tried to keep my love of words light, fun, unburdened. He bought me a word-a-day calendar every year for Christmas. The last one is still sitting in my desk drawer. It's stuck on June 15. And the word is "callipygian" (definition: having shapely buttocks).

Striker for the soccer team, class vice president, beautiful and smart girlfriend since puberty—I mean, Joe was basically a textbook case of popularity. But he wasn't like what you read about in bad teen novels or poorly scripted shows. He was nice to everybody. He liked to read. He spent two days during his junior year home on the couch, leaning against my mom because some friend made a comment about Joe's "orphan card."

Mom held him tight and said orphans don't have family, and that his friend needed to invest in a dictionary.

"Or an Anna," he'd said.

I'm convinced it was lines he read aloud, lines like "For every atom belonging to me as good belongs to you" that made me a believer. Made me think words could mean one thing, but also, something much bigger than any dictionary could hold.

I sent him every piece I wrote when he was at school, before anyone else saw it. He was my best editor. Words tied us together. When he died, the thread was cut. No matter how much I wanted to, how hard I tried, I couldn't reconnect us. Earth to sky. Here to gone. I failed him.

Even if I tried writing again, my ideas for good first lines have vanished. And a first line makes or breaks a work. More than last lines. More than the stuff in between. Because I once thought I was a superstar in this arena, I can say with absolute certainty you've got about two punctuation marks to bind someone's eyes, mind, soul to a story.

For my life, I claimed one first line: "The universe is made of possibility."

I wrote no less than 361 poems and stories using it. I won a lot of awards. You can do amazing things with such a simple, wide-open sentence. Until you stop believing in what those words mean.

In my mind, no more first lines means no more good writing. Gramps, on the other hand, says he doesn't buy it.

He tells me at least once a week I need to be doing something productive with my time.

"Forty-five solid minutes of word purging would be much better for you than lying around playing dead," he says, peering up from whatever stereo or laptop he's fixing for a friend. Gramps owned an electronics repair shop for like, four decades. It was down in old town, where I'm only allowed to hang out during daylight hours. He closed his business a few years after Gran died, but he still gets lots of calls at home. He's a fixer.

He tells me Gran stories, about how she was this brilliant artist and if she couldn't paint she would have gone crazy.

"Even when the painting felt dark. Even when it was scary. But mostly, she had to paint because she liked to do it. If you don't like writing anymore, then find something else you do like. You aren't just one thing, Anna. You can redefine yourself without needing to copy another person's life or spending part of every day acting like you no longer exist. It's wasteful, what you are doing."

Gramps might be a retired electronics repair guy, but I'm pretty sure in a past life he was a monk. A monk who talked way too much.

But before I went to bed last night, I pulled an empty notebook from under my bed. Scribbled on a corner of the page until the dying pen I found started leaving its mark.

Rain clouds hang low and sluggish, ready to burst the minute their bellies hit a building corner or church steeple. I will them toward downtown, where angles are sharp, rusted. I want it to pour. I want to hear water pound down against the roof and windows and pavement. It has been one year since Joe died. I was sixteen, and now I'm seventeen. He was nineteen, and he'll never be twenty. No one but Sameera said his name today. Not Mom. Not Dad, who didn't even call to see if I went to work as promised. Not Gramps or Bea or Nat. I spent today proving to everyone I can start over and that they can stop worrying I'm a Sylvia Plath in the making. This seems oddly hilarious, considering Bea's the only one who has ever stuck her head (shoulders, arms, legs) in the oven.

10

Whatever cohesive feeling Mom and I shared last night has vanished. She's sitting across the table, fiddling with a spoon left over from Bea's late-night ice cream raid. I stare at my breakfast/lunch bowl of cereal, eating tension with every bite.

"I want to make sure you are feeling okay. I understand what you've been going through more than I think you realize."

The way it comes out, I know the lines have been well rehearsed.

"You disappeared upstairs and didn't come down until you left with Nat, which is why I didn't talk about it with you yesterday, like I'd planned. I just don't understand why you haven't been able to say it to me, how this whole makeover is about not dealing with grief. It's so obvious to us, Anna, and you can't seem to see it. We're all going through it too, and you need to talk to me about it…You and I, we can face it together."

Sure. Because "it" is a topic so easily broached, "it" can be discussed without even using a name. I want to scream, *JOE IS NOT AN IT!*

Instead I chew my organic Cheerios-like cereal. Tap out a beat on the table with my fingers. Hope the noise will drown her out. No such luck.

"There's a lot I wish I could change…about everything…after you found out…I'm not sure what happened next was 100 percent tied to you not getting to…to say goodbye, like all the therapists have suggested."

Her words are paralyzing darts. I can't leave. Can't tell her to shut up, right now, please and thank you. I can only listen. And hold my breath.

Her gaze shifts out the window. The leaves on the big maple in our front yard shift back and forth, a thousand hands waving.

It wasn't just about not saying goodbye. No kidding.

———

The night Joe died, I'd promised my parents I would stay home with Bea. They, in turn, promised Joe was improving. But Bea was restless and I couldn't get her pajamas buttoned straight, and finally we both looked at each other and understood what we needed to do. She walked wordlessly into her room, grabbed her big bunny slippers (which were mine before hers, and Joe's before mine), and went to the car.

On the way to the hospital, I told her a story about a land of stardust and bright colors, where all the buildings were made of origami just like Gramps creates. I don't remember the point of the story, but I do remember the first line: "Birds sat on a wire, fluttering paper wings."

I also remember Bea fell asleep by the time I pulled into the parking lot. I sat there, my head against the wheel, knowing the right thing to do meant going back home. I'd already started the car and clicked it into reverse when I saw Nat getting dropped off near the entrance.

Sliding back into park, I jumped out and waved my arms under the dim parking lot light.

"Nat! Nat!" I hissed as loud as possible without yelling.

She paused for a second before realizing it was me. Looked up toward Joe's room, which was lit, but just barely. "I was just coming to check on you," she said, jogging over and giving me a quick squeeze. "Everything okay?"

"Yeah, my parents wanted Bea to have a night away from all this." I swept my hand toward the hospital. "But I hate sitting there, waiting. We decided to come anyway. And then she fell asleep. I guess I have to go home."

"I'll take her," Nat said, pulling the keys from my hand. "Go on inside."

"Um, you don't even have your license yet."

"Details. I drove the car here. My mom didn't have to yell at me about a rolling stop once. Honest."

"I don't know." I peeked in at my little sister, sprawled across the seat, bunny ears flopped against her ankles. "I mean, Bea's in the car."

"It's less than three miles to your house. I will keep my hands locked at ten-and-two. I will go five miles under the speed limit, without the radio or my cell phone on, and when I get there, I'll tuck Bea in and hang out until someone can run you back home. Besides, I told my mom I was having a sleepover. Other option would be you driving us. Or I could go up and check on things in your place, if you'd rather not get into it with your folks."

I must have known deep down that he'd stopped breathing. Because I sent Nat and Bea home, but couldn't step away from the empty parking lot space until long after the taillights disappeared. I remember glancing up at Joe's room. It went dark. Then light. I craned my neck to watch his fifth-floor window as I walked.

I never made it all the way to the front door.

Halfway up the sidewalk, I saw Gramps stagger out and sort of fall against a bench. A bunch of moths flitted around a beam of light above him. I didn't have to get any closer to know. His head rested almost on his knees. His body jerked back and forth, muffled with sounds of pain and loss. I'd come to know these signs well in the three weeks Joe was in the hospital. Physical manifestations of what happens when hope ceases to exist.

I closed my eyes. My lids were made of bricks. I stepped backward again and again until my foot fell off the curb.

Above me, the biggest meteor shower in a century started dropping stars into the light-polluted sky. I stood in the middle of the street, trying to breathe. I thought about the end of a poem, how we are here, but not really, no different than stars.

There were too many words tumbling, stabbing, pounding against my skull. I had to start walking.

Joe
Gone
My father's family, wiped away
Gone
Joe
Empty
Forever
Erased
Joe

I followed traces of light, away from the hospital, away from the bent silhouette of my grandfather, away from the truth.

I walked five miles, to the highway.

I moved past the "motorized traffic only" sign. Walked down the C-shaped on-ramp. Down to the four lanes of Friday-night traffic zooming north.

The short yellow lines between lanes reflected against car headlights like stars on the ground. I wanted to lean down and touch one. I wanted to stand on an island of yellow paint, a thing whose only purpose is to keep people moving forward, in the right direction, a safe distance apart.

So I stepped onto uneven asphalt, pocked with filled and refilled potholes. Cars honked. Swerved. But I never flinched. Not once.

Yes, Mom. I remember.

And no, we don't need to talk about it.

11

The rest of today hasn't been much better. I stayed (un)locked in my room cranking Patti's record "Piss Factory" until I heard Mom scream. I ran downstairs just in time to see her pull Bea out of the washing machine. She unfolded my drenched little sister like a beach chair with busted hinges.

And then I had to go to Liza's office, and she wanted me to tell her a story about Joe. Any story, she said.

So I told her about the time when he was ten and I was seven, and his appendix burst. He had to have emergency surgery. Gramps came to babysit but he never found me because I was hiding in an oven. At this point, Don't-Call-Me-Doctor Liza stopped to say I needed to tell a real story, not one with bits recycled from Bea's perpetual games of hide-and-seek.

"Fine," I snapped. So I told her about when he came home from surgery—he really did have a burst appendix—and Dad bought us a tent to set up in the living room, and Mom let us eat bright-colored Popsicles for breakfast, lunch, and dinner. We stayed up late watching movies. At some point he looked over with his goofy grin and said my mom and dad got married all because of him. I didn't believe it, because my parents were the lovey-dovey kind, so I yelled for Mom.

"It's true," she said, and beamed at Joe like he was Cupid or something. Then she hummed, kissed my dad extra, and everything was warm and perfect and right.

"Is that good enough?" I asked Liza. "Because that's how it went with us. It sums up everything. Joe was the universe. And he made us all stars, twinkling and sparkling like we'd never burn out."

———

The shrink said I did well, but I've spent most of the minutes that followed our session staring at the words on my arm. *You can't let emotions consume you.*

Bea is standing in my room while I get ready for work. She looks so innocent it makes me want to smack her for pulling what she did this morning.

"Why do you keep putting yourself in these idiotic, dangerous places? I mean, you could end up seriously hurt, or worse, hiding this way. Haven't you ever heard stories about cats who end up—"

"The cat stories are always about dryers. I was in a washer."

"I'm not kidding around, Beatrice."

She stares at me with hollow blue eyes. The same as our mother's.

"I just needed to take a break."

I'm still searching for the right words to tell Bea that I understand when Dolores shudders up the driveway.

"Nat's here," Bea says, her head tilting toward the window. Dolores's stereo is blaring the last song off the *Wicked* soundtrack.

"You better go," she adds, not looking at me.

Nat doesn't come to the door this time. She doesn't even honk. She rolls down all the windows, opens the sunroof, and cranks the music so the words of Glinda the Good Witch, singing about people who come into other people's lives for important reasons, echo right into my room.

"Coming!" I shout into the open window.

The music follows as I move down the stairs.

"Bea, stay out of dryers and dishwashers and anything else that spins, heats, or potentially suffocates!"

Mom is walking out of the garage just as I get in the car, and Nat slams into reverse before there's a chance to strike up a conversation. She gets something like stage fright whenever there's a reason to be near my mother for longer than two minutes. Mom and Dad found Nat and Bea asleep in Joe's bed the night he died. They'd come home to tell us he was gone. But then, they found out I was gone too.

Mom turned vicious within seconds. She shook Nat. Grilled her about where I could be, and then later, after I was tucked into the sixth floor of the hospital (while Joe grew colder in the morgue), the interrogation turned to what I tried to do (walk, that's all, walk with a little star-dust under my feet). Were there signs? Were there warnings? Could my parents count on Nat to swear she'd tell all my secrets in order to save me?

12

There's always tension after moments like this. We don't talk about why. Nat doesn't ever ask what I was doing in the middle of a four-lane highway on a Friday night, knowing without knowing that Joe was never coming home (walking, just walking with stardust beneath my feet). We don't talk about what followed: six days in the hospital, one evening at the funeral home, one morning of some stranger making promises of eternity, and then me puking and screaming and refusing to leave the family car at the cemetery.

We don't talk about the pressure I know Nat still feels to bear witness to every one of my moods, waiting for a warning sign.

So I tell myself to make small talk. Ease the tension.

"I met that boy last night, while I was hiding from Mrs. Fala. The one from the kitchen. You know—the cute one?"

"Good for you."

"His name is Mateo. But you probably know that. It's a pretty cool name, don't you think?"

Nat doesn't answer. She grips the steering wheel with both hands. Her knuckles are white.

"You okay?" I ask, although it's clear she's not.

"Fine. I'm in a bad mood, that's all."

"What is it? Play troubles?"

The volume on the radio gets jerked up.

"Uh-oh. This looks more like trouble in lovers' paradise." There's a hint of mean in my tone.

Nat's lip trembles. She takes a turn with too much speed. I hold on to the door handle.

"You guys didn't break up again, did you?" I ask, counting in my head the number of times Nat and Alex have called it quits over the last three years—thirteen maybe? Drama kids.

Nat cranks the music up even louder. She lets out a bitter laugh.

"I don't want to talk about it."

Since I'm the queen of not wanting to talk about things, I take her words at face value. We listen to a sappy Broadway mix the rest of the way to the local university, where we're working some fancy dinner ball. It's my first foray into formal service, which means two extra hours of pay to practice synchronized meal delivery. How very exciting.

The kitchen is huge and metal and cold, but it still feels warmer than the Fala house.

"You didn't go all addict on me and start smoking a pack a day, did you?"

His voice in my ear. His body heating the right side of mine.

"No. Two packs, actually," I say without turning around, hoping he doesn't notice the Pavlovian reaction I'm experiencing.

Mateo helps dish up dinners. It's clear I'm not the only one watching him drizzle demi-glace onto steaks, moving a ladle up and down, painting. A line of waitresses—lowly underclassmen from my school and Catholic Central girls who know how to tighten uniform shirts and skirts in all the right places—gather around him. They're practically drooling, elbows up on his counter as he fixes sprigs of parsley on beds of brown rice. They giggle. They ask where he goes to school, if he wants to party, if he has a girlfriend. I know this because their voices are loud. His, on the other hand, is quiet. A low rumble. I try not to strain to hear his answers. I try not to look over, but when I do, he's sneaking a spoonful of vegetarian pasta into his mouth. His eyes meet mine. I swear I hear a click.

Just before our last five-count plate drop, Nat's phone vibrates. She pulls it from her skirt pocket and frowns.

"What?"

"Alex," she says, stuffing the phone back and picking up two strawberry shortcakes.

"You want me to tell him to leave you alone?"

She gives me a surprised look and shakes her head.

"You were crazy pissed at him four hours ago, remember?"

"Oh." She moves the plates like a seesaw. "Yeah, well, he always knows how to weasel his way out of trouble. He wants me to meet him at the drive-in; there's a Fred and Ginger marathon until 1 a.m. My parents would probably let me break curfew for it, but—"

"You can't get out of here, take me all the way home, and make it to the drive-in," I finish for her.

"No worries. Might be better to just go home anyway."

"Go," I say firmly.

Nat looks around.

"There's nobody here to give you a ride."

"There's Charlotte, the sophomore. I'm pretty sure she lives only a few blocks from my house. And I used to play softball with a couple of those Catholic Central girls. Besides, I can always call my mom. Who can call my dad. Who won't leave me stranded, despite his mid-life decision to become the world's biggest ass. Go. Make up with your Romeo."

Nat chews her cheek for a second and then nods. I scan the kitchen, taking in the clumps of girls who look like me from the neck down. I'd rather walk.

By the time I'm done cleaning up, the parking lot is almost empty. The night air is perfect. Like, literally perfect. It isn't warm and it isn't cold, but I still feel it brush my skin. A full moon is halfway to the top of the sky. Planes of light shoot out, vertical and horizontal, and in two small diagonal peaks.

It's the kind of night I used to wait for all year. The kind when I'd drag a sleeping bag and pillow to the flat overhang of roof just outside my window. It covers the front porch, and it goes under Joe's window too. Our secret fort. I learned all the constellations sitting out there. Or thought I learned them, until I had an exploratory astronomy class in ninth grade and discovered there is, in fact, no cluster of stars designated as a constellation for the Little Prince's airplane. Joe said being gullible is a rare and admirable quality in teenagers.

It's at least seven miles to my house. I know I'll have to call Mom at some point, or she'll call Nat's mom looking for me. And that will be a great big mess. But I want to stay outside a little while longer. So I start walking down the road. On the grassy shoulder, not the yellow lines.

I've probably only made it a mile or so when an older green Jeep blasts past. The brake lights blink twice, then stay on as the Jeep kicks up dust pulling to the side of the road.

I freeze.

The college is off the main drag of our township's sprawl, but close enough for me to not question if it's safe to be walking alone. At night. I try to remember self-defense moves Nat taught me two years ago. I try to remember, although I'm not even sure I'd want to use them.

"Hey!" A boy leans out of the driver side window. His voice sounds familiar.

I walk a little closer.

"Anna? It's Mateo," he calls, opening his door and holding up his hands as if I need to see he's safe.

I don't answer or speed up, but I keep moving in his direction, and he keeps moving in mine. In my head, chefs are always pudgy. The shadow walking toward me is lean, athletic. He reminds me of one of those 1950s boys in white T-shirts and jeans. Cool. Confident.

When we're only a few feet apart, he nods his head once. Studies me for a second.

"Nice night," he says.

It makes me laugh. We're standing next to an empty road and Mateo is dead serious, looking up at the moon and its beams of light.

"Ah, yeah," I say. "It's, um, lovely."

"Do you need a lift?"

"No." I can tell there's an edge in my voice because Mateo shakes his head a little, the same way he did when I told him I *parle français*.

"Okay, let me try again," he says with a smile. "Would you like a lift? May I please give you a ride?"

He has a perfect chin. This is what I notice while I'm thinking about how I don't like chivalrous smartasses. I make a big show of blowing a puff of air in his direction while stomping past him, but then I'm stopping next to the passenger side and pulling the door handle and all of a sudden I'm buckling the seat belt and saying, "I don't really feel like going home yet."

Mateo makes a noise I assume is akin to a smirk. I don't really know though because I'm looking everywhere but at him, all light-headed from the spice and boy smells filling the Jeep.

"You need a shower."

"What?" Mateo laughs. "What kind of thing is that to say to the person nice enough to pull over and give you a ride—"

"I was walking! You stopped. I didn't flag you down. Besides, you do. Need a shower."

"Well, if that's the case, I guess I better take you home now, so you don't have to smell me. Although you were in the same kitchen. And had to run around a lot more. Just saying."

He sniffs the air like a hound. I smack him, as if we know each other.

"Since we both stink"—he grins—"where do you want to go?"

I savor this, just for a second.

"Anywhere."

We drive for a few blocks without talking, and I'm wondering if he regrets picking me up. This is a bad idea. Everything about his mannerisms indicates he's "that" boy. He's too comfortable with the quiet, and with me in his passenger seat. He's too relaxed, one hand on the wheel, like he expected I'd accept the ride.

"Where do you go to school? How come we've never met?" I ask after waiting out the silence as long as I can stand it. "Are you at Catholic Central?"

"No, I go to Gerald Knoll," he says, checking to see my reaction. It's smooth as butter. The Knoll is deep inside city limits.

"Oh, cool. I don't know anybody who goes to school there."

"Yeah, no surprise," he says. "I'm guessing you go to Ancestry?"

"Am I so obvious?" I ask in mock horror.

"Well, you don't look like any carbon copy of the bleach blondes with fake tans, if that's what you mean," he says, sweeping his eyes up and down.

No, just a carbon copy of a 1970s punk rocker. A copy all the same. His lips are full, sort of pouty without being too big. I can't stop looking at them.

"There's no way you're a church-school girl. And I'd definitely remember if we went to school together." The way he says this, it makes me ache and feel filled up all at once.

He knows nothing about me.

Then Mateo touches my knee. Light. Like almost a non-touch. I hate the word swooning. But I might be doing it. A little.

"How 'bout a little greasy spoon dessert?" I want to stretch this ride home into one, or five, or five hundred minutes more. "Or are your culinary tastes too highbrow for the world's largest banana splits?"

Banter, spiked in his direction.

"Oh, those are fighting words. Just tell me where to go, 'cause I don't mess around when it comes to dessert." His free hand draws imaginary squiggles on the center console between us.

I text Mom to say I'm getting some food with a new friend after work, and promise to be home by 12:30 a.m. She sends back a ":)" and I don't know whether I'm irritated or glad I got her hopes up about day 366 being the turning point.

"So…" I drag the word out as we approach a stoplight switching from yellow to red. If we don't talk, I'm afraid I'll forget to breathe.

"So?"

"So, um, tell me five things about you."

I visualize how many lights are between the college and our all-night diner destination. Three. And another four before we get to my house. That's a total of thirty-five things I could know about him before I have to say goodnight. I know plenty of girls who make out with boys they only know one or two things about, and those things aren't even good.

Mateo lets out a one-syllable laugh. Oh, God. I hope I didn't say that out loud. In an effort to not die of embarrassment, I give myself specific tasks. Tasks I make sure to only say in my brain: Breathe. Watch the road. Stop blushing.

"One: I was accepted into the tri-county culinary program for my senior year. You ever heard of it?"

I nod. I've read about it in the paper. A guy named Julio Revolio, who grew up in Drisdale, which is the town next to ours, is a famous chef in California now. He started this program for seniors in high school who are super talented cooks. They go to school in a little kitchen classroom right in the middle of town, doing regular classwork part of the day, and spending the rest of the time learning from a bunch of superstar chefs Revolio brings in for a month at a time. The success rate for getting full rides to the top culinary programs around the country is like, 99 percent, and I think the other 1 percent is just because some of the kids have gone straight to work.

"Wow," I say.

He nods.

"Yeah. My folks were pretty psyched."

"Okay, so that's one." He rolls his left hand to crack his wrist. I notice a tattoo, in small cursive letters. It reads, "Val." My stomach flops. A girl. A love deep enough to leave a permanent mark.

"Hmm. Two: My favorite color is yellow."

"My car is yellow. And also in the shop for a broken axle. Curb jumped in front of me the other day."

"How about that. Meant to be," he jokes, reaching over to poke my side.

"There is definitely no 'meant to be' in my world," I

say, trying to get my voice hard while I scoot closer to the door.

"Three: I have an older brother named Valentino who still lives at home, because he's..." Mateo stops, smacks his lips together.

"Valentino?" I repeat. I don't dare ask, but my eyes flick to his wrist.

"He's...different," he finishes with a shrug. I see his face falter. He holds up three fingers. "That's three."

Popping a fourth, he tells me both sets of his grandparents moved here from Mexico when the auto factories were still fresh and gleaming, and most of the time his parents still speak Spanish at home, because his mom freaks about losing cultural identity.

"Actually, I can count that info as things five and six, but I'll give you another fact as a bonus: I think you're interesting," he says.

Interesting. Interesting is not like being, say, hot. Or funny. Or smart. Interesting is the kind of word one uses to describe a stinky-cheese science project or a bad one-act play (starring your best friend). Which would make sense. This guy is gorgeous and talented and friendly with everybody. And I'm me. It's just a ride home. It doesn't mean anything.

For the next two stoplights, I don't say a word, and when we near the Cowboy Grill, I flick my hand, indicating where he needs to turn, then cross my arms and push back into my seat.

"Did I say something wrong?" Mateo asks when he parks and I still don't open my door.

"No. Just something... *interesting.*"

He lets out a whistle.

"You are, whew. I don't even know. Tough." He hops out and jogs to my door, opening it for me. "Or are you just afraid to get busted for bluffing about this being the world's largest banana split? Because I gotta say, I'm picturing a pretty wimpy, limp banana and double scoop of ice cream."

Inside the restaurant, the lights are almost orange and hang from wagon wheels above all the booths. A waitress with dark black circles under her eyes and huge boobs bulging out of her uniform comes up and says, "what'llitbe," like the entire question is one syllable and she's too tired to bother peering down to get our answer.

"Can you eat a whole one by yourself?" Mateo asks me, raising his eyebrows like a challenge.

"Only if you'd like me to explode. Gross. No."

"We'll have one banana split, please," he says to the waitress, returning our menus. She gives him a kind smile. There's a quality in his tone; it's soft, slow, and I can tell she feels like she's been spoken to, not at, for the first time all night. She flushes a bit when he adds, "Thanks so much, Darcy." Her name is embroidered across one of her boobs. I automatically look at my pathetically under-developed chest, and feel heat rise in my face too.

I spend most of the five minutes we're waiting ripping

apart a cheap paper napkin. Silence has never been a good friend of mine. It makes my chest tight. Mateo asks me a few questions about school and how I ended up waitressing. (I explain my best friend and I want to hang out as much as possible during our pre-senior-year summer. Not a lie. Not a full lie, anyway.) I try to think of witty things to ask back, but it's been a year since I've tried to make small talk.

The banana split serves as a good icebreaker. Mateo falls to the side of the booth cracking up when it arrives: four bananas topped with a half gallon of ice cream, chocolate sauce, nuts, probably a whole can of Reddi-wip, and six cherries dotting the top.

"Holy Mother—"

"I told you."

"Wow."

"I know. Dig in. It gets pretty disgusting within seven minutes or so."

We stuff ourselves to such a point I can't even look at my spoon, let alone pick it up for one more bite. I realize I don't have any cash on me. And I want to sink under the table.

"Um, I'm really sorry, but I just remembered I left my purse in my best friend Nat's car."

I start laughing again when I say this, and it makes Mateo laugh too. I'm pretty sure my stomach might seize up any second. My giggle-related muscles are way out of shape.

"Wouldn't be a date if I let you pay, right?"

I'm caught off guard and say the first thing that comes

to mind, which is needing a bathroom, while tripping over myself getting out of the booth. Instead of the restroom, though, I walk straight out of the restaurant and into the night air. I shiver and my flesh goes to goose bumps. Mateo comes out a few minutes later.

"Hey, sorry, I didn't mean to—"

"No, it's okay." I wave like I'm waving away smoke, which makes him seem to remember he wants to light up.

I watch him suck in and blow out ten or so puffs before he's crushing the cigarette against the ground and walking it over to the outdoor ashtray.

"Why do you do that? I mean, nobody smokes anymore."

"If nobody smoked, I wouldn't have these," Mateo says, patting the pack of Kools in his pocket.

I wrinkle my nose.

"I sort of picked it up a few weeks ago," he adds. "I don't know why. Must have a death wish. Ready to go home now?"

"Yeah," I say out loud. *No. No. No*, I repeat in my head.

Everyone on my street is sleeping. All the cars are tucked into their garages. Houses are only shadows. A rabbit darts into the road, and Mateo slows down. It pauses, blinking in the headlights before diving back onto a lawn.

"This is me."

The windows are dark, but I catch a faint glow from the kitchen island light. Mom used to leave it on when Joe was a senior and got to stay out until midnight.

Mateo moves the gear shift to park. He looks at the closed garage door, then down at his lap, then over to me.

"Thanks a lot," I say.

I know I need to get out, but I just keep sitting here, watching him blink.

"Sure," he says. "Would have taken you 'til tomorrow to walk home. Besides, it was nice, hanging out with you."

Watching his lips fold into themselves, I don't want to want him.

I unbuckle my seat belt. Instead of pulling the car door open, I sit statue still. Coffin still. I need to get out of here. My eyes keep shifting toward him. Those lips.

"Well, good night," I say, opening the door.

"Night," he says, not putting the Jeep into reverse.

I count breaths. Seven. Eight. Nine. Ten.

Mateo clears his throat.

"Right, well, I gotta get home before my mom wonders if I got abducted by some vixen waitress."

He flashes a dimple. His thumb grazes my cheek, traces one side of my jaw. I freeze. Except for my heart. It's echoing into my ears at a maddening pace.

"Night, Anna."

And...nothing. He straightens up and shifts into reverse.

I scramble out, standing in the middle of the sidewalk leading up to my front door until every last trace of red taillight is gone. My skin thrums with a buzz I've read about, a buzz I've witnessed but never experienced. Rush. Heat. Ache.

I lie down on cracked concrete, fold my arms across my stomach, stiffen my muscles, open my eyes so wide the stars and moon blur with the black sky, watercolors of light and dark running together. I start counting seconds, then minutes, until I reach nineteen. Because here's a universal truth: You never feel more aware of what it means to be alive than when you're falling in love.

Or dying.

13

I can't sleep. It's 3:45 a.m. and I've gone through every possible solution for insomnia: warm milk; counting sheep (only sixty-four wooly critters jumped a fence before I got too bored, but still); reading passages of *20,000 Leagues Under the Sea*, one of those classics no one could have ever possibly enjoyed; coffin yoga to an old Cowboy Junkies record, with my eyes closed, twice. Still awake.

The moon casts a hazy light inside my room. I untangle from the covers and get up, throw on one of the sweatshirts my dad left behind, and go to the window. We haven't put the screens back on yet, probably because it's always been Dad's job. I didn't even notice until now. Guess we haven't opened them much.

Before I can think about it, I grab my cell phone, yank up the window, and crawl out onto the roof. Last time I was up here was two Christmases ago. It had snowed, so the shingles were full of fluffy white flakes, and Joe and I bundled up and watched the sky. I mean, I was fifteen, so it isn't like I believed in flying reindeer. At least, I claimed I didn't believe. I didn't want to be teased about my secretly-not-meant-to-be-ironic Rudolph Christmas sweater.

Even though the roof is bone dry, I'm unsteady on my feet. So I sit down and look up. Then I crawl to the left, toward his window.

For a few minutes, I debate whether or not to text Nat. I start typing a couple times, then hit delete. I start writing, "I'm sitting on the roof outside Joe's room," and hit delete again because she'd think I'm about to hurl myself off, even though I'm pretty sure the one-story over-hang wouldn't be enough of a fall to kill me (plus I was only walking that night on the highway, walking with star-dust beneath my feet). Texting might not be a great idea.

I stand up. Turn and face the blackened glass. Put both palms against it. And wait. It's not as if I expected a ghost to reach up from the other side and match his hands against mine, but I did maybe hope I'd imagine him there. I've read lots of books with people who see their dead friend or relative in a familiar spot. I know, fiction.

When nothing happens, I push up on the glass. The window cracks open. My hands fly off like I touched a hot stove. Then they go back again, palms against glass, pushing up until there is enough space for me to crawl through.

Joe's room is locked from the outside. There's a high little latch Mom had Gramps install one day after Bea hid for three hours by simply sitting on top of Joe's bed. I could reach up and unlatch it if I wanted to, but the day Gramps locked it was the last time anyone stepped foot in here.

The air still smells like Joe; it delivers an invisible punch in the gut. My eyes adjust to the familiar shapes of his room. His clothes hang in the half-open closet. A little pile of his laundry sits in a heap on the floor. His bed is made, but everything else is exactly as it was the day he went into the hospital.

I tiptoe over to his bookshelf, afraid if Mom hears movement in Joe's room and gets up to find the door still locked, she'll go right over the edge. His shelves are crammed with books that Dad wanted to donate to the local library and Mom insisted we keep to be divided between Bea and me someday. It's tricky to navigate without making noise. I want the biggest book on the shelf, his *Anthology of American Literature*, still dog-eared in a hundred places. When I free it, I flip through, tracing imprints of notes written in the margins.

Nineteen minutes go by. I count the seconds. I sit perfectly still until I say "sixty" under my breath for the nineteenth time. It's like I'm a cuckoo clock striking midnight. I stop counting and start ripping pages from his book. I tear slowly at first because I don't want to wake anyone up, but at some point I stop caring and I'm thrashing around like the book and I are in a fight to the death, and there's a confetti storm of paper floating around me.

When there's nothing left but two ragged covers, I curl up on the floor amid the mess.

I wake up to my phone ringing. It's still out on the roof. It takes me a second to realize where I am. The window is wide open. So is the bedroom door.

The ringing stops and then starts again. I get up and lean out to grab it.

"Hello?" I say, rubbing my eyes. Everything is still dry and fuzzy, so I can't see the number.

"Hey."

Pause.

"Um...hey."

"It's Mateo."

"Right. Hi. Uh, how'd you get this number?"

"It's on the waitress board that goes to all the catering jobs—you know, in case one of you flakes and we need an immediate replacement."

I'm pretty sure it only takes a second to recover, but in that time I've worked out (a) I am standing in a sea of shredded pages in my dead bruncle's room, (b) I am talking to Mateo, who just called me, which means (c) he took down my number before pulling over and splitting the world's biggest dessert and not kissing me. And this means (d) he might...wait, (e) I have no right to even be thinking like this or feeling a flutter of happy when I'm in Joe's room and Joe's gone and—

"Anna?"

"Ah, yeah. I'm here. So did you need something or did I forget some—"

"I just wondered what you are doing after work tonight."

"I'm…I'm busy. Sorry."

I hang up without saying goodbye.

I was always looking backward. It took me a long time to appreciate the present.

14

I stand. I walk toward the hallway. I head down the stairs. I do not prolong the inevitable.

Logical deduction: open door means Mom knows where I slept. Which means she knows about the shredded book mess. Which means she knows I'm a bigger disaster than ever. Deduction part two: I'll be packing my bags for Hell very, very soon.

Jazz plays in the kitchen. Gramps must be here. I slink into the room and await my verdict. Gramps glances up from his paper. It's the *New York Times*, and the cover photo is of people screaming and running. It looks like a Hollywood movie set behind them, one where a bomb just blew up a fake coffee shop or something. Except, of course, the people in the picture aren't in a movie.

I wince a little, waiting for what comes next. Tick. Tock. Tick. Tock.

But he gets up, tucks the paper under his arm, and walks past, slowing down long enough to kiss my forehead.

"Morning, sunshine," he calls back.

I turn around like a girl in boot camp and follow him.

"That's all you have to say?" My eyes narrow. I don't like sneak attacks.

"What else would you like to hear?"

"Where's Mom?"

"Believe it or not, she's out back. Pulling weeds."

This stops me dead. I scan our living room to make sure I didn't fall off the roof last night or get sucked into some parallel universe. Blue couch, worn spot on the left arm. Floor-to-ceiling bookcases full of books everybody has read and books nobody will ever read. Flat-screen TV, on without volume. Scratched wood floor. Fuzzy cream rug with a faint red stain in the corner from when Nat laughed so hard at Joe's suck-tastic charade-playing skills, Cranapple juice shot out her nose.

Yup. Same house as yesterday.

Mom's clients used to brag about her horticultural genius, like she's a fairy yard-mother or something. Dad joked a lot, before, about our own backyard "garden." He always made air quotation marks when he called it that. He said Mom put in every perennial that was impossible to kill, like daisies, black-eyed Susans, oregano, and thirteen varieties of mint plants.

The problem? Everything requires some level of care. The mint plants got zero love this spring. A person could argue they're thriving (because those things spread like green wildfire). Except in reality they're one giant, tangled mess of suffocating roots.

Mom's bent over in the middle of the mint and oregano jungle when I step outside. She hears the sliding door open, and pulls her big brown sunglasses to the top of her head as she turns around.

She isn't wearing makeup, and the half-moons beneath her eyes are the color of charcoal.

"Can you go get me a pair of garden scissors from the garage?" she asks. "I think you'll find them behind the tin tubs of work gloves."

I stare at her.

"Well, can you?" she repeats, bending down to pull a monster pricker weed.

I come back a few minutes later, scissors in hand, sharp part pointed down. When she takes them, I catch a glimpse of my arm. Yesterday's verse is still there, barely faded at all.

Yesterday's words are still there.

Coffin yoga. My arm. My morning. I spin around and reach for the door so I can run inside and up the steps and into my room and onto my bed and stretch out, eyes wide, trying not to breathe. But Mom grabs my other wrist. She holds on tight.

"Help me out here for a bit, please?" Her voice is

unsteady but she smiles, and it almost feels real. I try to pull away. She doesn't let go.

I'm really hot and then really congested and I need to get away but I don't want to go to Hell (at least not while alive). I stoop over to yank a bunch of weeds and mint shoots as tall as my knees.

We work like this, not talking, for a long time. We move from overgrown herbs to perennials to shrubs. Bea comes out, hands on her hips, grumbling about how Gramps went fishing and she's been hiding inside the couch forever and nobody even noticed she was gone.

My shirt clings to my back and my lips taste salty. Mom glances at her watch and hops off her knees, a huge pile of wilting weeds in her arms. She says she needs to get Buzzy to her doctor (read: therapy) appointment. I follow her inside. Wait while she jogs up the stairs, wait until her bedroom door closes and the steady thrum of the shower is going.

Then I slide back into my room. Settle into my coffin. I can't seem to get comfortable or hold my breath longer than fifteen seconds. Maybe I need to find my verse first.

The words pop up on my computer screen like a story from the other side: *I was always looking backward. It took me a long time to appreciate the present.*

The ink is still wet when I creep into his room. Shredded pages are still everywhere, but there's also the white plastic tub we use for paper recycling. Gramps.

I pick up handfuls of words until the carpet is free of

scraps. The hollowed hardcover is still on the floor. I push it into the hole of space between his copy of *The Catcher in the Rye* and *Harry Potter*. That's when I see it.

The sharp angle and pointed tip of a paper crane's tail. It's smooshed against the back of the shelf, cream paper almost blending in with the cream paint of the wood. I have to pull *The Chamber of Secrets* out before I see the rest of the bird. Cranes are the first origami design Gramps teaches, because they're his favorite. He and Joe had a goal of making a thousand cranes every year, starting the year Joe went to college.

They were playing off some lucky marriage story, where a thousand paper cranes meant a life of happiness and love. There's a box of cranes sitting in the basement. Joe was still trying to finish his half when he got sick. Gramps tried to encourage him in the hospital, bringing in some of the five hundred he'd already finished. He lined them on the windowsill of the hospital room. A red one, a green one, three yellows, and a blue.

This crane's a little lopsided, made with regular paper. Inside has a bunch of scribbled lines, probably notes from one of Joe's classes. I open it up to see.

And then it's clear: this paper crane was folded up and tucked in the back of a bookshelf because the words on the page were not to be found or read by anyone else. I have to sit down. I have to read the first paragraph ten times before I can process what it is saying.

*I WISH YOU'D HAVE PICKED UP YOUR PHONE
THE 100 TIMES I TRIED IT TODAY. OR MAYBE
I DON'T. MAYBE I SHOULD STOP TRYING TO
WRITE THIS AND JUST LET YOU GO ON HATING
ME. BECAUSE IT'S BETTER IF YOU DO. BECAUSE
THEN I CAN'T TELL YOU HOW I REALLY THINK
I FEEL. THERE ARE SO MANY REASONS THAT
WHAT'S BEEN HAPPENING IS WRONG, AND WE
BOTH KNOW IT. BUT IT DIDN'T FEEL WRONG. IT
FELT MORE LIKE THE MOST RIGHT THING EVER.
WHAT ARE WE SUPPOSED TO DO?*

He cheated.

He was cheating.

He was with someone. With someone who wasn't Sameera.

A part of his life was a lie. A secret. Kept from his best friend in the universe. Me. I blink to bring the words back into focus.

The next two paragraphs suck every bit of air from my lungs.

*I TOLD YOU IT WAS A SCREWUP. THAT WE
WERE STUPID. THAT I DON'T—CAN'T EVER—
TRULY FEEL THAT WAY TOWARD YOU. I KNOW
IT'S THE RIGHT THING TO DO, TO MAKE YOU
HATE ME. YOU WANTED ME TO MAKE A CHOICE I
WASN'T READY TO MAKE. SAMEERA AND I HAVE
BEEN TOGETHER FOR SO LONG. I NEEDED SPACE*

TO GET MY HEAD AROUND WHAT WAS HAPPENING BETWEEN US. THERE ARE SO MANY OTHER FACTORS AT PLAY, AND NO WAY TO KNOW IF WE'D WORK OR IF IT WOULD BE WORTH EVERYTHING WE'D LOSE. EXCEPT WHEN I SAID I WISHED I COULD TAKE IT ALL BACK, IT WASN'T BECAUSE I REGRET IT. YOU DESERVE MORE. THAT'S THE BAD LINE EVERY SCUMBAG JOCK IN THE UNIVERSE USES. I'M TRYING TO EXPLAIN HOW BEING WITH YOU—I'M AWARE IT'S WRONG. BUT IT DOESN'T STOP ME FROM WANTING IT. IT'S KILLING ME NOT TO DRIVE RIGHT OVER TO YOUR HOUSE AND CRAWL THROUGH YOUR BEDROOM WINDOW.

SOMEDAY I HOPE YOU UNDERSTAND, HOW I NEVER MEANT TO HURT YOU. HOW THIS THING WITH US, IT JUST HIT LIKE A TRUCK. YOU KNOW IT DID. NO ONE WOULD EVER, EVER BELIEVE THAT. NOTHING WILL EVER BE THE SAME, BUT WE DON'T HAVE TO MAKE THINGS WORSE. WE CAN'T, EVEN IF I WISH WE COULD.

Joe's sloppy scrawl is unmistakable. So is his adherence to letter-writing etiquette, because the date is in the top right-hand corner: May 24. Twenty-one days before he died. Two days before he started to get sick. There's no name at the top.

He didn't give it to whomever it was meant for, obviously, but he saved it. Hid it. Hid all of it. I pull another book off the shelf, and another and another until there are books flipped open, books in crooked piles, books sagging sideways on their spines. Six shelves emptied onto the floor. No more cranes. No more hints. This is all he left behind.

"What are you doing?" Bea asks, leaning against the doorframe. She's sucking on a round lollipop and makes a puckering noise, pointing to the new mess.

I shake my head and hold up my hands in a silent plea to be left alone. Instead, Bea says "criss-cross applesauce" and plops down, blocking the doorway. The one time I want her to, she refuses to disappear.

I stuff the crane in my pocket. Pick up the books one by one. Hold their covers like wings, shaking each to make sure there are no more secrets tucked inside their pages. He was a liar. He was a cheater. He never told me.

I need to get out of here. Need to get anywhere else.

Stumbling out of his room, I get to mine and slam the door.

The words "He never told me. He never told me. He never told me" crash through my head and I need to do something, anything, to get it out. I want to scream. I want to break. I want to burn that crane and never, ever know it existed.

How could Joe—the person who shared everything with me, the guy who was so good and honest and true—also be a total douche bag? Maybe a friend wrote it. But then he wouldn't have folded it into a crane and saved it. I can't slow my brain down. It's like the only thing I have left of him, the picture of who he was, is suddenly splitting into a 1,000-piece jigsaw puzzle.

I can't get answers. It makes Joe feel more gone than ever. Because how do you hold on to someone you've lost, if maybe you didn't really know him, the real and true him, in the first place?

"I'm going for a run! See you later," I call into the hallway. I don't run. Not even when chased. But my car is still in the shop and I need to leave fast before Mom catches a glimpse of me.

"Whoa!" She's standing at the top of the stairs. I turn, but bend over and act like I'm scooping up all my hair into a ponytail.

"You're doing what?" she asks. There is clear concern in her voice. I hear Bea whisper something behind her. She pauses and then says, "Gramps wanted to take you to lunch in about an hour."

"I'll—I'll be back by then," I stammer and open the front door. "I just…I want to run. Or jog, or fast walk or whatever."

I don't wait for a response. My legs are burning before I get around the block and the back of my throat's on fire. Patti's words on my arm pump in and out of view. The phrase means something different, harsher now.

15

Twenty-one days before he died.
Two days before he got sick.
He'd drive to her house.
People wouldn't forgive them.
No one would have guessed.
Who?
Who?
Who?

16

I run and run and run. Stopping only to hack, heave, gasp for more, more, more air. My shin muscles push away from the bone or wherever they belong. My side cramps and throbs and cramps again. But I keep going until I reach Nat's house, four miles away.

Nat's subdivision is named Willow Brook even though there are no willow trees (not even chopped down) and no brooks nearby. The houses are enormous and look like they are different arrangements of the same set of Legos. Identical circle driveways cut through bright lawns that are adorned with identical collections of dogwoods and crabapples and hydrangeas and bright-colored annuals. Mom hates this kind of cookie-cutter landscaping, but never says so in front of Nat, who believes the sameness is kind of nice in a disorderly world.

I walk in the side door without knocking.

Nat's sitting at the kitchen table, one knee propped up on the chair. Her forehead is tucked against it, but I can tell her eyes are closed and she's listening to some musical I'm not familiar with. She does this, closes her eyes and dissects every note, the way a sculptor might inspect every chisel mark in a great masterpiece.

"Hey," I say extra loud as I open the refrigerator and pull out one of the water bottles Calandra, Nat's mom, keeps full and chilled at all times.

Nat opens her eyes and nods, holding up one finger and listening to the last rising and falling notes of the song. When the soundtrack stops, she answers.

"Hey. What are you doing? Why are you so red? And sweaty?"

"I ran."

"You ran here?" Her eyebrows disappear under her bangs. "From where? Were you being chased by a pack of wild dingoes?"

I planned to fork the letter over to Nat the second I got to her house. Nat's years of being in plays make her a classic detective. She can imagine the motivations of any character you throw her way. But when I reach into the tiny pocket of my shorts where I stuffed the folded and re-folded paper crane, I can't pull it back out. I can't bring myself to share what it says.

So I make up a story, kind of.

"I slept in Joe's room last night," I begin, talking faster

right away because I can tell by Nat's face she's about to bombard me with questions. "And I found something under his bed, this note written on the back of a receipt for a motel that he stayed in on May 24, and the note said sorry it won't work out, and I know Sameera would have told me if they were fighting right before he got sick and so now I'm, like, sure he was cheating on her and—"

"Hey, wait a minute. Back up. Slow down. What are you talking about?"

"Joe was…he was…"

"What did it say? It was written on what, again? Was there anything else? Did you look?"

Nat is leaning against the table now and the side of her hand hits the wood with every question. I want to pull out the crane, but instead I keep saying this lie.

"On a motel receipt. It said, 'This wouldn't work out.' Oh, and that too many people would be mad. It said that too. And there wasn't anything else—"

"Do you have it with you?"

"What?"

"The receipt! A motel? What motel? In what city?"

"Um, I flushed it down the toilet."

"You flushed it down the toilet?"

"Yes. I didn't want Mom to find it or something."

"Do you really want to know?" Nat's eyebrows are scrunched with worry. Her hand is on my back. "I mean, are you sure it was even Joe's handwriting? It could have been some scrap that was blowing across a gas station parking lot. You have no idea. It probably means nothing, Anna. Joe loved Sameera. We all know that."

She is so final about her last statement. I try it out in my head. Joe loved Sameera. Except the paper crane is hot against my thigh. Why can't I tell Nat?

Because then she'll know all of his secrets too. She'll know the words he said to this mystery girl. She'll know exactly as much as I do, and that isn't fair because he was my family and my other best friend, not hers. I need her help, but I want to get at the truth of the situation without giving her the truth of his letter.

"It was his handwriting. Obviously I know what that looks like," I say with more righteous indignation than should be allowed when lying to your oldest and dearest friend in the universe.

Nat begins biting both her thumbs, which is what she does whenever she's nervous or thinking really hard. "Okay," she says slowly. "Okay. So he went to a motel and wrote a note on the back of the receipt saying it wouldn't work out. That people would be mad. So why wouldn't he leave the note there?"

"Maybe he wrote it in the bathroom when the girl was sleeping. Maybe she woke up and he told her to her face."

"What motel?"

"The Riverside."

"That's right out of town!"

"I know," I say, nodding gravely. "And the credit card was his so there is no denying he was there on May 24.

Plus, it has to be someone we know. I mean, why else would he say no one would have ever guessed?"

While I'm talking, Nat gets up and starts pacing furiously around the square slate tiles in her kitchen. When I say this last thing, her head flicks up like a hunting dog's.

"Wait—what? You didn't say that before."

"Yes I did."

"No, you definitely didn't."

"Oh. Um, well I thought I did. Yeah, it also said no one would have guessed they were together. And something like, 'People would be mad.'"

"I'll be right back."

Nat tears out of the room too fast for me to ask what she's doing, but I can hear a bunch of commotion coming from her dad's office. A minute later she returns looking flushed and carrying a notebook, pen, and highlighter.

"I knocked over two of the globes in my dad's collection trying to reach his pen holder," she says. "Before we get into this, Anna, I think we have to decide if it's worth it. Because he's not here. And we might learn things that he'll never be able to explain away. We might never find the truth."

She frowns and exhales noisily.

"If you really want to go there, then we have to decide how to go about this. Like, do we want to go tell Sameera—"

"No! Are you crazy?"

Nat holds up her hands in surrender.

"All right, all right. I'm just asking. Don't bite my head

off. You know we need to have a plan and you know I can help you organize it, which is why you're here. So, no Sameera. At least not yet. Then we have to start at ground zero. Make a list of possible suspects."

"Let's make the list," I say, settling the decision.

Nat waits a second, the end of the pen clattering between her top and bottom teeth.

"I'm not going to change my mind. I have to know."

"Why?"

I can't answer. How do I explain? Because I need to believe the Joe I knew and the Joe who wrote the letter I found this morning are the same person? Ever since I found the crane, there's been this stir of excitement hanging in the shadow of all my shock and confusion. It's like as long as I have this mystery and this story of Joe's world I never knew, he's alive again in some way. Even if that way is bad.

"Because I just do," is all I say.

17

Sarah Sallenton—because she's been obsessed since their fake marriage on the playground in third grade, and came over with Sarah Gerber on the deadaversary.

Sarah Handy—nicest of the Sarahs (which isn't saying much). Talked on the phone with Joe sometimes. Good at soccer. Brought stinky roses to the house.

Sarah Gerber—likes to conquer the unobtainable ones.

Joanie Anderson—Joe's seventh grade girlfriend for a week. Also was valedictorian and is playing field hockey for University of Michigan.

Liz Whitehouse—cute in a girl-next-door way and always volunteered for same stuff as Joe. Has a long-term boyfriend.

Helen Petrovsky—Joe said she was the prettiest girl

in the whole school when we played two truths and a lie once. He also said his favorite food was a dill pickle. He puked if he even smelled dill pickles.

Layne Trotter—quiet, beautiful, and generally not interested in boys. Would fit the total shock factor.

———

Two hours of arguing, dissecting possibilities, and scouring Nat's yearbook left us with seven sort-of-solid possibilities. We've moved to her room, which is still princess pink and has a fake zebra rug, loads of Broadway musical posters signed by cast members, and more tchotchke than any one person should be allowed.

Sandwiched between three families of matryoshka dolls, Nat has this prehistoric-looking plant with thick stalks and wide, shiny leaves. The flowers have long, angular orange and purple petals. It's called a bird-of-paradise, because the flowers look like paper cranes. I shove the note deeper into my pocket.

"I hate that plant," I say, glaring at it.

Nat doesn't look up from the list. She's repeating the names out loud, running through them again and again.

"We need to see who was around, back when Joe was home right before he got sick," she says. "Five of the people on that list were just finishing their freshman year too. Maybe some of the colleges went later?"

"Yeah, but Sarah Handy went to community college

here. So it doesn't matter when she got out, and Joanie Anderson was at Michigan too."

"Well, we have to start somewhere. So we'll check the schedules of the other five and see if we can cross them off the list. I mean, Liz goes somewhere in, like, Maine or Massachusetts, right?"

We get on the computer and cyber-stalk. Liz goes to a little college in New Hampshire. The school's website says classes start in late September and don't get out until late June. We put a line through her name.

"A motel receipt," Nat repeats for the tenth time. Her eyes are slits. She glares into blank air and says, "Really, Joe? Really?" as if he can answer.

She chews the end of her pen. Taps it against the paper. Twitches her mouth back and forth.

"I think we need to go back in his room," she says, spread out on the floor in a position one could mistake for coffin yoga.

"I know."

"But not today, okay?"

Nat also reads minds.

"Good plan," I agree, and slump down into an over-stuffed fluffy white beanbag that resembles a sleeping baby yeti. Wisps of white hairs float near my face, and I bat them toward the floor.

"My mom cleaned up the mint jungle this morning."

"Wow. That's a good sign, right?"

"I guess. I think so. It was weird. I sorta thought I'd

be in trouble for sleeping in Joe's room, but nobody said a word."

"Why did you go in there?"

It's my turn to bite a nail.

"I don't know. I guess I wasn't thinking. I got a ride home from Mateo last night."

This gets Nat's interest.

"What? Why didn't you call me? What happened? Did you talk? Did he make a move? Did you just go up and ask him for a ride? Did any of those Catholic Central girls see you? I bet they were freaking pissed!"

Nat and I have become masters in the art of other conversations, like who we think will win the presidential election, or who will be homecoming queen, or how good the sushi is at the new sushi bar in town and how bad it will suck when the owners figure out they can make more money someplace like Birming Pointe, where more people still have good jobs. We don't talk about what—or who—could be important to me. I wish I wouldn't have said anything.

"Anna!"

"I was just getting ready to call my mom." White lie. Almost not even a lie. "And he just came up and offered me a ride. Nothing happened. We went to the Cowboy Grill and ate a banana split. How was the movie with Alex?"

"Movie was great. But seriously, can we please talk about you getting a ride home with the mysterious hottie that every single waitress—me excluded, of course—is totally longing to have a summer fling with?"

"It didn't mean anything."

"Oh yes it did. Who paid?"

"For what?"

"Don't be like that! Who paid for the banana split? Those things are like, twelve dollars!"

I groan.

"Don't remind me," I say, shaking my head. "My wallet was in your car. So he sorta had to pay."

"Oh." Nat thinks on this for a second and then breaks into a grin. "No, it still means something. He offered you a ride. And he didn't want to take you right home. Do you know how many times I've heard girls ask him to hang out in the month I've been doing these catering jobs?"

"Well, until a week ago, you only did them on weekends because we were still in school. So it couldn't be that many."

She ignores my reasoning.

"I knew it. You two totally had a spark."

She gets up and claps her hands, beaming like she does for an audience after her final bow. Then she disappears into the bathroom for eight minutes. I count in an effort to stop replaying the end of my night with Mateo. Specifically, the part when he didn't kiss me.

When Nat comes back, she's quiet.

"Are you OK?"

She nods yes, then pauses and looks at me. "I'm worried this thing with Joe will make you backtrack or whatever and I just really want you to start getting better."

I remember Nat's face when she came to my hospital room during supervised visitation hours and saw my new haircut. The same gullible nurse who let me download Patti songs also agreed to help me cut it in huge, chunky pieces. Her reasoning ("it was a healing expression") didn't go over too well with my mother and father, who needed me presentable at a funeral in the near future.

"Why?" she asked, picking up one angled piece of still-mousey-colored hair.

I tried to tell her. I tried to explain how Joe was dead and I was locked up and how the echo of Patti Smith's music and words might save me. How latching onto a crazy-strong stranger was the way I'd make it through.

"I don't get it," Nat said, shaking her head. "I just don't get it."

She always got it. I didn't know how to respond.

I went through this conversation with the first eight shrinks too. I told them that part of the truth. They didn't understand. Instead, they handed me books or papers or pamphlets with soft blue and gray tones.

The therapist before Liza explained, in his radio-ready voice, that copying a 1970s beat poet turned punk rocker had no correlation to dealing with my feelings about death or my family falling apart.

He said I should be journaling.

I said, "Therapists aren't supposed to say 'should.'"

He said I needed to snap out of my costume so I could begin the real work of getting my mind back on track.

I fished a watermelon Jolly Rancher from a sea of sour green apple in his candy bowl. When I'd sucked it into a tiny sliver, I opened my mouth and said he was ignoring the possibility of me being a teenager who simply figured out who she is. I said, "I am not what happened to me; I am what I choose to become."

The shrink made sad eyes through his Buddy Holly glasses and replied, "Yes, that's what I'm most afraid you believe."

Idiot didn't even know a good Carl Jung quote when he heard one.

We moved on to Liza the following week. And I don't tell her anything except what she wants to hear.

So sitting in Nat's room, I say, "I'm good," over and over again. Her dubious expression gets wiped away the second I add, "Mateo called this morning. He asked me out."

I'm pretty sure the whole neighborhood heard her squeal in delight. In fact, I'm a little worried Mateo heard it, clear across town.

Got to love a drama queen, I suppose.

18

Nat drives me home because running is not an option. Neither is walking, considering the quarter-size blisters I have on my heels. And the button-size ones on top of my toes.

"Let's wait a few days to go through Joe's room," Nat says as she turns into my driveway. "In the meantime, you've got to call Mateo back."

I start to protest but she's already reciting the lines she wants me to say.

"Hey, Mateo," Nat practically coos, "it's Anna! Sorry I rushed off the phone this morning, I was in the middle of drying my hair" (Nat flips hers as she says this). "Anyway, I'm busy tonight, but I have a free afternoon tomorrow, if you want to go with me to see my best friend's boyfriend's soccer game. You know Nat, right? She's the most fabulous friend in the universe, super talented and beautiful and—"

"Oh, yeah." I nod. "I am totally going to say all of that."

Nat smiles and shoves me out the door before stalling the car, twice.

Once I'm alone, I pull the phone from my pocket. Play hot potato with it. My blood is running flood-river style through my body right now. I decide I'm not calling. Decide I am calling. Decide he's probably figured out I'm a hot mess. Decide I need to know if this is true.

He picks up on the first ring.

"Hi," I say, too fast to hang up.

Silence. I pick a frayed thread on my shorts.

"Hi?" I try again.

"Yeah, I'm here," Mateo replies. "Just had to double-check who was calling, because after this morning, I didn't think I'd be hearing from you."

I set my jaw. This was a bad idea.

"But I'm glad," he adds. "That you called."

"Yeah, well." I stall as much as Dolores. "Even though you ate way more banana split than I did last night, I figure I either owe you six dollars or can drag you to watch my friend Nat's boyfriend play soccer tomorrow, where I can pay six dollars for you to experience the concession stand's equally enticing hot dogs and fake-buttered buckets of popcorn."

"You've got a weird sense of balancing out a debt," Mateo says. I can tell his dimple is showing.

"Well, I know it's slumming—" I cough to cover up my faux pas. It's not that I assume Mateo lives in a ghetto, it's just, well, us township kids aren't well versed in his area of town. And vice versa.

"How do you know I haven't already experienced those delicacies?" he asks. I twist a chunk of hair around and around until my finger turns purple.

"Do you play travel soccer?"

"No."

"Do you have friends that play travel soccer? At the field on my side of town?"

"Your side of town?"

"That's not what I meant."

"Uh-huh. I've never been to this snack shack of yours, so how about I pick you up tomorrow and allow you the pleasure of introducing my fine palette to such preservative-rich treasures."

I can't help laughing.

"You sound ridiculous when you talk like that," I say after snorting.

"How do you know this is not how I carry on a normal conversation?" His words come out like a slow current.

"I just do," I say, trying to match his tempo.

DAILY VERSE:
You can always count on me to be
just yapping away.

19

I opt for a thin purple (pre-Patti, to appease Mom) long-sleeve shirt, cut-off jean shorts, black Converse high-tops, and three leather cords draped around my neck. The one hanging closest to my twined gold key has swirling glass beads on each side of a Celtic cross. The designs carved into the metal used to be tinted green, but the whole thing is stained black with permanent marker now. I stare at the Patti photo grid and frown. Sometimes it would be nice to just have a mirror.

The doorbell rings. I hear Mom get up, and listen to her exchange cautious pleasantries with Mateo. I wonder if she's running through a catalogue of faces, trying to recall if she should know this boy from school plays or games or field trips. I wonder if she is afraid my heart will be on my sleeve, or if she'd rather see it broken than not beating at all. I wonder if she's hoping he's a promise of better days.

I don't let myself wonder anything else.

"We're watching Alex's game. Back later," I say without stopping, pulling Mateo outside with me. His hand stays in mine a second too long. My skin tingles like a new lifeline was carved with the trace of his finger.

"I like soccer," he says to break the silence. "I played when I was younger. But then I got too busy with cooking and school, plus I play basketball too. Still like to watch, though…"

His head bobs with the beat of some pop-ish love song on the radio. The window is down. I let my hand surf waves of warm air. This is what life felt like, I think, back before it happened. This. Normal. Happy.

We pull into the parking lot just as Nat is stepping out of her car.

"Natalie, right?" Mateo says, flicking his head in her direction. Her hair is pulled back in a high ponytail. She's wearing a green and yellow Hornets T-shirt, which is what all the girlfriends on Alex's soccer team wear to games. She waves.

"Mateo?" she asks, and I'm reminded just how talented of an actress she is. "Nat. Nice to see you outside of a kitchen. Hey, Anna."

I give her a quick squeeze, like this is what we do.

"Yeah, nice to see you girls in Technicolor," he says with a grin.

Nat throws back her head and laughs. It reminds me of Sameera.

"I like him," Nat says, as if Mateo isn't standing right next to me. She winks and walks ahead of us. I shake my head and make a mental note to strangle her later.

The team is already on the field, doing their ritual warmups. I know the whole sequence from when Joe used to play. They lift their legs in a sort of high march-skip, moving toward the bleachers and then dropping to the ground for five push-ups before gathering into a circle to dodge and weave in place. I look over at Mateo and roll my eyes.

"I used to find this hilarious. They look ridiculous out there."

"Used to?" He cocks his eyebrow. "Come to a lot of games with Nat? Or did you have a boy on this team too?"

"Nat. I don't have another connection to soccer," I say a little too quickly. I don't glance over, but I know Nat's shot me a curious look. We've always been able to do this too—feel what the other is thinking without having to confirm it. I lean against her as an answer.

"Nat and Alex have been together a long time. That equates to a lot of 'Go Hornets' cheers along the way. It's like a prerequisite of being a best friend, you know, to be the supportive wing-woman. I could probably go out there and play as good as those boys just from watching. Or not, since I spend most of my time buying popcorn, eating the popcorn, buying more popcorn, and then running for a slushie because salt levels have caused my body to go into full dehydration mode. Yup. Love soccer games."

I pull my sleeve up for a second, glance at the reminder I wrote to keep from yapping away.

And what I don't want to say is this: sitting beside Nat on the third row of cold metal bleachers brings me back to last year, when Alex's team broke out of its normal warm-up to form a human version of the number four. They stood there, staring straight ahead, while the speaker above announced a moment of silence for Joe O'Mally, whose old jersey number, four, would be retired from the summer league forever.

My parents were on the field. Dad accepted a frame with his brother's jersey, or a replica of it anyway. He shook hands with the coach. Walking back to the stands, Mom stayed a step or two behind.

Nat didn't see any of this because she squeezed her eyes shut tight. It's what I wanted to do, and she knew so without me saying it. I did coffin yoga sitting up that day. It was the only time I made it to three minutes without breathing. I passed out against Nat just as my parents were walking off the field.

"Take me to this divine popcorn you keep speaking of," Mateo says, offering his hand. He pulls me up and bumping his hip against mine, we walk toward the concession stand.

"But I'm paying," he adds.

Damn that dimple.

DAILY VERSE:
I think now it's time to get serious
about my work.

20

There has to be an explanation," Nat says. She's sitting on my unmade bed with a bag full of chocolate chips in her lap. Between bites, she continues pursuing all possibilities for why Mateo didn't try to kiss me (again) yesterday. I continue proving her logic is flawed.

"He's nervous because you're wild-child hot."

"Not possible: (a) I'm not, and (b) have you looked at him? Clearly he hasn't had a shortage of pretty girls batting their eyes in his direction."

"Whatever. Maybe he's suffering from severe halitosis."

"Nope. Breath smells like cinnamon. He leaned over to tell me what position he used to play in soccer, and I got a good whiff."

"Okay, he mentioned he knew the goalie on the other team from church. And then when you asked where he went, he said St. Mary's. So he's clearly Catholic. Maybe he's like, saving himself until marriage."

"Saving himself to the point of no kissing?"

"It happens."

"Doubtful."

"Girlfriend?"

"I don't think so." I get the feeling Mateo is about as honest as they get. He wouldn't omit information like that, not when he keeps saying things like "Thanks for the date." Of course, I believed in Joe's unwavering honesty. And that made me blind to his truths.

"Maybe he's getting over a cold and—" Nat stops dead. "Sorry," she says, tripping over every letter. "I didn't mean—"

"It's fine. And maybe. Doesn't matter. Should we get started?"

The real reason Nat is here has little to do with dissecting my non-existent love life. We're going to sneak into Joe's room while Mom is running errands and Bea's in summer school. (Bea's teachers let her hide a lot last year—under her desk, in the supply closet, coat room, etc.—but her vanishing acts left some serious holes in her necessary-for-third-grade skill sets.)

"Right. Yeah, okay. But I had this epiphany last night and I'll totally forget if I don't say it."

I roll out my hand for Nat to take the stage. She pops up and starts pacing the room, ignoring the cascade of tiny chocolate chips falling from her lap to the floor.

"So." She rubs her hands together. "Remember how we used to talk about the future? How we railed against the traditional zombie student apocalypse of stacking résumés to get into the good colleges to get the good jobs to make money and have babies and repeat the whole cycle as parents? We knew our passions. We knew ourselves. I think it might help now. To try and have a real conversation again."

Partly because she sounds like she's performing an impassioned monologue, I don't interrupt. I do, however, click on the small TV slumped against the bottom of my bookshelf. It's a Gramps special, with an old-school antenna and rounded screen. He rescued it from a dumpster and got it to work well enough to plug in an also-rescued Atari. Gramps hates waste. He hates the idea of TVs or typewriters or computers or radios exceeding their usefulness the minute something better comes along.

Nat exaggerates a sigh and sits cross-legged on my bed, waiting. I pick up the control and turn on Pac-Man. It doesn't take long for a red ghost to eat me. I match her sigh and toss the controller back into the bookshelf.

"Fine. What deep, philosophical musings would you like to discuss before we go pull my dead bruncle's room apart in search of clues to solve this mystery I-can't-even-think-of-without-wanting-to-puke?"

"Really, Anna? Do you have to be so mean?"

Part of me wants to scream YES. Part of me wants to

curl up next to my best friend and draw invisible elephants and sheep and airplanes with our fingers, like we used to do with Joe on lazy afternoons. Back then, I could see the nonexistent with ease.

"Look, I'm sorry. I don't have anything interesting to say, I guess. I don't have a passion anymore. And I doubt you want to talk about how life is basically a grenade with the pin half-pulled."

I don't tell her I wish it wasn't this way, or how much I'd love to rediscover the old me. I don't tell her I sometimes want to find a new first line. I don't tell her I want to believe that any of this, anything at all, matters.

Nat's face is hard to read. She comes over and plants a kiss on my temple.

"Come on," she says, holding out her hand. "Let's get this over with."

We creep into Joe's room even though no one is home. We're both jumpy and whispering.

"You do this side," Nat says, hushing as I trip over the one stack of books I didn't put back the other day. "I'll take the closet."

We work without speaking. His dresser gets rummaged. His books get pulled again. Rifling his closet, Nat discovers a ten dollar bill in a shirt pocket, a super violent video game I distinctly remember him telling Mom he got rid of, and a copy of a literary review that printed one of my stories.

It feels like we've been at this for two weeks but the clock in Joe's room is telling me it's been twenty minutes.

"This is crazy," Nat says. "We're never gonna find anything. We'll never really know."

"My counselor thinks I need a hobby."

"This is not a hobby."

"It's like a quest."

"It's like stupid."

"You don't have to help."

She stands in the middle of the room, her bare feet sinking into the ugly blue shag rug Joe insisted on keeping when we first moved into this house. Hands on hips, eyes in slits. Ah, yes, Nat's don't-mess-with-me face.

I'm half under Joe's bed, groping around for anything that doesn't feel like a stray sock or gum wrapper. As I pull my hand back, empty, my pinkie touches something cold. Snatching it into the light, I hold up a plain silver linked bracelet for Nat to see. There is a tiny bird charm attached near the clasp. Her eyes grow wide with surprise. We both know Sameera owns one piece of jewelry: a skinny leather cuff she wears only on special occasions. She is a big believer in the "no fuss, no muss" rules of getting dressed every day.

"Maybe the trail isn't cold after all," I say, swinging the bracelet like a hypnotist's pocket watch.

"Do you know who it belongs to?" Nat asks, arms crossed.

"Not yet," I say. "But I have an idea how to find out."

Daily Verse:
You can't ever let yourself think any-
body's too interested.

21

Three days later, Nat and Mateo and I are sitting around a small, square table in Third Eye coffee shop. My latte is getting cold. Mateo's hot chocolate was gone ten minutes ago, and Nat's still sipping her green tea with two squirts of honey. I recheck the buttons on one of my dad's old white Oxfords. I'm only wearing one extra twine necklace today, its black feathers matching the raven patch on my ripped-up jeans.

"Is whoever we're spying on here yet?" Mateo leans over while he whispers this. Nat rolls her eyes and flicks the bracelet on my arm.

I shake my head, but keep watching the front door. Thanks to some serious social media searches, I flushed out the schedules of four potential suspects. This is stop number one.

Mateo doesn't know the bracelet is evidence of Joe's cheating, though, because he still doesn't know about Joe. I told him Nat's worried Alex is messing around and that we found a bracelet in the backseat of his car. Today is supposed to be about trying to catch the owner by surprise. Nat wasn't pleased that I used her as cover, but she forgave me because that lie was only a tiny fraction of the words Mateo and I exchanged during our three hours on the phone last night.

"Here she comes," Nat says, twitching twice in the direction of the front door. Five minutes early for her shift, Helen glides into the Third Eye looking every bit like the perfect, hip coffee-joint barista. Flowing skirt, jingling anklet, black hair held back by a flower headband, tiny silver ring in her nose. She's obviously not allergic.

"Hey, Helen," I say, waving her over. She jingles toward us, hips swaying.

"Hey, y'all."

I forgot this about Helen. She talks like she's from the South, but she was born in Czechoslovakia. Her smoky eye makeup and bright-red lips have Mateo leaning back in his chair, just taking her in like some painting in a museum. I accidentally step on his foot. Hard.

"I was hoping I'd run into you," I say, sticking with the script. Nat, to her credit, is sulking. Her suspicious stare sells the whole thing, I think.

"I was in here the other day and I picked this up off the floor," I say, unclasping the bracelet. "One of the dudes behind the counter thought it might be yours, but you were already gone for the afternoon. I told him I'd just hold on to it until I saw you next."

Helen takes the bracelet from me, but she's already shaking her head no. "Nope, not mine. Pretty, though. I can tuck it into our lost and found box—"

"No, no, that's okay. Now that I think about it, I actually remember my friend Sarah has one just like this. She left here before me. It must have fallen off her wrist." I snatch the bracelet back and smack my forehead. "I'm such a space case."

Helen touches my hand.

"No worries. How is your family? How are y'all doing?" She uses the I-feel-sorry-for-you tone and I wince because Mateo is tilting his head and blinking like he's trying to figure out why she's asking.

"Oh, fine. Fine," I say. My hands are doing this weird manic waving thing. I can't get them to stop. I bump the table with my knee. Latte splashes on my shirt.

"Uh, I just remembered I have a voice lesson in ten minutes," Nat says, hopping up.

"Right. We better go." I give Nat a silent thank you.

Outside, a car is stopped in the middle of the road. The driver leans over the right front tire. There's a dead something at his feet. A cat. White with one black paw. The driver scratches his head and gets into his car. Backing up, he arcs a wide turn around the cat.

"Okay, that's awful," Nat says, her hand on Dolores's door handle.

"Don't you wonder why there's never a big pool of blood?" I ask.

Nat stares at me. "Don't be weird," she mouths.

"What?" I shrug.

Nat glares and thumbs toward Mateo. He's not paying any attention, though, because he's jogged into the street. He waits to make sure the white Cadillac cruising toward him slows to a stop. He reaches down, picks up the dead, half-squished cat, and carries it to the curb.

There is blood on his hands when he gets back to us.

"I'm going to run inside and wash this off," he says, flipping his palms up for us to see. "Do we have time?"

"Huh?" Nat says, glancing back and forth from the curb to Mateo. "Uh, oh. Yeah. I don't have a voice lesson. I just said that so we could keep going, since, eh, she obviously isn't the one."

"Ha. I figured."

He opens the door with his elbow and disappears inside.

"What just happened?" Nat asks.

"I have no idea," I say, shaking my head. "He has soft spot for roadkill?"

"That wasn't like a squirrel or a rat or something, Anna. It was probably someone's pet."

"Or a starving stray."

Her face starts to fall, like she's just remembered how

screwed up I am. But then she stares at the empty space in the road and smiles a little.

"Remember when we tried to start a roadkill cemetery in your backyard?" She laughs. "Here lies Chuck, his life cut short by a semi-truck."

"And here's Daisy, a chipmunk who didn't realize the middle of the street was a bad place to get lazy," I add, glancing over at the limp shell of the cat. "We were weird."

"You were weird. I was precocious."

"Hey guys," Mateo says when he reaches the car. "Want to take a little break from super sleuthing?"

"No," I say at the exact same time Nat says, "Yes!"

"I think this lady wins," he says, nodding toward Nat, "considering we're on the chase for her possible…you know. Problem."

Nat sort of snorts, before adding, "Yeah, Anna. I think that's only fair. So do you have something else in mind?"

"Anything else works for me," he says. "No offense."

"None taken. I can only imagine how boring it would be to spend a day trying to prove my boyfriend is cheating on me."

I give her laser beam death eyes.

We end up driving in circles. Or squares, since we just keep going around and around different variations of the same city blocks. Nat hums along with the radio. Driving with no destination like she doesn't seem to mind one bit.

"Okay, how is this better than solving our Very Important Mystery?" I ask.

"Because sometimes solving the mystery isn't a good thing?" Mateo tries.

"No. Wrong. The 'Very Important' part clearly makes it necessary to solve."

"Did you guys ever play Clue growing up?" Mateo tries. Again.

"I love Clue!" Nat says. "I always want to be Miss Scarlett."

"Dude. She's kind of a hussy," Mateo says, laughing.

"What? She's Hollywood glamour at its finest."

"Are you guys kidding me right now?" I bite down hard to keep from yelling.

"What's wrong with a little cruising?" Mateo asks, reaching forward, between the seats.

He brushes his fingers against my arm.

I hold firm.

"It's not like there's anything interesting to see. I know every inch of this city already, thanks, and all driving around does is remind me I don't want to be here anymore."

"Whoa. A little harsh." Mateo sits back when he says this. "Anna, you really think you know this area? Every part, huh?"

"My Gramps used to have a shop one block over. And I've lived in this town my whole life. So, yeah, I'm sure. Every part."

"If you say so," Mateo says, leaning up again to push my shoulder, like a challenge. To Nat, he says, "We're only two blocks from the coolest spot in town, and I bet neither of you even know it exists. Think Anna will allow me the pleasure of proving her wrong?"

Nat clucks her tongue. Looks at me an extra-long second, and says, "Show me the way, my friend."

He gives Nat directions to go two blocks east. It takes us into Old Town's gut, past The Repair Shop. My Gramps is a literal guy. Since nothing else ever went in the space, his gold lettering is still in the window. Except the R and E are peeled away, so it looks more like The Pair Shop. Underneath, someone spray painted what appears to be big white boobs.

"Stop here," Mateo says, motioning toward a line of empty parking spaces. He jumps out and opens my door. On one corner, there's a guy painted metallic silver. When I say painted, I mean, like, painted from his top hat to his wing-tip shoes. He's standing statue-still on top of a milk crate. Mateo digs a couple crumpled dollars from his pocket and drops them in the bucket next to the crate. It only has one other dollar inside it. For a moment, it seems Mr. Living Statue is having an epileptic seizure; he shakes and convulses and twitches, but never falls from his silver box. A flow of crazy dance moves follows. And then, as abrupt as those shimmies started, they freeze. His closed eyelids glitter like metal beams after a rainstorm.

"Cool," Nat says behind me.

"Yeah," Mateo agrees.

"Except it's not like this is a super busy part of town. Why would he waste his time?" I ask.

There are pages upon pages of art tacked into the glass-less frames. The one I'm standing next to has a watercolor farm on top, with a tall tree and a tire swing and tiny specks of wind visible in the sky. When I go to pull it off, Mateo pulls my hand away.

"Unwritten rule." He smiles. "No peeking. The past is the past, you know what I mean?"

"She might not know what you mean," Nat calls from a little way away. She reaches up and traces some of the spray-painted sky above her. "But she could sure use a lesson."

"You could spend a lifetime here and not see everything," Mateo says, not pressing the point. "Or you could come back tomorrow and it might look totally different."

"What makes you such an expert in the underground art world?" I ask. I walk to the next frame. Inside it is a pencil drawing of a guy a few years older than us. He's got this unfiltered mischief in his face, the kind that disappears after age ten or so in real life. I can't help matching his smile.

"Wow," I murmur, stealing Nat's phrase. "This one is so…real. I almost feel like this guy is going to open his mouth and crack a joke."

I motion for Mateo to come look, but he stays rooted where he is.

"You don't think I know art, huh?"

"What do you mean? You cook. You're a chef." I stare at him.

"He can hear you, you know," Mateo says, walking away. "Come on, we're going to the alley over here."

I hear them leaving together, chatting like old friends. Nat laughs three times. I don't turn around and follow, though. I'm staring at statue dude. Not because I think he's cool. Truth be told, he looks ridiculous. I stare because I want to see him blink. I wait to see his chest rise or fall. I stiffen too, open my eyes wide.

But then Mateo is beside me again, and his fingers are warm when they lace through mine.

"Come with me. I want to show you something," he says, lips against my ear.

I hesitate, searching the statue's face. The blank stare I've been trying to master is there, effortless. Instead of staying and trying for nineteen minutes at least, to find the same emptiness, I let Mateo pull me away. And that's when it hits me: no matter how much I want it to be true, I can't be dead and alive all at once.

22

"Wow. Wow. Wow. Wow. Wow." Nat's a tape recorder stuck on one word as she walks up and down the alley.

Both sides are covered with graffiti, from ground to rooftop. It isn't gang tags or boobs on a window. It's blended color and portraits of people. It's the dirty brown river cutting through town. Giant, empty auto factories cast shadows against painted waters. Cars once made here are reborn on brick. There are full moons and silhouettes. Street dances. This is a story, mapped across walls, created by many different hands.

A row of real picture frames, sprayed white and drilled into the bricks, runs along at eye level. Inside, art is stacked on top of art: paper drawings and charcoal smudges and acrylic canvases and dimpled watercolors. Each frame has something in it—a sunset; a girl standing by a tree; an abstract piece my Gran would love; a couple, eyes cast down and toward each other. The frames run the length of the wall.

"What is this place?" I ask when I find my breath.

"Ha. Told you."

"Yeah, yeah."

"Admit it."

"I don't have a clue what you mean."

"Is 'wrong' not a word that exists in your vocabulary?"

I roll my eyes. Mateo grabs my hand and holds it to his chest. My skin glows, matches a painting of sun on the river. I try to pull away, but he holds tight.

"Fine. Okay. I've never been here."

"It's the best spot in town," Mateo says with obvious appreciation. He stops and catches my eye. "And right now, it's more beautiful than ever."

As I walk, Mateo stays a few steps behind. He's telling us how the alley got transformed from some garbage-strewn, no-nothing place. A bunch of street artists got together and did a blitz paint one night. More and more people started coming and adding all their best and most detailed works, and then the frames got added and now all these non-spray-paint artists come down and tack up their work.

"It's this totally organic, anonymous art show. Every so often someone else comes and covers up what was there before," he says.

"Right. Okay."

"Huh?"

"Maybe I know about this place because art is art. Cooking. Painting. Drawing." He stares past me, to the alley's dead end. His hands shove deep in the pockets of his jeans.

"That sounds stupid," he adds. "Look, we better go. We all have to be at work in an hour."

I watch him walk away, wanting to memorize everything. But he turns the corner before I get the chance.

———

We drop Mateo back at his Jeep and dash over to my house, where Nat left her work clothes. My dad's red Corvette is in the driveway. It's the most clichéd part of this mid-life crisis he's having. Normally, I don't miss an opportunity to tell him so.

"Shit." Right now, I don't feel like telling him anything. "Ten bucks says he's been here an hour and still can't find Bea. Will you just go get our clothes? Or go change and grab mine? I don't want to see him."

Nat doesn't say anything, but she gets out and walks toward the front door. When it opens, I see my dad give Nat a quick hug before ducking his head outside. His shaggy black curls are unkempt. His green O'Mally eyes lock on the car, and me. I drop my gaze to the floor. When neither of your daughters will show their face for you, it's time to take the hint.

"Well, that was fun," Nat hisses at me ten minutes later, tossing a shirt, skirt, and shoes in my general direction. "Your mom followed me into your room peppering me with questions about how you are doing. I was so flustered I accidently stepped on Bea's hand. She was under your bed, and gave me a good kick in the shin for busting her hiding spot. And then, to top it all off, your dad invited me to Sunday dinner at his house next week, adding it would be very nice to bring you along. He looks sad. I know that's not what you want to hear, but it's true."

"You're right, I don't. But thanks. I know I owe you one," I say, shimmying out of my jeans as she pulls away from Dysfunctional Central.

"We'll never be even," she replies with a sad smile, pulling a fistful of bobby pins out of her tiny skirt pocket and tossing them into my lap.

DAILY VERSE:
What I feel is not in the human
vocabulary.

23

I needed two consecutive rounds of coffin yoga this morning, my eyes burning more from exhaustion than the no-blinking rule. I only got three hours of sleep because of a back and forth text-a-thon with Mateo, filled with stupid questions like "If you could be any animal what would it be?" Me: armadillo, him: chameleon. Which isn't even an animal. I curled up with my cell phone when the battery died, and when I plugged my phone in this morning, a new text from Mateo popped up. It said, "I'm still here."

I have to get back into balance. The yoga didn't do much. The pressure I use pushing ink into skin as I write my daily verse isn't helping either.

I'm still fogged between night and morning when the

phone rings. I check the caller ID two seconds too late, after I've already hit "talk" on the portable phone.

"Hey, honey."

"Don't 'honey' me, Dad." I keep my voice cool.

"Anna." He says it firm, like he gets to still be the parent. "I know you are angry with me, but—"

"But nothing, Jack."

"Don't call me that."

"I won't call you anything if I have my way." I slam the receiver back into its cradle.

"Who was that?" Mom asks, coming in from the backyard.

"It was a sales call," I say with a shrug. "Nothing we want to buy. I'm going to the park with Nat, okay—"

The phone starts to ring again, and I grab it before the call even registers.

"Hell-o?"

"Is that a way to answer the phone?" Gramps scolds. "You sound like a prison inmate."

"Oh, hey, Gramps. Sorry. Thought you were going to be someone else."

"Well, I'm not. Are we still on for lunch today?"

I swear under my breath. Mom swats a hand in my direction. I have to work early, and I found a perfect timeline for Sarah Sallenton. She updated her status last night saying she'd be playing with her dog at the park from 12 to 1 p.m. today, if anyone wants to join her. It's already noon. If I go with Gramps, I'll never catch her in time.

"Uh, actually Gramps, I sorta double-booked. Do you care if we go tomorrow instead?"

"Is 'double-booked' code for going back to bed all day?"

"Nope," I say, aware my mother is leaning in the doorway, pretending to dig dirt from her nails. "It means I made plans. Plans involving leaving the house and hanging out in a park. With people."

"Well in that case," he says, his voice bright, "tomorrow works great. I haven't been fishing in two days, so I think I'll head on out to the river instead."

"See you tomorrow."

———

The park proves status updates can't always be trusted. The Internet isn't able to predict when someone named Sarah might change her mind on how the hours between 12 and 1 p.m. might be spent. I don't feel like going home, so I pull into Nat's driveway and honk twice. Our horn code for "want to get sushi?"

The huge oak tree next to Nat's window blocks her from view, but after my second round of beeps, I hear her yell down, "Fine! But you're buying!"

During lunch, Mom calls six times. I ignore her. I'm not in the mood to check in.

One hour and several yaki-nori rolls later, I drop Nat back home with plans to meet her at work by 3:30 p.m. We have to drive separately since she's going to Alex's cousin's bar mitzvah later.

When I pull onto my street, the first thing I notice is our garage door. It's open, but Mom's car is gone. Mom's kind of a freak about locking the house since Dad's not around. She won't admit it, but I know she sometimes sleeps with the phone already dialed to 911 at night. I wonder if Dad's been here. He still has a garage door opener. And a key. I wish Mom would take both away, and I make a mental note to tell her this.

I don't have to step all the way inside the front door to understand something is wrong. There's nothing but silence. The heavy kind I know too well.

A note with handwriting worse than Bea's is taped to the end of the banister.

"Gone to hospital. Bea next door with Mrs. G. Gramps is there."

Gramps is where? Mrs. G's? The hospital?

I pick up the phone and dial, taking my time to punch each of the seven digits.

"Mrs. G? It's Anna—"

"Oh, honey, God. So much has happened to your poor family, to you girls. Are you okay?"

At this point, it seems the answer is a definite no. I bite the corner of my lip because I refuse to say it.

"Your Gramps, honey, he fell into the—"

"Go ahead and send Bea over here, please." I don't want to hear any more.

Two minutes later, Bea bursts in like a stray dodging a dog catcher.

"Gramps is gonna die," she sobs through a fountain of snot and saliva. I know it's true because even in the worst of situations, my sister does not ever choose to acknowledge heart hurts.

When our dog, Danny, died, Bea found him all stiff in the backyard. Joe ran out and scooped his beagle up, but Bea just pointed to the swarming flies and said, "Did you know flies puke and eat it every time they land?" When her best friend, Georgia, moved (weirdly) to Georgia, she stood in the driveway watching their car go. Her only comment? How car exhaust smells like rotten Easter eggs. And when my parents told us they were going from legally separated to officially divorced three months ago, she honed in on the china cabinet and asked where dust comes from, and how it decides where it wants to settle.

"He didn't breathe for like, twenty million minutes or something!" she wails, tearing away from and back into my arms over and over again. "Was underwater! He was in his, his, his fishing boat, you know, the one that always looks like it might sink, and something happened and he, he fell in the river…and…and…"

I clutch my sister tighter and tighter and tighter. I shake my head hard, as if that can push back my own hysterics. Air won't reach deeper than my throat. It's dry and every breath burns and chokes me. We sway back and forth, not talking. Acid keeps rising up from my stomach, a rolling burn that comes from the kind of crying Bea's doing. It's different than sweaty toddler tantrums or the sobs of bitchy girls who don't get their way. It's raw and lost and frightening, and it reminds me of broken promises and the moment when you start seeing the world for what it really is.

It's just pure pain…not a bad thing.

24

Gramps.
I close my eyes.

"Are you going to start the car?" Bea asks. She's sitting in the front seat, which may be against the law. It definitely breaks one of our mother's cardinal rules of safety.

Gramps.

The new words on my arm are shaky. The letters aren't quite straight. I didn't have to look up a quote. I know this one by heart. I need this reminder. I need to carry it with me. To physically see it and feel it and—

"Anna, are you gonna start the car?"

I turn the key.

When I told Bea we were leaving, she didn't ask any questions. Instead, she tucked her feet inside the bunny slippers that are a half size too small now, and got in the car. While we drive, she folds herself into an accordion position, legs and knees tucked against arms, tucked against stomach. Her eyes are squeezed shut. I can see her fingers popping. 1, 2, 3, 4, 5, 6, 7, 8, 9, 10. Again and again and again.

Gramps.

He's our rock. He's the only person who didn't sink when the lines and anchors of our family were severed in the last year. He's the one who taught us kids how to fold origami, how to deliver words inside airplanes and stars and jumping frogs. He's the one who knows what to say to my mom. When Dad left, she abandoned any pretend ability she had to still be the glue for our family. We're all broken eggshells, but he knows how to step light. He keeps us from being crushed into flecks too tiny to see.

He knows to say things like, "We all hope to lose loved ones the same way we are supposed to lose our children: slowly, in small pieces, as time goes by. But no matter how it happens, no matter when we have to let go, we aren't ever ready. To feel all of that, it's okay."

Gramps.

Drive. Breathe. Put on turn signal. Stop at stop sign. Drive. Breathe.

Gramps.

He doesn't get to die. He doesn't get to leave. He doesn't get to become another reason people look at us, then look away, because our level of suck is toxic. Because we are the people who make others whisper thanks for their own tedious lives.

We pull into the hospital as an ambulance blasts by, lights and sirens still going strong after parking outside the Emergency Room.

"Don't, Bea," I groan as she shimmies out of the passenger-side door and slides immediately to the ground. By the time I get over to her side, only an errant bunny ear peeks out from under the car. I drop down to my hands and knees. Little chunks of gravel dig into my palms.

"Bea, it's okay. I'm going to set you up in a family waiting room. Remember those? They're smaller and have toys and beanbags and giant stuffed animal pillows. You were okay here, when"—deep breath—"Joe was sick."

The bunny ear disappears.

"I already know where you are," I say, reaching my hand out and tugging on her heel. "Besides, who knows what is under there. Parking lots are disgusting."

"Two wads of gum. One pink and one blue. The blue one still has a smell, like raspberry maybe." My sister's voice is matter-of-fact. "Oh, and I think there's a dead one of those crawly insects with a million legs next to my ear, but I can't turn my head enough to check. I don't wanna come out."

A handful of people walk through the parking lot. One woman starts coming our way. She only sees me slumped against the car. I watch as she stops short, acts like she's digging something out of her purse, and makes a sharp turn in the opposite direction.

Under the car, Bea is quiet.

A few years ago, I used to beg to put Bea to bed at night, because she loved to listen to me recite my poems. She loved this one poem about the moon best, because she liked the sound it made against her ear. When Mrs. Risson was still my favorite teacher—and not just Mom's frequent let's-talk-about-how-messed-up-Anna-is lunch date—she made me listen to recordings of writers reading their work. My whole sophomore year was a lesson in listening. In picking up ways to make words become music.

A poem of my own will make Bea come out, I'm sure of it. I'm desperate enough to try, so I clear my throat. Crack my knuckles, one finger at a time.

Moon was the first word I learned.
Hitched to a fencepost,
luminous hole in
infinite night,

The bunny slippers reappear. I pause. So does Bea.

your hand in mine
secrets of a mother, daughter
pass between us, puckered kiss
of sound—

Legs, torso, shoulders. She twists back into view, resting against my lap for the final verse.

a single syllable. Moon.

"Okay," she says, resolved. I give her a hug. This one isn't so tight. I'm trying to say it will be okay, without having to use any more words. Without having to lie.

We walk through the hospital's revolving door. I know we need to keep the forward momentum going, but the smell of sick people hits and we both misstep.

"I don't want to," Bea whispers, her clipped fingernails digging into my skin. I drag her over to the Emergency Room waiting area. We slide into pale peach plastic seats.

"We'll take our time," I say. She leans against me. The whole of her weight shifts onto my side.

"I'm going to make a phone call." I announce this to myself as much as to my sister. She nods and closes her eyes.

I can't talk to Nat right now. I'm not ready. I wait a second, and then push hard against his number.

"Hey, wild child," he answers after two rings.

"Hi."

"Are you okay?"

The way he asks, like he knows something must be wrong, it kind of breaks me. All of a sudden I'm vomiting sentence fragments. And tears.

I'm crying. For the first time in a year.

I let it all spill. The things he didn't know about me, the things that made him different, for not knowing. I purge and purge and purge, even if it will ruin everything. Even though I need to hang up and find my mom and need to not let Bea see me falling apart and lock this shell of a girl I am up tighter than ever. But I don't want to stop. I tell him about Gramps, his paper hobbies, his bushy eyebrows, his ability to forgive my dad. Saying his name is razor against wrist.

Words and sobs tumble, slam, flood out of me. I almost tell him what I did. I almost tell him why Joe's death is my fault. But I hold that one secret inside. I bury it deeper than ever.

Surge after surge of pain grips me. There's no order to how much awful can happen, I cry. No rules about how many people you can lose or how many ways you can be torn apart. Nobody gets piled with so much unless it's a soap opera or melodrama. If I'd only gone to lunch…I say this too, over and over and over and over again until the words become threadbare and I go back to saying we all stop existing and none of it matters and maybe that's great because what I really want, what I really need, is to have it stop, to stop for five minutes—

He silences me with a hush. Not the mean kind. More like his voice is making his body reach through the connection, holding me close.

Mateo keeps hushing. My sobs slow to sharp gasps. I suck in and exhale, suck in and exhale until I can find a rhythm.

Then I whisper goodbye and he whispers back, "I'm still here."

The chair next to me is empty. My sister is gone again.

The front desk lady meets my panicked expression with a matched look of pity and flicks her super-long red fingernail toward the gift shop.

———

A half hour later, Bea and I sit in the smaller family waiting room on floor five. The Intensive Care Unit is located one floor below the crazy people unit. We've been in this room; it hasn't changed. Kleenex boxes on almost every chair, it reeks like funeral home, old-lady perfume, bleach, and invisible, already-sobbed tears. I turn on the television and hand the remote to Bea, who is clinging to her new teddy bear. Her new $25, five-inch-tall, plastic-eyed bear. Gift shops are such a rip-off.

"I'm going to go find Mom, okay?"

"That sounds funny," Bea mumbles through a mouth full of $4.99 Kit Kat. Rip-off.

"What are you talking about?"

"It sounds like Mom's playing hide-and-seek."

"You'd know," I mutter, walking out of the room.

I don't have to look long. One corner later, I almost run into my father. His back is turned to me. Mom is behind him, facing the hallway wall. She leans into it, forehead touching the cream-colored paint. Her blonde hair is only half held back; clumps of loose curls stick out every which way.

I want to back up and grab my sister and drive home. The way my dad bends toward her, the way their hands almost touch; it's too private, like conversations falling silent whenever one of us kids walked into the room after Joe died. Or maybe like walking in on the thing you don't ever want to catch your parents doing. So raw and close. I blush at their unspoken communication, the knowing that comes with being together for twenty-two years.

It's also the first time my mother looks old.

DAILY VERSE:
I wanted to take responsibility for
my own actions.

25

The four days that followed ran together in a sea of blurry moments, all smeared between hospital and home. Time stops in waiting rooms, only restarting at dark, when visiting hours are over and I trudged back home. And every night, I pulled into my driveway to see Mateo sitting on my front porch. Sometimes, he rested his hand on mine. Mostly, we just sat without talking.

Last night, Mom caught me standing in the hospital's fifth-floor hallway staring into space like a ghost. Then she had a long, whispery talk with Liza and decided I need a normal routine. Which, I said, means hospital. home. eat. sleep. repeat. She does not agree.

"I am not going," I say with such force my swollen eyes start burning again.

"Oh yes you are," Mom snaps back. She's rifling

through Bea's closet, pulling out pajamas and T-shirts and pants and underwear. Bea's already strapped in Dad's bucket seat. She went without a fight.

"Your sister is going with your father and you are going to work. I don't want to hear another word about it."

"Well, you don't have to hear anything. You can watch me shake my head no."

"Anna, I'm not doing this. For once, it is not about you. Go to work. I'm going to the hospital. Go. To. Work."

"Not happening."

I walk away.

She grabs my arm, right across the words I wrote this morning. It seems so long ago now.

"Go to work, or I put you in the car with your father and he drives you straight to BrightLight. I cannot—I cannot—worry about you. In fact—" She pauses and yells out Bea's open door for my dad. "In fact, your dad will drop you off at your job site. And pick you up."

"Don't open your mouth to argue," Dad says, thundering up the stairs. The two of them stand next to Bea's dresser, staring at me. I turn and sulk out of the room. My dad's voice follows, asking Mom if the suitcase is ready and if Bea still sleeps with Larry the one-eyed penguin. And then he pauses and asks if she remembers frantically packing the same suitcase in the middle of the night Joe's first weekend at college when he got caught drinking and proceeded to mouth off to campus security. How Mom brought four toothbrushes and no pants, and how she walked into the police station the next morning in her neon green pajama bottoms, which Joe claimed made his hangover worse.

Mom laughs a little. I shut the door to my room. I remember that weekend too. We woke to Gramps and his skyscraper plate of pancakes. Except he told us Dad and Mom went to parents' weekend. Joe never told me the truth.

Silence is beginning to say more than I ever imagined it could.

————

Nat's afraid to talk to me. She keeps staring and looking away when I catch her. Then she glances over and smiles, shy and nervous. She hasn't called once since she heard about Gramps. I'm her best friend, yet she has no clue how to deal with this because I'm that big of a freak. A freak who should wear a "Don't Get Too Close or You Might Die" sign around her neck.

But Gramps isn't dead. Not yet. They don't know what happened. Maybe a heart attack. Maybe a seizure. Maybe a stroke. Maybe a granddaughter who ditched out on lunch. Lots of tests. Medically induced coma. At least he was only in the water a minute, not twenty million. Someone fishing nearby watched the whole thing happen and pulled him out.

I shouldn't be here, shouldn't be working right now. I need to be at the hospital.

"How are you?"

I turn around and Mateo catches my elbow.

"I'm fine. I'm fine."

He lets go and I move fast in the other direction. Do a lightning round of appetizer deliveries before Nat nearly bowls me over in an effort to get the empty tray from my hands.

"I'm sorry," she blurts.

"I'm fine."

"Oh my God, Anna. No you aren't. I'm just...I didn't know what to say."

"I'm. Fine."

"I should have called. I tried a ton of times but I kept hanging up and—"

I shove the tray at her, not sure why I'm so mad.

"Let it go, okay? I'm FINE." I storm in the other direction, opening the first door I see and ducking inside.

This event space is a defunct restaurant that's now rented for weddings and reunions and company parties, like the one we're working tonight. I'm standing in a big closet, probably originally built for bulk dry goods like flour and napkins and straws. Now it's empty and dark. Not even a shelf left. I lean against the cold wall.

I don't know how long I'm hiding before the door opens. I squint. The door shuts. Someone else is breathing.

"I saw you come in, and I thought maybe you needed a minute. But...you've been in here a while."

"Why are you so nice to me? What is it about me—

me out of all these flirty, happy, bouncy, beautiful girls out there—that's so interesting?"

Mateo is quiet.

He moves closer without making a sound. Presses his body to mine, trapping me against the wall. I tense. He's warm. I shiver.

Our lips are almost touching. He smells like garlic and basil and something I can't quite place. Sorrow, squeezed like lemons? I hold my breath, afraid to move.

He still doesn't answer. I close my eyes, let the dark get darker. Let this boy I don't want to want but want all the same set his lips against mine. They rest there, a question, waiting. I press back.

When I pause and bring an inch of space between us, Mateo slides his hand behind my neck. His breath hitches with want, with the pull we both feel.

Then his mouth meets mine again and everything gets very fuzzy and exploding and wonderful for a minute.

Until the door flies open, a pair of hands reaching into the closet, dragging us into the light.

"You," the head chef snaps, her gray ponytail swinging as she whips away, and back to, Mateo, "are fired. Get. Out. Now."

We both stand there, assimilating into undarkness. A body, electrified, sends every bit of oxygen to lungs and limbs, like trying not to drown. Words stop making sense because no neurons are firing to help process them.

Mateo comes around first.

"Please. Nancy—please. They could take away my spot for this—"

"Out."

"I'm sorry," he pleads.

I am rooted beside him, willing my particles to rearrange themselves into part of the wall.

"For what?" Nancy says, flicking her hand in my direction. "Getting to know the anatomy of a girl you shouldn't be messing with? I told you already there's a line of kids waiting to take your place. I don't do second chances, no matter who you are."

"Please—"

"Out."

Without so much as an exhale, Mateo pulls off his apron and pushes out the restaurant's back door into the light of early evening. I watch his back from the slit window.

"Forty-five applicants for a student chef position, and the one I pick, the one with the most promise, ends up trying to get in a waitress's pants, and burns an entire batch of tortes in the process. He doesn't deserve to be—" Nancy pauses, as if just remembering I'm still standing here. She lets out a disgusted snort. "Get to work. You aren't my problem."

For a minute I stay cemented to the tile floor.

Mateo is already out of sight. The window is empty. Its view shows only brown, weedy grass and the corner of a green Dumpster.

I want to go after him, but I don't move. His Jeep roars to life. Tires burn against pavement as it squeals away.

Like I said, there should be a sign around my neck: Stay Away. Life Wrecker.

I don't care about what will happen to me anymore. I walk up to the head of the wait staff, an always bubbling college-age girl named Mary. I tap her on the back, and announce without second thought: *Hi, Mary. Sorry, but I quit.*

Outside, while I wait for Dad to get me, I think about Mateo's lips against mine. I've never been very good at letting go.

I'm not hung up on anybody's idea of who I should be.

26

We are sitting at Sabroso, a Mexican restaurant in Old Town. It's near the hospital. Rays of sunlight filter through windows hazy with soap residue. The teal vinyl booth in the front is faded in crooked streaks. I pick at the corner. There is a knife-like slit with foam pushing out of it. A plate of nachos quite possibly twice the size of my head and towering with a questionable meat substance sits on the table. Are cats supposed to be used in place of chicken in Mexican or Chinese restaurants?

"You can't call emergency intervention because my grandpa is currently a vegetable and I am now using this as a diversionary tactic."

Nat's eyes go wide and her mouth hangs half-open even though some semi-chewed nacho chips are still in it. She swallows with exaggerated effort.

"Awful. Seriously. That was cross-the-line awful. You are sitting here refusing to talk about anything but an accelerated plan to find Joe's secret girlfriend—"

"Not girlfriend," I say, pointing a fork at Nat's face.

She looks pained, and pushes the utensil back to the table.

"Here's the thing, Anna. You don't have a dash between your born date and death date, but everything you are doing right now—obsessing over this thing with Joe, quitting your job, practically living at the hospital—it's flashing warning signs. You can't go there again. You can't do this to your family."

"My family. Right, Nat. Let's review what I've already done to my family: one member is dead. One is dying. Plus, there's one divorce in progress. I can trace all of those things back to me. So thanks, but I don't need you telling me what I can and can't do."

Gramps can't open his eyes, can't squeeze Mom's hand. Things keep shutting down and nobody has an answer. Life support is beginning to feel like death avoidance. It's only been a year and some change since Joe. And now, here I am again, waiting, trying to stop hoping. And drowning in what I could have done to save someone I love.

Nat and I glare at each other until the short waitress who isn't a ton older than us comes up and pours water in our empty glasses.

"*Mucho gracias*," I say.

"Um, you're welcome."

A fly lands on Nacho Mountain and I think about Bea and our dead dog and insect barf. My fork twirls in my fingers. Nat is frustrated. She pushes back against the booth and crosses her arms.

"Let's try again. It's good that your mom said you can watch Bea for the rest of your 'summer job' so long as you agree to relocate from the waiting room to home. So, no crazy Bible camp. That's a positive thing." She's letting me know we can drop the subject.

Nat stirs her ice water with a spoon. She tucks hair behind her ears. Glancing around the near-empty restaurant, she tries to come up with more common ground.

"Maybe you should add Laura to the list," she says in this resigned tone.

I ought to be glad she's trying to help, but come on. I mean, Laura and Sameera are practically sisters. That goes well beyond everyone being shocked Joe and the mystery girl were together. A Laura + Joe combination would be more like a mushroom cloud of destruction.

I may not have known Joe's every secret, but I do know it isn't her.

"Seriously? I am not wasting my time there."

"All right. Whatever. Just trying to make conversation. What are you going to do about Mateo? He hasn't tried calling?"

I rip the paper napkin on my lap and roll the pieces back and forth. I stare at the clock on the wall. It's one of those generic office-looking ones, black rimmed with a grease-spattered plastic half-bubble covering the numbers and sharp, spiked hands.

"At least answer me."

I sigh. She's not going to give it up.

"No. I haven't heard from him. I got him fired, Nat. Fired from a job that he needed to keep in order to stay in good standing for the culinary program he's supposed to attend this fall. The program he's supposed to attend in order to be basically guaranteed a spot in a top culinary institute or restaurant, post graduation."

"You have to stop doing this," Nat says, sitting up straight. "You have to stop blaming yourself for everything bad that happens. He kissed you. Not the other way around. What happened after wasn't your fault."

I stab the center of the nacho pile. My fork stands up all by itself. Nat groans.

"I wish I'd paid more attention in statistics and probabilities class so I could give you some hard and fast truths about how this last year has been a huge, random accident," she says.

"Joe's death—the odds were 1,728,234 to one."

Nat stares at me.

"But that's not taking into account the Anna factor," I add. "I'm sure if we add what I did to Joe, or how I cancelled plans with Gramps, or how I kissed Mateo back, the formula's results for odds of trouble when spending time with Anna O'Mally would be more like a three to one ratio."

The way Nat twists her mouth makes me wonder if she's calculating the risks of being my friend. It's like playing with matches in the middle of a gas station, and we both know it. I pull money from my pocket and motion for the bill.

"No worries, Nat. It's all good. I'm on a mission right now that doesn't require backup. I'll get lunch. You go ahead and get out of here."

She doesn't argue. I can see her pause when she's outside, though, digging in her enormous red purse until she finally produces her phone. It's decorated with gold star stickers. When she starts walking again, it's three huge steps in my direction, until she's standing on the other side of the dirty window, knocking on the glass. Holding up the phone, she points and smiles.

The screen says, "Mateo."

27

She's still leaning up against the orange stucco building when I come out ten minutes later.

"You totally want to hear what he had to say."

"Nope. I totally don't," I respond, plugging my ears for good measure.

"I'll sing it at the top of my lungs, operetta style, if you don't listen to me right this second."

"You wouldn't."

Four glass-breaking notes later and I'm yelling, "Okay!"

"He only hasn't called because he feels bad. He said he was pissed at first, but then realized it was stupid to be pissed."

"Wow. Impressive vocabulary."

Pinching my lips shut with two fingers, Nat tells me to button up and let her finish.

"He said he thought it would be best to leave you alone. But then he told me he couldn't leave you alone. Because you've been on his mind, like, constantly. Honest to God, that's what he said. In fact, he said he's never had this happen—where he couldn't get into cooking or whatever and just tune everything out—until now. It didn't sound cheesy, by the way. He didn't even ask to talk to you when I said you were right inside. He just asked how you were."

She hops up and down a little, triumphant.

"See! Something good! He really likes you, and hello, he could have any freaking girl in Chef Nancy's kitchen. Or could have had. When he still had a job. Eh, this is beside the point. He likes you, and you like him, and together that equals something good!"

"How did he have your number?" is all I say in return.

Nat shrugs. "We exchanged digits when he took us to the alley. And we talked a couple times right after your Gramps…when I was being an awful friend and not calling. He's a good guy, Anna. Don't make trouble exist where it doesn't."

"I'll keep that in mind," I say, walking away. I can tell she's standing there, maybe perfecting her sad fadeout shot, but I don't look over my shoulder. Instead I pull out my phone and call Sarah-of-the-stinky-roses.

Above me, thunder rumbles, long and loud. The sky hangs thick with greenish-gray clouds, like it has the flu. Sarah answers just as rain starts falling. And within two minutes of talking, I've got her. The nervous laugh. The fast "yes" to coffee. The way she held the "o" too long when she said Joe's name. And the last words she says before hanging up: "There's things I want to say."

It's like he's right here, watching me unfurl his little riddle, wing by wing. Maybe this was his intent all along. To make me guess. To tell me his secret by way of clues, not sobbing confessions.

Maybe there's more I don't know about Joe. Maybe there's more to discover about a person I thought I knew so well, but didn't really know at all.

28

Sarah's already at Third Eye when I get there. She's wearing her blonde-streaked hair in two braids that reach to the top of her tank-top dress. She's also wearing a bunch of silver and beaded bracelets on one tan arm. Three silver rings on her hands. There's a splash of freckles across her nose, which she's twitching a little while fiddling with the string of her tea bag. She's got that *au naturel* prettiness Joe loved and she's nervous. Strike two.

"Hey, Anna!" she says, and then looks around because we both realize her voice came out all rushed and loud and off key.

"Sarah," I say with a tight-lipped smile. "Thanks for meeting me. It's nice to see you."

I stretch out my hand to give hers a squeeze and catch

her checking out the bracelet dangling from my wrist. She meets my eyes and quickly looks away.

"I was surprised you called," she says. "Can I buy you something?"

"Huh?"

"To drink. Can I go order you something?"

"Oh, no. I'll get it. Thanks."

When I get back to the table with my latte, Sarah's brought over a game of checkers and is stacking the pieces in two neat rows.

"My brothers and I always called checkers smoke and fire," she says without looking up. "Because the pieces are black and red."

I sip the frothy milk and tell her I prefer chess.

"Joe was on my mind the other day when my sister-in-law and I were at the mall. One of those all-Christmas, all-the-time stores just opened."

I raise my eyebrows and nod, to say both "go on" and "so what?"

"Didn't Joe ever tell you the story of Christmastime our junior year?" Sarah's getting animated now, giggling and leaning forward.

"We were partners for a history project on the Constitution. Crazy boring work. So we decided to take a break and went for a walk around my block. One of our neighbors goes a little nutty with plastic Santas and snowmen and nativity scenes. When we passed the house, Joe got a wicked grin and snuck onto the lawn and snatched light-up baby Jesus. We took off running, and eventually ended up driving over to Laura's and sticking it into the top of the snow fort she built in her front yard. It ended up becoming this thing—we stole like, fifty-nine different yard ornaments and 'rehomed' them. David Paschel? He alone got thirteen Santas one night. We even made it into the *Township* newspaper, as the 'Christmas Decoration Deviants.' We never got caught. But I'm probably boring you. You knew all those stories, right?"

I take a huge swig of latte. It burns my throat.

"On the phone, you said you wanted to say something to me." I cut right to the chase. I'm not here to pave a memory (or fake memory) lane for her.

"What?"

"On the phone," I repeat, trying to keep impatience out of my voice.

"Oh. Right."

Sarah pulls both braids down and and rocks side to side a little. Then she wraps both hands around her cup of tea and sighs.

"How come you asked me here?"

I'm aware there is a table of sophomores sitting a few feet away who went from hysterical giggling to silent in the last thirty seconds. I can almost hear their ears popping from eavesdrop strain. Hanging out with Mateo made me forget how much most people from my school know about me. I shift in my seat and cast the girls a punk rock-worthy glare. They straighten up, lean together, and whisper.

"I don't know. I guess because no one thanked you for the roses you brought over on the dea—uh, on the anniversary. I just haven't seen you in a while."

Sarah tilts her head to one side and bites the corner of her lip.

"Don't laugh or hate me," she says finally, "but I was kinda hoping you had, like, a message for me or something. From him. Maybe like something he never got to tell me…" Her voice drifts off, retreats into the dream she's playing in her head.

Bingo.

"Why would you think—I mean, you know he and Sameera—"

"I know," she interrupts. "It's just, well, the last night we stole Santas, I slipped on the ice. He caught me right before I hit the ground, but then we both slipped and sort of fell together and…"

"Yes?"

Before she can speak again, my phone beeps. I hold my hand up to pause her. It could be Mom.

Except it's Mrs. G from next door. Who apparently thinks all texting must be done in capital letters.

ANNA HI IT IS MRS G I AM WATCHING BEA AT YOUR HOUSE RIGHT NOW AND SHE SAID TO SEND YOU THIS MESSAGE BECAUSE THERE IS A BOY HERE WITH A PLATE OF FOOD. SMELLS GOOD. THE FOOD. NOT THE BOY. I DIDNT TRY TO SMELL HIM. BEA SAID I SHOULD WRITE LOL.

WHAT DOES LOL MEAN? IS IT A SWEAR? ARE YOU COMING HOME? HE SAID HE WOULD WAIT.

I look from my phone to Sarah's eager, waiting face. A scream builds because she needs to finish the story but my fingers have already moved to hit reply: Mrs. G—I'm on my way.

"I gotta go," I say to a bewildered-looking Sarah. "Something came up. We do need to get together again, though. Maybe next week. There's some stuff I think I want to say to you too."

I take my cup to the counter and ask for it to go, and then duck out the door, energy from what I maybe almost learned rushing through me. It's pouring now, and my hair is dripping across my bare shoulder by the time I get to my car. I curse Patti for giving me the idea of cutting the neck out of my black T-shirt, and lean over to the passenger seat to ring out fabric and hair and emotion.

Mateo's at my house.

His Jeep is parked at the end of the driveway, as if he wasn't sure he wanted to be there once he arrived.

The three of them—Mrs. G, Bea, and Mateo—are sitting in the living room. He stands up when he sees me. He's wearing a white T-shirt that hugs against him just right. He wipes his hands on his jeans, like he's nervous.

"I brought some tortillas made from my mother's recipe, and fillings—beans, cheese, some chicken—for your mother, because of your grandfather being ill." He's formal, nodding toward the kitchen. I walk in and he follows.

There's a large dish covered in aluminum foil sitting on the counter. The dish has little green vines running across it.

"I also brought some extra masa, with instructions, in case your mom doesn't know."

I take it and try to peek under the foil, because I have no idea what *masa* means. He steps closer and thrusts a sheet of paper, folded once, into my hand. The writing is neat and slanted. It's the complete opposite of my haphazard scrawl. Penciled illustrations line the sides. Onions and cast-iron pans, peppers and a plate heaped with steaming food, a hand reaching out to it. I'm about to ask who drew these things when Bea pounces in behind us.

"My gramps isn't ill. He's a vegetable. Not like a carrot or broccoli but like a guy who can't eat or walk or talk or even blink. He's got machines that breathe for him and they sound like Darth Vader, or at least that's what I heard Anna tell her friend Nat on the phone this morning. I wouldn't know because my mom doesn't let me see *Star Wars*. But I haven't asked her in a year. She probably would now. Maybe I should see it before I go see my gramps, so I know what to expect. They haven't let me go past the waiting room yet, because they are afraid I'll freak out. I heard Mom say that to my dad."

She nods and puts her hands on her hips, like she's the most astute seven-year-old on the planet.

Mateo lets out a laugh.

"You're pretty smart, huh?" he says to her. I notice how he bends down so they are eye level.

"Yeah, even though I have to do summer school, I'm smart," Bea says with a proud grin. The way she smiles at Mateo is shattering my heart, glass against pavement.

"Do you want to see my rubber band collection? It's in my room," she says, holding out her hand.

He takes it without pausing. They are about to walk up the stairs when the front door opens, and I hear Bea's little feet pound up the stairs at lightning speed.

"Beatrice!"

Super. Dad's here.

"Hi, Gloria," he says. It comes out as a sigh.

I hear Mrs. G introducing him to Mateo and decide I'd better shuffle out into the front hall.

"Jack," I say through gritted teeth.

"Anna, don't call me that." Everything he says, it seems, comes out as a sigh.

He turns back to Mrs. G, who is standing beside Mateo. Mateo, who is standing a little taller than normal. He's got a good three inches on my dad, unless you count Dad's eternally out-of-control hair. Most guys his age would kill for a tenth of Dad's locks. I notice he has on my mom's favorite shirt—a vintage Detroit Tigers one with blue sleeves—and I wonder if he remembers she gave it to him, with a pair of behind-the-plate tickets, for their anniversary five years ago.

"Gloria, I'm sorry I'm late picking Bea up," he says, rubbing his temples. "I was at the hospital with Tess and I just lost track of time."

"Why were you there? What's going on?" I ask. "What is it?"

"Calm down, honey," Dad says. "Your mom just has a lot of decisions on her plate. She called and asked me to come help her sort through some of the options."

"What decisions? What options? She could have called me. I told her I'd watch for her text or call if she needed anything."

"Sweetie, it's grown-up stuff."

"Oh, of course," I snap. "So you can swoop in and be part of our family again? Lori okay with that?"

Mrs. G sucks in her breath, fidgets with the book in her hand, and quickly excuses herself. When the door shuts, Dad is still staring at me.

"What?" I ask him. It's a dare.

He doesn't take it.

"So, Mateo, you're a friend of my daughter's?" he asks, thumbing toward me.

"I am, sir," Mateo replies.

"Sir, huh?" Dad's eyebrows rise. He used to tell Joe to always call Sameera's dad sir, out of respect for the girl he adored. And also, so Sameera's dad didn't want to punch his face in for, you know, sweeping his daughter off her feet.

I blush.

"Well, it's nice to meet you," Dad says, reaching out to shake Mateo's hand. "If you'll excuse me, I have a little Houdini to find."

He disappears upstairs, and we're left alone again. I

walk back into the kitchen and sit on the counter, next to the food Mateo brought us.

Mateo steps close.

"You're here."

"I'm here."

"You brought me food."

"I brought your family food."

"After I got you fired."

"After I got me fired."

I stare at him for a long minute, searching for an explanation. Why would a boy like this want a girl like me?

He moves in a little, draws a circle against my knee with his fingertips. He smells like mint and smoke.

"You're here."

"I like to help. With food, you know? It's my thing or whatever."

I wrap my legs around his, and take his hands into mine.

"Your dad," he says, pulling back a bit.

"Is inconsequential in my life."

"You don't mean that." He lifts my hand to his mouth. Kisses my knuckle then moves to the opposite side of the counter.

"You don't know what you're getting into."

He shoves his hands into his pockets and rocks back on his feet. The window beside him is streaked with rain. Everything outside is bleeding together, a watercolor painting.

"I think I do," he says, not meeting my eyes.

"Do you know Pablo Neruda?" I ask.

"No, should I?"

"He's a poet. He's dead. But he's from South America."

"Where?"

"Chile."

"You know that's nowhere near Mexico, right?"

I look at him and smile a little, because that is exactly what Joe would have said to me.

"Yeah, I know."

We stand there not speaking. Mateo's waiting for me to finish what I started, to explain why I brought it up in the first place.

But how do I say this without sounding crazy? How do I tell him about Mrs. Risson—how she brought me a book of Neruda poems the day after the funeral? How do I explain the way she sat with me on the front porch and read each one while I watched blades of grass bend with the breeze?

How do I say Mateo reminds me of the poem that cut deepest? The one so full of fear that one break in stillness is enough to bring joy and hope and life?

I don't.

"Never mind," I say, sliding off the counter and taking his hand. "I should probably go help find Bea. It's a special talent of mine."

We sort of fall together in a slow, careful way. His forehead rests against mine.

"I'm not going anywhere," he whispers, before walking out the door.

I had been working on the surface for so long.

29

Coffin yoga. Daily Verse. Think about Gramps. Think about Mateo. Think about how weird it is to feel broken and mended all at once. Sad and happy. Sappy.

Bea is sitting on my floor, pounding the wood like a strung-out drummer and singing totally inappropriate lyrics about not getting laid but getting in a fight.

"Um, you can't say that kind of stuff. Where did you learn that song?" I recognize it from when Nat and I used to go to the '80s night at the bowling alley, like way back in middle school. Or tenth grade.

"Lori. She was playing it at Dad's when I had to sleep over the other night. She said it was a slumber party kind of song."

Bea stops drumming and looks up at me.

"She's kind of dumb."

I can't help but laugh.

"Do you want to make stovetop s'mores for breakfast?" I ask.

Bea hops up and starts dancing around my room.

"Okay," I nod. "But then we're going to call Mom. I know she's nervous about you being in the room with him, but I think you can handle it. We need to give her a break, and I can bring cards and some stuff to draw with too, so we can almost pretend he's just taking an afternoon nap. It will be like we're hanging in a hotel room."

I'm pretty sure Bea stopped paying attention after I suggested the stovetop s'mores at 9 a.m., because she's bobbing her head up and down as she skips right out of my room.

––––––

The ICU floor is empty for a Saturday. Fluorescent light bounces between the ceiling and fresh wax on the floors. Our shoes squeak and Bea begins twisting with each step to magnify the sound. I don't tell her to stop. It makes us walk slower.

"Hi, Mom."

We stand in the doorway of Gramps's room. A single paper crane, which I recognize to be his first origami attempt, sits on his tray table, frayed and lopsided. In his stories, my grandmother's engagement ring was tucked inside it many years ago. There is also a potted fern with a card sticking out of it. I walk over with Bea on my heels. It

says, "I love you, George. Fight the good fight. Jack." My
father.

When I turn around I feel sick to my stomach because
everything seems yellow. Yellow, not black, is the color of
death. Gramps's skin is yellow. The florescent lights make
the whole room yellow.

Mom offers a thin smile, asking Bea if she's okay and
if she'd like to come closer. Bea shakes her head no but
puts on a brave-enough face that Mom only nods and says
it's good of us to come. She fidgets with her ringless ring
finger, twisting skin instead of a wedding band. On the
nightstand beside her chair are four empty plastic cartons
of red Jell-O and two crossword books without a single
crease in the spine.

"We thought you could use a break."

"No thanks."

Mom shakes her head. Stands up to stretch, twisting until her back answers with a sharp crack. Laying one
hand on her father's, she turns to Bea and me like she
wants to say something but can't. Emotional lockjaw. So
Bea steps in for her.

"Mom, I got 100 percent on my spelling test this week.
I even spelled the bonus word right, so technically I got
101 percent. It was 'necrophilia,' the bonus word."

Newsflash, Mrs. Lovack (Bea's summer school teacher):
bonus words about sexual attraction to corpses on little kid
spelling tests offer a pretty unflattering glimpse into the
reasons the youth of America are falling apart.

All things considered, I'm thinking Bea's attempt at small talk might make Mom lose it. But that's the thing about having a conversation with a griever. Everyone waxes poetic about spiritual and philosophical and psychological boo-hooey, as if the emptiness can be filled with something as worthless as words. But Bea and her ability to properly spell a vocabulary word that's meaning boils down to an affinity for doing it with dead things, that makes Mom's mouth twitch and give way to great gasping chokes of laughter. Tears stream out of her eyes.

"Oh, Buzzy," she finally says, throwing her arms around my sister. "Girls, I think Gramps will be okay with some quiet time. Why don't the three of us get out of here and go to Guido's for lunch?"

Guido's is right across the street from the hospital and serves the best tomato basil soup from here to outer space in handmade bowls that sit crookedly on the table. My memory of the place and the place itself match up to perfection, like we never left. Like we've discovered a wormhole in which time stands not still, but together, and one year ago is also right now. The black painted wood floor planks, hot waiters wearing vintage ring-collared tees, mismatched furniture, and stereo blasting the next coolest indie rock band albums—it's all the same.

This was my parents' spot when Joe was in the hospital. They walked across the street for lunch and took turns going back to pick up takeout for dinner. Pretended they were on dates, not waiting for my father's only remaining relative, his best friend/practically own kid/little brother, to get better. To get better, she stressed. Not to die. We never thought that would happen, Mom said once, voice breaking a little. If they'd known, she said, they never, ever would have gone for lunch.

I wonder now if she thinks Gramps is going to get better.

There are only three other occupied tables. All of the people glance up, and then back down at their food. A man who looks like he usually shaves, but hasn't, tucks a newspaper under his sport coat, drops a five dollar bill on the metal table, and walks out into the sun. A waitress steps out from the kitchen, wiping her hands on a dish towel. She does a double take at my mom and smiles.

I wonder if they have lots of customers like us: ghosts of those waiting for people to become ghosts. The hospital is so close, after all.

"Are you sure you want to eat here?" I whisper as we take our seats.

Mom cocks her head to the side as if I'm speaking a foreign language.

"Why not? I'm tired of hospital cafeteria food and we can have a quick bowl of soup. Soup is so comforting, don't you think?"

I used to.

But now soup reminds me of what I did. When everything went down with that London writing program and Joe kept ditching me, I got sick. Like, got-the-flu sick and

I started wishing he'd get it too, because then he'd have to stay home. I got it in my head he needed to get sick. He needed to stay home and eat Mom's chicken noodle soup.

So I did everything I could to pass my germs to him. And it worked. He wasn't able to listen to my stories and poems, or tell me one stupid writing program didn't matter. He couldn't say he still believed in me because he got so sick so fast.

I know I didn't kill him on purpose. But he died because I thought I needed to play the "nonsense words only" version of Scrabble we'd created when we were kids. I thought being quarantined together would give him time to tell me about all the hope and otherness existing beyond high school, beyond hometowns. The promise of a wide-open future. And then I got better and he got worse. My stupid plan put an end to his life.

The day he went into the hospital because he couldn't breathe, I took his pillow into my room. It smelled of old sweat and sickness but I buried my face in it, breathing his smell and his germs and wailing until my eyes were swollen and it hurt to blink.

Bea didn't understand. In the hospital waiting room she kept asking when Joe could play, as if he were only hiding.

Mom and Dad kept saying we needed to stay home. One evening, I left Nat coloring get-well cards and watching Psychic Friends Network infomercials with Bea, so I could sneak up to the hospital for a few minutes. I brought a stack of Kurt Vonnegut books and *The Catcher in the Rye* with me, because they were Joe's favorites. Through Joe's cracked-open door, I could hear beeps and blips and hisses of the machines. Heavy curtains drawn together, it seemed like night had already arrived.

"They ran to get coffee," our family's favorite nurse, Betty, said as I peeked down the hall for any sign of my parents. Betty was nearly Gramps's age, with thinning, frizzy white hair and huge boobs. She wore her scrubs like a business suit. She also wore white sneakers and a scowl mean enough to make a baby cry. She doted on Joe, and Mom and Dad too. She liked to rush in all bossy and thunderous, saying things like "Rise and shine, Joseph. It's a brand new day and you are missing all these ridiculous Bambis"—that's what she called young nurses—"peering in, wanting to be the one to give you a sponge bath."

"Go on in and see him," Betty said that night. "Fifteen minutes. Then you scoot your fanny right back home and get your little sister into bed."

She ushered me into Joe's room and gently closed the door. He was already in and out of consciousness, but not on a breathing tube. Not yet.

"Hello?" his voice rasped. I shuddered.

"I'm here," I said, rushing to his side. I was afraid to turn on the light. I could tell in the green glow of machine numbers that he was getting worse.

"You came." His clammy hand clamped down on mine. Earlier, it had been ice cold.

"I'm right here," I said again.

We sat together for what seemed like a year. It was probably ten minutes. Every blip the machine made accused me of hurting Joe. I wanted to tell him I was sorry. Instead, I sat still and quiet. I thought about death, and how people will forget each other, and eventually how no one will think of us at all. I sat by Joe's hospital bed and thought about the pointlessness of life. He must have sensed this, because all of a sudden he shot up coughing and crying.

At first the sounds coming out of his mouth made no sense. Garbled bits of half-words, coughs, wheezes. But then he gripped my hand tight. He wasn't looking at me. He wasn't looking anywhere, really.

"You have to let me explain. You have to know," he said. "Don't you see? Everything hurts. Everything. I want to go. I want to go. I need you to tell me it's okay. I need you to say it!"

Betty came rushing in, because Joe was shouting. His eyes were bugged out but not focusing, and sweat dripped from his forehead. Then he started to hack and gasp and cry out in pain. Betty's hambone arm shoved me back as she fiddled with an IV drip and smoothed a mat of hair against Joe's forehead.

"Go on home now, Anna. He needs to sleep. He's delirious. You understand? He's fevered and talking nonsense."

I tripped over my shoelace, landing against the cold linoleum floor with a thud. I don't remember getting up. But I do remember standing in front of the window at the end of the hospital hall. Hues of dusk filtered inside. The kind of color and light where, under different circumstances, a person would feel infinite. I watched a black bird with orange-tipped wings fly straight toward the glass. It shot skyward right before hitting. In the distance, fading sunlight glittered across the river, as if the water were a steady current of fire.

30

What I also remember: the next day, Mom's head bent against Joe's arm. His eyes were closed. Not conscious. She wept. It made my stomach hurt, her mix of gagging and crying and moaning. It told of a fear too big for a mom to hold.

"Stay. Stay. Stay. Please, stay with us," she begged.

DAILY VERSE:

The worst that could have ever
happened to me had already
happened.

31

Laura showed up at the hospital today. Bea and I were in the middle of Twister when she walked into the family waiting room. My left foot was twisted under Bea's right hand, her left foot entangled with my right, when Laura's familiar snicker echoed in from the doorway. I tipped over in surprise. And waited a second to look up.

Joe's friends rotated through this waiting room a lot, the last time. Nobody stayed long, except Sameera and Laura. They came almost every day, bringing Bea and me ice cream or new movies. Sometimes, Sameera got too sad. Laura stayed then, held her friend's place with us O'Mallys. It's jarring, seeing her here now. Like we've gone back in time. Like we have to live it all over again.

"Figured I'd find you two here."

"Hiya, Laura. Wanna play Twister?" Bea says, recovering first and skipping over to give her a hug.

"What are you doing here?"

"Geez, Anna. Bad hair and bad manners makes for a really crappy combo. I'm done with my summer class, so I'm home for a few weeks. My folks told me about George. Thought I'd come see if you needed a break, or wanted me to hang with Bea so you could, you know, sit with him."

She casts her eyes down when she says this. I can tell it's not just me remembering now.

"Thanks," I manage to say, sitting on the edge of a fake leather couch. Seeing Laura here also reminds me of something else entirely.

"Hey"—I snap my fingers—"I heard this story the other day, and I think it's a lie, but whatever. Did Joe ever stick a fake baby Jesus—"

"Upside down like a flagpole in my awesomely huge snow fort?" Laura interrupts with a laugh. "Yeah. And he tried denying it for a week. What a dork. You never knew about all that?"

I don't answer.

"Hey, really, I'd love to hang with Bea for a bit," Laura says.

I nod and slide away. In Gramps's room, Mom is asleep in the chair. I stand over him, watching tubes and machines chug and pump and hiss.

He isn't waking up.

It makes me ache for all the words I haven't heard him

say. Our relationship still has too many blank spaces, and I'm sick of people I love being defined by stories I haven't heard firsthand.

Gramps isn't coming back and I wish, just for a second, we could trade places.

Never let go of that fiery sadness
called desire.

32

It's been a week since Bea, Mom, and I went to lunch. A week of balancing where we were with where we are now. I've started doing coffin yoga in weird places. I can't make it to nineteen minutes without getting distracted or letting my leg do this constant nervous bounce. I'm a top wound too tight. Especially right now, because I'll be away from the hospital for a full evening, and the outside world already feels like a foreign planet.

Mateo begged me to take a night off from the waiting room. He offered to make a picnic. For some reason, I insisted on cooking instead, even though my skills in the kitchen match my ability to solve Fermat's Last Theorem (which is the most difficult math problem in existence). I can't even compute cook times. I tried baking lasagna but set the smoke alarm off (twice).

Just before leaving for Dad's house, Bea asked why I was going on a date with a boy I didn't like, because I'd never make a boy I cared about eat my cooking.

"That stuff smells even worse than the last batch of burned gunk," she said of my last-ditch attempt at pesto pasta.

Good thing I stopped by the bakery and bought cupcakes as big as our heads before picking Mateo up. Chocolate can make up for just about anything. I think. I hope, since we're officially picnicking now, and I'm about to serve a chef some of my cooking. Pretty certain our definitions of what passes for food don't match up.

I kneel on the orange-and-yellow-and-brown quilt he brought. His mom got it at a neighborhood garage sale, to use for picnics. Except they don't go on picnics, he said, so it just sits folded on the floor of the linen closet.

"Do you hang out here often?" I ask, pulling the glass container full of pesto-slathered noodles from my backpack. We're sitting by the bank of the Grey Iron River. The East Side of the Grey Iron, which is a place as famous for its constant violence as it once was for the gleaming new automobiles that rolled off its assembly lines.

"I hang out here sometimes." He looks around, turning his head in slow motion, taking in the patchy grass littered with mystery metal, broken boards, faded beer cans. He follows the long line of empty factory buildings with his eyes. They go on and on and on along this side of the river, rectangles and smokestacks stretching far enough to get small in the distance, like perspective drawings we did in eighth grade art class. I say so, and it makes Mateo smile.

"Do you like art? That kind, I mean?"

"Perspective drawings from eighth grade?"

"No," he laughs. "Visual art."

"I do, but I don't understand it very well. You'd think I would, because of the whole word thing…"

"What do you mean?" He's trying not to wrinkle his nose, because I just opened the pesto dish I made. It's like a garlic bomb exploded between us. Maybe one clove only meant a piece, not the whole bulb. I root around in my backpack and pull out the cupcakes.

"Dessert first?"

"Nah. I like garlic. Besides, cooking for us doesn't really fit the tough-girl image, so I gotta at least try what you made. It makes me…I don't know. Want to know what other secrets you're hiding." When he says this, he leans into me. Like we're sharing a joke.

I stare at him hard. I want him to see I'm still a shell of a girl. I want him to understand there's nothing beneath the surface to discover.

"So you were saying," he says between bites. "About not understanding art?"

"My Gran was an artist. She did all these beautiful abstracts. I like to look at them, but honestly, I have no clue what any mean, besides brush strokes on canvas. I guess it's always kind of bugged me, because I'm supposed to be this deep…" I catch myself. "I mean…"

"What do you mean?"

Mateo twirls some pasta onto his fork. He watches me push mine around my plate. I try not to meet his eyes, but then I start counting his blinks. Seven. Eight. Curtains closing, opening, drawing me inside.

I shrug.

"But that's the thing about art, isn't it?" he says. "I mean, maybe the meaning you take from your grandmother's paintings *is* her brush strokes. Like the story of the painting is more about the painter for you, the person who made color move across the canvas."

"Whoa. You're pretty deep." I nudge his knee.

"I'm only saying I think some people get too caught up in trying to find big, dramatic messages in art. And I like how you're cool admitting you have no clue what a lot of it is supposed to say about life. I don't think there should be pressure when you look at something like a painting. There should just be you and the art and the moment. Even if it doesn't mean a thing."

I've never heard Mateo talk like this. Not even last night, when he called to tell me about how he scored a job at Table, the fanciest restaurant in our area. The chef held a sort of audition, letting him craft the asparagus salad that accompanied a Kobe flat iron steak with red onion jam, herb yogurt, and Parmesan lavosh. I asked if lavosh was even a word, and we spent the next forty-five minutes talking about flatbread (lavosh, apparently, is a flatbread that originated in the Middle East). He went on and on about ingredients and cultural menus and fusions and the million ways to slice, dice, and chop an onion—which he claimed as the only skill set he'll need for the next "million years" until moving up on the line.

When he repeats "just you and the art and the moment," I want to curl into his arms.

"I used to feel like that about writing."

I say it before I can swallow the words. My lips pinch together too late. Mateo takes my plate away and pulls me toward him. My back against his chest, he circles his arms around me. We fit like spoons. I draw invisible infinity signs on his hand. It's better this way, not looking at each other.

"Tell me."

And so I do.

I tell him I wrote poems and stories because I liked the way sentences could become music. I admit out loud, for maybe the first time ever, how exhausting it was when people started analyzing every single line to find hidden metaphors or allegories or anything, really. Writing became less mine, I say, and turned into something I had to do because there were expectations to meet and awards to win and adults to make proud. My dad said some folks go through their whole lives without a passion, and he loved knowing I found mine so early. But I didn't even know if I felt passion or just obligation, and then I lost this one big contest and I thought because I'd been so self-ish maybe my talent was gone. I thought maybe I did love words but didn't know it until it was too late. And not long after, it stopped mattering.

I tell him things I've never told anybody. Not Nat. Not Joe.

When I stop, we sit without speaking. This time the silence isn't as bad. Mateo leans to one side and turns my wrist gently. Then he kisses all nine words inked on my arm. Today is the first time I've worn a short-sleeved shirt around him. It's my favorite Patti tank, white ribbed. I don't have any jewelry on other than my key on thin twine.

I wonder if he's going to ask about my daily verse. I wonder what I'll tell him.

He kisses up my arm, around the twine on my neck, rests his lips on top of my head, and asks me nothing at all. My chest explodes. Red and yellow and orange sun-bursts blast inside, reverse meteor showers. Empty dark-ness has been there for so long, and now it's suddenly, unmistakably, filling up with light, with Mateo.

Reaching across my lap, he tugs at the camera sand-wiched between my legs. He moves until we're face to face again. "Don't smile," he says. "Just…look at me the way you do…"

I imagine his words in typeface, font size growing smaller and smaller until "do" is barely visible. And so I look. The shutter clicks. This moment is good. It's almost enough.

33

The heat of day has long disappeared. We sit by the river's edge, a few feet from the orange-and-yellow-and-brown quilt. Behind us, the cracked parking lot is empty but buzzing with a handful of still-working lights. They come on at dusk every night, Mateo says, waiting for workers to return.

He's been telling me about his grandmother's house a few blocks away. She refuses to move even though there are gangs and drug lords around, because it's her home. She is too proud, he says. I say maybe she's hopeful. I have to pause mid-sentence, though, because a bunch of sirens are blaring for the fiftieth time, which makes Mateo laugh in a sad way.

As the sky gets darker, so does the river.

"I don't know why I didn't think about this before

now, but are you okay, being here? With your grandfather...and the river?" Mateo asks. His eyes are fixed on
slow-moving currents.

I trace lifelines on my right, then left hand. Above us,
a crow shatters sky with its cawing.

"Why wouldn't I be? It's not like it intentionally sealed
my Gramps's fate. It's just a river. And we all die. We all die
anyway."

For a long moment, we watch the water. Watch the
same noisy crow swoop down to pick at a glittering piece
of garbage on the bank. When it flies away, I think I hear
its wings flapping.

"He's not gone," Mateo reminds me. His voice is
quiet, warm.

"But he is," I say. "He is. The ending for this story has
already been written. It just hasn't actually happened yet."

"Do you do that a lot?"

"Do what?"

"Write other people's stories for them?"

I try hard to follow a branch as it flows downstream.
It's getting too dark. The brown water has turned black. I
tell myself to watch the shadowy branch. I shake my head
back and forth a little too hard and say no, no I don't write
anyone else's story. Not ever.

34

It's too dark to stay, Mateo says, packing up. He stays close as we walk across the parking lot, and holds his finger to his mouth twice, yanking me to a stop. We listen in silence before moving a little faster toward the car. I don't notice I'd been holding my breath until we drive back across the bridge. Air sort of hisses out of me like a flat tire.

Mateo shakes his head, but he's grinning.

I ignore him and turn on the radio. The song "Landslide" is playing. I turn it up and wish I wasn't driving, so I could close my eyes.

"The tattoo on my wrist," Mateo says, holding up his left hand. "I got it last year for my brother, Val. He has this thing called Fragile X syndrome."

When I glance over, I see he's leaning his head against the headrest. His eyes are closed. I want to be a good listener, so I stop making up images of what Fragile X is in my head. Instead, I ask what it means.

"It's a genetic disorder. I probably carry a pre-mutation of the gene, but my brother, he got the full deal. It basically means he's different. A lot of people call him retarded. I hate that word. You know?"

I nod, because I do know. "Retarded" is a terrible-sounding word. It's full of sharp edges.

"Anyway, he sees things differently. Doesn't process stuff like everybody else. It's not like he needs full-time care, but I'm not sure he's ever going to be able to get it together and live all alone either. On the whole Fragile X scale, though, he's one of the lucky ones. He's got a job through this post-high school program. He folds towels for a hotel. He really likes it because he loves the smell of the detergent they use."

Mateo starts to laugh a little and I laugh a little too.

"That doesn't seem too bad," I say. "To be happy folding towels and grateful for the scent of detergent."

"He's definitely happy most of the time. But when he gets upset, it's wicked. Last year, he got arrested because he saw a guy in our neighborhood kicking a cat. He went up and started kicking the dude hard enough to put him in the hospital. Anyway, I got the tattoo in his honor. He just sees stuff the way it is. Or maybe I got it to remember not to ever be a kick-worthy asshole."

Mateo pulls a smushed pack of Kools from his back pocket. The windows are already down so he lights up and sticks the cigarette out to keep most of the smoke from coming into my car.

"You know, you haven't had one of those things all night."

Mateo cocks his head to the side, thinking. Then he does his little head shake, the one I replay like a one-scene black-and-white movie when I'm falling asleep.

"I guess I didn't need to take a deep breath," he says.

"That might be the weirdest reason for smoking I've ever heard."

"Or the most truthful. I mean, think about it. When do you feel yourself breathing more than when you are inhaling smoke? It goes in and it goes out and poof! There's proof you are here."

"Or proof you are trying to kill yourself."

I half expect him to say "pot calling the kettle black" (except he doesn't know about me walking, just walking, with a little stardust beneath my feet). He flicks the cherry out of his cigarette and puts the half-smoked stick back in the pack.

"Hey, pull in there." Mateo points to a gas station with only half its sign lit. The building is spray-painted to look like it's underwater. Sunken junky cars have fish floating through broken windshields. The long green stalks of seaweed look so real, I swear I see them sway in the breeze or current or whatever. Two kids lean against the bottom of the building, which looks like the bottom of a river.

They're drinking two liters of Mountain Dew and squint against my headlights.

"Be right back," Mateo says before jumping out and jogging into the gas station. He comes back a few minutes later with two cups of coffee and a bag of almonds.

"You are not like any boy I know," I say as I sip the too-hot coffee, wondering how he knew I wanted it with a little sugar but no cream.

"Ditto, but switch the word 'boy' for 'girl.'"

"Is that a good thing?" I ask before I cannot ask.

"You tell me."

When I don't, he goes ahead and answers. His hand brushes against my hair.

"All the girls I've ever gone out with are all really... what's the word?"

"Beautiful?"

He frowns and tells me I'm beautiful. I chew on my bottom lip, but don't tell him to shut up.

"They were all...I don't know. The same? Like they want to hear about cooking, but what they really want to hear about is where cooking will take me—like will I get to be on Iron Chef or will I get tables at the best restaurants for free or will I get to meet celebrities and see inside their kitchens. Same with basketball. They want to wear my jacket or have me wave to them when I'm on the court, but they don't care about the game. It isn't even that. It's more how they fake care about things. All the girls I've dated want to be somebody they aren't. I don't normally tell people about Val because I don't want them to fake feel bad or get weird about it…but I wanted to tell you."

"Hate to break mit to you, but I'm just using you for the best tables in town and so I can wear your varsity jacket."

"Well, at least you're honest about it." He kisses my cheek.

We drive and park and park and drive, but not for the typical reasons. At my old elementary school, we swap funny way-back-when stories.

Underwear frozen stiff and raised on a flagpole for snitching on kids who were stealing lunch money. (his)

Detention for eighteen days for breaking eighteen No. 2 pencils as a brilliant but failed attempt to keep an entire third grade class from taking the Michigan Educational Assessment Test. (mine)

Telling Steve Williams kissing was a necessary part of playground marriage, but must be done with no-tongue-or-I'll-punch-you. (me, again, because pencil breaking apparently isn't that funny)

In the Masonic Temple circle drive, we circle back to favorites.

Food: Nopalitos (this gives away the "him" factor, since I don't even know what Nopalitos is); book: *The Outsiders*; song: I already forgot because I'd never heard of it; movie: some 1990s flick called *Poetic Justice*.

I can't stop giggling about that one.

He liked my food choice (chocolate) and said he'd never read my favorite book, *A Tree Grows in Brooklyn*. I admitted I haven't read it either. It was Joe's favorite and I worried I wouldn't love it as much as I was supposed to. I said my favorite song was "Be My Witness" by the Bahamas, but quickly retracted that and replaced it with "Dead City" by Patti Smith.

Behind the church my family used to go to we talk about our friends. I tell him I'm a floater who sort of turned into a sinker. He says maybe I just floated a little out of reach. I want to cry so I eat a bunch of almonds and ask a lot of questions about his friends. They play basketball and soccer and have plenty of girls hanging around and work after school and are generally pretty chill, but aren't into the township crowd because we have a reputation for being sheltered and stuck up.

"Fair enough," I say.

"But you aren't stuck up."

"No. But I'm not sheltered either."

He doesn't ask, but the air gets thick all the same. I start the car and creep back onto the empty road.

"Basketball players are all good at jumping, right?" I ask like I might not remember him telling me a week and a half ago how he made varsity as a sophomore.

"Yeah—why?"

"No reason."

We stop at a big-box store, but I ask Mateo to wait in the car. Standing in the checkout aisle with a giant can of red spray paint, I smile. It's a mischief kind of night. When I get back in the car, I crank up the radio volume until my car speakers rattle. We head out of town toward a giant blue cylindrical shadow in the sky.

"The water reservoir," Mateo says, half like a question, when I pull in and turn off the engine.

"Get out. We're going up!"

I point to the enormous round silo's metal ladder, which starts about seven feet off the ground. As if that's a good enough security measure for a bunch of bored kids. Please. It's almost insulting.

"I'll need a boost to the bottom rung, but you can just jump and grab it I'm sure."

"Are you crazy?"

"Do you have to ask?"

"Is this okay?"

"No one has died yet, if that's what you mean. And I've been up here a zillion times. Come on, chicken!"

As with any other American teenage boy, this last dig is enough to make Mateo walk beneath the ladder and lock his hands together like a step.

"All right then, hop on."

He throws me high. I almost miss the second rung.

"Easy there, Tiger! Now wait till I get up a little more, then get a running start and pull yourself up."

It only takes Mateo twice to get it, which I know is impressive but don't tell him. I'm already sitting on the particle-board top, feeling the echo of feet against metal as he climbs up to meet me.

"Welcome to the unofficial Lovers' Lane of Grey Iron

Township," I say, eyebrows raised and suggesting things I won't say.

"Really?" Mateo takes a few steps, listens to the hidden sea of water sloshing beneath his feet, and promptly sits down.

"And this board stuff is, like, safe for people to stand on?"

His doubt is cute.

"I think so. I mean, it used to have a metal roof but there was some problem with it rusting and contaminating the water, so they removed it and this is the temporary fix. But I've been up here plenty of times—"

"Have you now?"

I roll my eyes. "Not like that."

"I bet that's what you tell all the boys."

"Maybe."

He stands up, making sure his eyes never leave mine. I can feel the buzz of his hands even before he reaches me.

I let him pull us together. He's warmer than the air. My fingers slide under his shirt. His back is smooth. Muscles tighten as I move up his spine, back down, over to where his hips meet his jeans.

I've never touched a boy in this way. In this moment, I never want to stop.

"Hey," Mateo says in my ear. His voice is honey and electricity all at once. My body hums in response.

"Hey," he repeats, tilting my chin up with one finger. He's making me look at him. Not just look at him.

Look into him, through those huge almond eyes. I let out a muffled whimper. This feels too close, too close, too...

His mouth meets mine. It isn't like the kiss we shared in the closet that day. No, this kiss was supposed to be the first kiss, the answer for each goodnight or goodbye when he didn't put his lips against mine. He was waiting. He wanted to show me the way it feels to be seen and wanted. It's like he's telling me, with his lips and without words, that I'm good. I'm a good person.

I pull back, swallow, step away. The heat whooshes between us, and I'm shivering.

"What's wrong?" he asks. His concern hurts as much as his kiss.

I sit down and wave him off like its nothing, pulling out my phone and searching through its extensive playlists. I settle on a Simon and Garfunkel song called "America."

"Dance with me," I say.

Mateo relaxes as I move toward him. He laces his fingers through mine. His other hand reaches under my tank top, settles against the skin on the small of my back. His thumb moves in circles, slow and purposeful. The music is faint, a whisper.

We're barely swaying when he murmurs into my hair. "It's good."

I try to pretend I didn't hear him.

"This thing with us. It's good. I don't know, I..." He trails off, scoops me closer with one hand. He's strong.

It's hard to remember how impermanent feelings, relationships, love, life, all of it is. It's hard to remember this makes no sense, this "us." Because his hand is on my back. His lips are on mine. Because right now, right now, right now.

I push away, twirl back to my bag, pull out the can of spray paint.

Mateo sits back down, legs stretched toward me, muscled arms holding his weight against the particle board.

"What are you doing?" His eyes widen when he sees the paint. "Nothing about that looks like a good idea."

To answer, I spray big cursive letters across the width of the particle board. Song lyrics. It's not an original idea—a real artist was on NPR for doing this exact thing all across the city—but I feel like I'm tapping into something genius.

"To being empty and aching and not knowing why!" I read out loud when I finish. Red paint is streaked across my thumb and forefinger.

"Will you stop messing around so close to the edge?"

Only now do I notice my feet moving heel-toe like a tightrope along the edge of the reservoir tank.

"Anna!" Mateo's voice is strained. "Knock it off!"

The tension doesn't leave his body until I'm close enough for him to cup my face. His thumbs embed in my cheeks. This time, his kiss comes fast and desperate. He locks against me, grip weaving into my hair. He roots us together.

Every move he makes aches with urgency, and even though my head is saying stop, there's something about his skin and muscles and bones and the way they all fit together with my skin and muscles and bones, something about his long black lashes fluttering against mine. Something about something about something. I can't help holding the back of his head, velvet against palm. I can't help crushing my lips against his.

He hesitates when, after a long while, we drift apart. We don't speak, probably because we're panting. I've never felt more alive. Every inch of my body is on fire but I'm trembling. I want to reach out and start that kiss all over again. Instead, I walk toward the ladder.

I don't love him.

Not really.

Water laps against the wall of the tank. Holding tight to the ladder, I lean over and put one free hand against the metal. I feel what's there without being able to see it.

Our date has stretched into its ninth hour, exactly 32 minutes past my curfew. Our moments are stacking up like bad dominos, so I'm grateful for a reason to call it a night. When Mateo slides into the passenger seat and says:

"So where now?"

"I'm already late for curfew."

"I know. Does it matter, by degree of lateness, how much trouble you will be in with your ma?"

The way he grips my thigh tells me too much. When people know they are losing someone, they take time to drink in every possible detail. It's what I used to dream about doing after Joe died. It's why I watch my grandfather so closely now.

"I'm not in the habit of going out at all, so I don't really know."

"Will she worry?"

I think about this. Mom would worry—would straight up panic—if Nat's mom hadn't informed her over lunch that I was having a date with a very cute boy tonight. She practically shoved me out the hospital doors, she was so thrilled to know I was doing something "normal."

"No," I say, looking out the window. "I think she's probably sleeping."

"Then please, will you stay out a little while longer?"

"Do you really want to keep driving around?" An exhaustion sweeps through me.

"I do, Anna."

He says this with such fierce conviction that I flash to a poem shaped like a bride and groom, words falling on top of words, moving from head to toe. It's like I've already fallen asleep. Like I am dreaming of a different me in a different life.

"So. Where to now?" He tries to sound casual, but his fingers are hooked in the pocket of my shorts like I'm a flight risk.

I shrug and start the car.

We drive away from endless rows of half-vacant strip malls, pit stopping only at this place called Tony's, where a lot of kids from school hang out. Mateo doesn't ask why when I request he be the one to go inside and order our chocolate milkshakes. He also won't take the six bucks I'm holding.

"This stuff is like heaven on earth," Mateo says, shaking his head back and forth, taking off the plastic top for a gulp.

"I'm kind of hoping God has higher standards."

"Are you crazy? This has to be divined from some higher power. I gotta say, you've introduced me to some seriously good junk food, Ms. O'Mally."

I stick my tongue out. He responds by lifting my free hand up, kissing each joint. I almost drive off the road.

"You know, those Simon and Garfunkel song lyrics you wrote, the guy who is painting those around town...well, he's making a statement," Mateo says after we've been quiet for almost three minutes. "He's saying something about art and healing and—"

"And what?"

"You kind of missed the point." He sounds like a teacher, the way he says it. Like when Mrs. Risson showed up at the house for the first time during my junior year with a stack of unfinished assignments tucked under her arm and an offer to help see me complete them.

"Don't act like you know what I was thinking," is all I say back.

We travel in the general direction of east, under the green cart bridge near the County Club, beyond the big homes lining the golf course. When I turn into a driveway made only of two lines of gravel with grass between, Mateo takes a turn, suggestively raising his eyebrows. Thanks to the stealth mode of a hybrid, my car creeps up the drive with no noise, and now, no lights. Not that it matters. The white house in front of us, covered in ivy, is barely visible in the dark cover of night. It's also empty.

"Where—"

"This is Theodore Roethke's house."

"I'll bite," Mateo says. "Who's Roekthke?"

I sigh.

"He was this poet from our town. Obviously, not super famous in most circles. He's been dead a long time," I explain.

What he doesn't know—what I won't tell him—is this: I actually have a key to this house-turned-museum.

The windows are up and it's steamy but I like the sound of Mateo's straw slurping the bottom of his milkshake too much to let the rest of the world in just yet.

The sounds of night still creep in, crickets tuning up, mourning doves cooing, cars on the four-lane road just behind us zooming this way and that way. I ask Mateo to lean back his seat so I can crawl over, and when I do, I forgo his lips and lay my head straight into the crook of his shoulder. We fit like sculpture pieces. I would stay here forever; his heartbeat a metronome in my ears, his hands moving in barely traceable lines up and down my back.

Except he wrecks it all, because when he opens his mouth he asks about Joe. Not about Gramps. Not about the person I love who is dying in the present moment. He wants to know about the person I loved more than anything. The person who is gone forever because of me.

And I want to bolt upright and start the car and break all the speed limits until Mateo is gone and I'm alone. He whispers into my scalp and I feel his words seep inside and he's saying it's okay. It's okay to talk to him. I try to stiffen. Try to conjure up the prison of a coffin, the empty stare, the frozen breath. I try and I fail. I open my mouth and I tell him everything.

I tell him about this house, this summer thing of Mrs. Risson's and how she offered it to me like the participation ribbons they give everyone who sucks at Track and Field Day. I tell him how I lost London, and how in that moment I lost everything I knew to be true.

I tell him how Joe always, always made things better.

When Gran died, Joe spent a month learning to make origami lanterns and took Gramps fishing one night so he could light them and let them float down the river. It meant so much to Gramps, who understood the language of literal things like machines and folded paper. And whenever my parents would fight, Joe would order pizza, set the table all fancy, crank up the "soft jazz," and use a fake Italian voice to call them into the kitchen for a date. They smiled and kissed and made up every time.

But when I needed him? He vanished. He was too busy going places he couldn't tell me about, places I'm now sure had to do with a not-Sameera girl. He wouldn't even look at me. He said I wouldn't understand. He said

I wasn't ready to grow up. How could he not see that betraying me when I needed him most, it forced me to grow up? How could someone who promised to always be there, to always put family first, just stop caring because of what...some girl?

Then I tell him the rest. The stuff I've never said to anyone but Nat.

How I used my bout of fever and lingering cough as ingredients in a foolishly simple recipe to make Joe stay home. I hacked all over his pillow. I backwashed in the water bottle he kept on his nightstand. I wiped my germy hands on his bedroom door handle.

I did everything I could to pass my germs on to him, because I wanted him to get sick. I wanted him to stay with me.

"I did that to him," I say, hoarse from letting a truth that big claw up my throat. "Joe's eyes were rimmed with pink from the very first day he got sick. His breath stopped at the top of his chest. You could see it get stuck there, the way his stomach distended and retracted and everything hurt. He got so much sicker than I ever could have imagined, moving from influenza-related bronchitis to a pneumonia so severe that no antibiotics, no treatments were strong enough to even touch it. It got worse and worse and worse and there was nothing I could do to take it back."

I say the rest into Mateo's chest. How later, Joe begged, in rasping, semi-conscious gasps, to let go. And then, how he died. How I walked up that center line of the highway with stardust beneath my feet.

I whisper this.

Mateo's arms tighten around me. He kisses the top of my head, strokes my hair, holds me like I might stop existing if he lets go. After a minute, he tilts my chin up. He's going to say he loves me. His eyes are soft and warm and see every bit of who I am.

I bolt up in a panic.

"Forget about the whole Joe thing." I scramble back over to the driver's seat. "I was just being dramatic. He got sick and he died and that's the whole story."

Mateo doesn't respond. The words were swallowed without so much as a cough. He unclasps the gold necklace he's been wearing lately and re-clasps it around my neck. It's one of those Catholic things—a saint medallion. I don't give it back even though I'm still shaking. Catholic accessories don't mean anything. They just look cool.

Until you go home and Google them, only to find out Saint Dismas is actually the patron of thieves, conflicted criminals, and jail inmates.

Oh, and liars.

DAILY VERSE:
We gave each other what the other
didn't have.

35

Mom is in the cafeteria, restocking her red Jell-O supply. Bea is with Dad (and Lori, but I try to forget this part). I'm sitting next to Gramps, fiddling with the saint around my neck. I tell him who Saint Dismas protects. I tell him I need to rebuild my walls. His machine chugs back a reply. It says, "I know. I know. I know."

My phone buzzes.

NAT: We've got the wise child complex

I can't help a half-smile. Nat's quoting *Frannie and Zooey*, the other famous J.D. Salinger book. We both read it, instead of *The Catcher in the Rye*. I play my line back.

ME: We're the tattooed lady

NAT: agreed. Now, can we try to not analyze everything?

This is how we make up. We speak with words that aren't exactly our own. It makes things less complicated.

ME: PS was with Mateo last night
NAT: I know. Called your house and your Dad answered.
ME: what?!?
NAT: chill. He was just picking up Bea from Mrs. G. Nice that she covered for you. Again. Was it fun?
ME: ...
NAT: Subject change?
ME: Yes.

My phone stops buzzing. I feel bad. We've been best friends for fourteen years, but there's nothing to say. When a new text comes in, it's from Mateo.

MATEO: Dinner with my family tonight? 6 p.m.?
ME (TO NAT): Can we go hang at Satopia Park today?
ME (TO MATEO): pick me up at home?
NAT: Pick me up at play practice half an hour...
MATEO: cool

I walk over to the window. A new dad wrestles with a car seat, then rushes over to help his wife, who slides in the back beside her baby. He checks them three times before driving away. In the distance, the river glitters. It's a sunny day. I don't know how I feel about any of this.

Mom is sitting in my seat when I turn back around. She watches me watch the world outside.

"Hey. I didn't hear you come back in."

"You were lost in thought." She says this with a tired smile.

"Is it okay if I head out for the day? I know Bea's not back until tomorrow, and if you are going to be here for dinner—"

"It's fine. Just don't break curfew tonight again, okay?"

"You noticed?"

"Of course I noticed."

"I thought you were already sleeping when I came home," I say with a shrug. "Sorry."

"You think a lot of things, Anna. Doesn't make them true."

She holds my gaze a long time.

"I better go. Bye, Mom."

Old Town Playhouse is just minutes from the hospital, so I slip inside and settle in the back row of the theatre to watch the rest of Nat's practice.

The Playhouse's summer musical is *Frankenstein*, and Nat plays Victor Frankenstein's wife, who gets murdered by the monster. She's very excited to die on stage for the first time.

I cry when I watch. I'm glad the house lights are down. When the run-through is over, I slip back outside and wait in the car.

"Hey," Nat says as she opens the door. "What did you think? I saw you sitting in the back."

"You were great."

What I can't articulate is how haunting it was, how it felt like Nat understands death more than me, despite a year-plus of coffin yoga.

———

Satopia Park used to be my favorite. It's a mix of baseball diamonds and hiking trails, and it's one of the few places in our town where the ground wasn't pushed flat by glaciers. Instead, small hills slope along a little lake. I've found six four-leaf clovers in this park. Kids come here to play Frisbee and hula hoop and sometimes get stoned. It's kind of the township's version of Neverland.

When we pull in today, Nat leans down and pulls a big purple bottle out of her theater duffle.

"Bubbles?" she says, holding the bottle and two wands up for me to see.

"Bubbles," I repeat. "Okay."

We stroll over the giant weeping willow near the trailhead and flop down. This is our tree. We've been coming here since eighth grade, when we used to hitch rides with Sameera and Joe and their group of friends.

"Remember the time we saw Rebecca Sanderson run out of the woods half-naked?"

Nat's bubbles float into the willow's stringy branches and leaves, popping one by one.

I nod as she hands me a wand with three circles. Rainbows of soap reflect inside them. "We were totally freaking out because we thought maybe somebody was like, hurting her."

"Especially since Bobby Fischer ran out two seconds later with only one pant leg on, swearing so bad Sameera got all frazzled and covered your eyes instead of your ears," Nat adds, rolling back with laughter.

"But then that skunk came trotting out behind him, with its tail held all high and proud." I can't finish because Nat's giggling too hard.

"That was a good day," she says finally, with a big sigh.

"It was. Remember how we got all the kids in the park together, post skunking, to play kickball on the baseball field? The stoners and Joe's group and the art kids who were doing a photoshoot—"

"Oh, I forgot about that," Nat squeals. "They were wearing thrift store wedding dresses that were covered in ketchup as fake blood. That was the best part, watching them try to run the bases in those huge, puffy getups!"

"I think the best part was just being there, with everyone."

Nat nods, moving out from under the willow tree. She blows another set of bubbles, and this time, they keep going up into the sky.

"I was thinking about your list of suspects this morning," she says. "And I don't think it could be Sarah Sheldon. I'm pretty sure last June she was at Camp Hiawatha.

Alex's brothers were there as soon as school let out, and she was a counselor. I remember Alex saying she was bragging about getting asked to be head counselor, which means she would have had to be there for a few weeks getting ready for campers to arrive."

My face is warm. It could be the sun. I burn pretty easily.

"I think it's the other Sarah."

"You called her?"

"We had coffee. A few days ago."

"Why didn't you tell me?" Nat's voice is a little shrill. She must not remember how self-righteous she was about me leaving the whole Joe's-cheating mission alone.

I shrug in response.

"Well, all right. Fine. I wanted you to take a break. Can you blame me?"

I blow a set of bubbles in her direction.

"I'm glad you can still do that," I say.

"What?"

"Know what I'm thinking so I don't have to say it."

Nat rolls her eyes.

"Can we get back to the discussion at hand?"

She's tossed her wand into the bottle and started pacing, weaving in and out of the curtain of willows.

"She said she had something to tell me," I recount. "But I don't know what it is, because I had to go before she could. Also, she was staring at the bracelet."

"Where did you have to go so fast that you couldn't

listen to what she wanted to say?" Nat's stopped walking. Her hands are on her hips.

"Home."

"Why? What couldn't wait?"

"Geez, Nat. Chill out. Mateo was there. Mrs. G texted, all tweaked out about a boy bringing food over and waiting on me to get back. So I left."

I expect Nat to break into a wide smile, because she's been so bent on playing matchmaker. Instead, she slumps against rough bark and frowns.

"I can't believe you haven't called her back. What if she changes her mind and decides not to tell you anything? What if you missed your window to know the truth?"

Behind us, a group of middle schoolers are gathering at the baseball field. I watch them circle up and divide into teams. They hoot and tease each other before the first pitch. A bat cracks, cheers erupt, and dust clouds rise and settle on the diamond.

I can't explain why I haven't called Sarah back. Part of me knows I don't want it to be over, back to the place where there's nothing new to discover about Joe. And part of me doesn't want to know because I hate believing he really did this. But there's another part too. It's like an out-of-focus photograph. This fuzzy knowledge that I may have to choose between days like yesterday and sitting across the table from a Sarah in the coffee shop.

I move to sit next to Nat. We rest our backs against

the trunk. Blowing a round of bubbles into the ground, I say, "I'm glad we're here."

36

My outfit is subdued for tonight: a boatneck black sweater and jeans without holes. I add a blue beret at the last minute, to hide just how wild my hair is, and also to pay homage to Patti's love of all things Parisian. Her poem, "Perfect Moon" is playing over and over inside my head.

When Mateo comes to the door, the first thing he does is pull me close. His hand is strong and sure around my waist. Like he is the moon and I am the tide and he pools light inside my darkness. I wish I could step outside my body, memorize how it looks to be held this way.

"Are you ready for this?" he asks with a lopsided grin.

"Why? Should I be scared?" I'm kidding, but his expression makes me pause. "Wait. For real? Do they not like me already?"

"No, it isn't that…it's just…well, they are a lot to handle. It's a big family. With a lot of strong personalities." His cheeks flush. My body warms in response.

The part of the city Mateo lives in isn't as rundown or ghetto as across the river, but it's a lot older and less managed than the township. The neighborhoods here are a mixed bag. Some homes have clipped lawns and only one letterbox next to the front door. Others are pocked with paint chips and overgrown shrubs. A few porches sag low, as if expecting good posture is too much to ask. One is boarded up completely.

When we pull up to Mateo's house, I have to do a double take. It's on a corner lot, and the yard is a mix of green grass and rose bushes. My mom would definitely approve. The house is three stories, with painted yellow gables and minty-green wood siding. It looks like a place with a lot of stories to tell.

"This is…"

"Yeah, my mom does a good job taking care of it. She loves this place."

"I can see."

We walk side by side up to his front door. Before he can turn the handle, it flies open and a skinny girl about our age with slippery black hair to her waist and bright red lipstick barks a hardened laugh.

"Oh my, Mateo. No wonder you haven't brought your little girlfriend around."

"Knock it off, America. Don't be such a—"

"Hey, hey, don't start calling me names just cause I call it like I see it."

I shift my weight from one side to another, trying to find the right I'm-too-cool-for-this stance.

"I'm America Veracruz. Loverboy's cousin," she says, flashing a bright white smile at me. "Our moms are sisters. I live a few blocks from here."

"Anna." I don't offer her my hand. It takes a lot more than this to get me rattled.

"Obviously. Tía wants you in the kitchen, Mateo. She's been bitching up a storm about you not helping and everyone else being useless and blah, blah, blah. I swear she doesn't even think anybody besides you can sort and wash the frijoles. She told me to keep your *gabacha* busy. Her words, not mine," America adds, holding up her hands in innocence as Mateo shoots her a look.

"Come on. I'll show you around," she says with a deep bow. I think Nat would like this girl.

Mateo mouths "sorry" and hustles off, leaving me to follow America, who is already halfway up the dark wooden staircase.

I run my hand along the banister. Three stairs from the top, my fingers snag on something rough. A messy carving in the wood spells "Mateo," with the "e" going the wrong way.

America stands above me, shaking her head.

"Mat got himself almost killed for that little incident when he was five. Holy steer, my Tía was so pissed—but now she gazes at it all lovingly, remembering when her boy was 'still little and needing her' and all that sappy mother/son reminiscing. You really like him, huh?"

America's sneaky. A question like this, tucked into an insider's story, was meant to catch me off guard. I try to ignore it.

"Where do you go to school?" I ask.

"The Knoll. I'm going to be a junior. You know there are a ton of girls around here who like Mateo, right? I don't mean to be rude, but I don't get what he's doing with you, even if you are kinda pretty. I mean, your hair alone is so...." She trails off, making a face. "This is the upstairs. His room is on the left. You can check it out, but if Tía catches you up here together, you're dead. Fair warning."

She looks me up and down one more time, frowns, and walks away. My eyes sting. It feels like the walls are closing in, and while I've never had a panic attack, I start counting backward from one hundred, following each breath to the pit of my stomach and back up again, just in case. When I reach Mateo's open door, I stop counting. I stop everything, and just stare.

The walls are covered with pencil and charcoal drawings. Crosses and abstracts, fluid rivers and row after row of portraits. Some of the drawings are cut out, edged with darkened lines. Some are ripped, obviously small pieces of bigger works. Some still have sketchbook frays on one side. There's a large portrait in the corner. My mind flashes back to the alley. It's the same boy, with the same mischievous grin and large forehead. His eyes are cast down.

"Aren't you going to step inside?"

Mateo's wrapping his arms around me, breathing into my neck.

"Who did all of this?"

"I did."

I whip around to face him.

"I…I don't understand. You never said you were an artist."

"You never asked." Mateo shrugs.

I'm trying to process the idea that Mateo could be a star in the kitchen and also be able to do this. He knows himself. He knows what he's good at—but it's clear by the detail and sharp pencil lines of these drawings, he loves this too.

As if reading my mind, Mateo shrugs again and says, "Cooking. It's my thing, being a chef or whatever. It's what we're here to celebrate. This is just…I don't know. Come on, Anna. Let's go back downstairs. I want you to meet my brother."

He reaches around and shuts off his light, closing the door as if it meant nothing.

Val is sitting on an Oriental rug in front of a large TV, playing a video game. I can tell it's him even with his back turned. I recognize his big ears from the drawing in the alley.

"Hey, Val, I want to introduce you to my girlfriend, Anna," Mateo says, lacing his fingers through mine.

Girlfriend.

Val leans closer to the TV, his thumbs working a million miles a minute to shoot all the zombies marching toward him on the screen.

"Val. For real, man, turn around."

"Hi, Anna," Val says, not turning around.

Mateo sighs. It kind of matches Mom's tired sighs. He walks in front of the screen and Val yelps. He drops the controller and starts waving his hands up and down like crazy.

"Pause it, dude. Just pause it," Mateo says, irritated. He snatches up the controller and hits a button so the zombies freeze in place. When Val still doesn't turn around, Mateo pulls me so I'm standing in front of him.

"Anna, this is my favorite brother, Val."

"I'm your only brother," Val laughs. His grin almost reaches his ears. It makes me break out in a smile to match.

"Nice to meet you, Val. Do you ever play old-school video games?"

He looks to Mateo, confused.

"Like Donkey Kong, bro."

Val lights up.

"Yes! I love old-school games," he says, trying out the phrase and nodding. "Do you play video games too? I don't know any girls who can play video games very well. I once made it to level 199 in Pac-Man."

"No way."

"Yup. 199."

"I've never made it past sixty."

"Ha! Mateo has never made it past eleven. I like you."

"You must be Anna," says a quiet voice behind us. I turn around to see a shorter, older version of Mateo—same dimple, same almond eyes—walking over with his hand outstretched. "I'm Frank Gomez."

We go through the standard getting-to-know-you questions while Val returns to his video game and Mateo returns to my side.

Girlfriend.

I bite my lip. I wonder what it would feel like to be a real part of Mateo's life. I don't have to wonder long. His mom steps out of the kitchen and looks me up and down with the same distaste as her niece. She's taller than I imagined, her hair sleek like America's, but it stops at her chin and is peppered with gray.

"It is time to eat," she says, casting Mateo a stiff look before disappearing into another room.

Mateo groans. His dad laughs. Turning to me, he says not to worry. A mother needs to let a girlfriend know who is in charge. Once that's established, she's quite nice, he promises. I nod.

"Let's wait a few minutes more," Mateo says, rubbing the back of his head. "Maybe if they start passing dishes, we can sit down without a big fuss."

"Won't that just make your mom even more mad?" I have a feeling the Gomez family dinners include everybody gathering at the same time, saying grace, all that stuff.

"You're right. Might as well make our grand entrance," he says, giving me a quick kiss on the cheek. "Let's go."

The minute I walk into the dining room, seven of Mateo's relatives or close family friends stop speaking in rapid-fire Spanish. Even the table noises—spoons bumping forks, chairs inching forward, the swish of napkins moving to laps—it all sputters out. Mateo squeezes my hand. He pulls out a chair for me and stands until I sit.

And just like that, the noise kicks back up again, although mostly in English now. There are lots of questions directed to me—where did Mateo and I meet, how many people are in my family, where do I live, go to school, go to church (followed by silence, then, "Oh, that's not Catholic?"), what are my interests and hobbies—Mateo steps in every few minutes. His relatives laugh and say they want to get to know this girl he's so taken with, which makes Mateo groan again.

When you're used to dinners being silent, crummy affairs where NPR or jazz no longer plays from the kitchen radio, where there are three instead of five, where the most distinct smell is toothpaste because your kid sister likes to draw the ghost of her family in permanent marker on the wood table (Gramps taught us toothpaste will remove the marker, again, and again, and again)...a dinner at the Gómez house is like being caught in an airport on a crowded people mover, going the wrong way.

And the only thing I know to do is get off.

Sometime between the salad and chicken tingas

Mateo's knee brushes mine. Our heads turn, and there it is. Heat rushes between us and even though I've never been in love I recognize it at once, as if this feeling has been waiting inside me all along. As if Mateo and I are mirrors, showing each other the truth.

There's a reason I keep a grid of photos above my desk, a reason I'd rather eat dinner on my bed than at the table, a reason I don't belong with a family like Mateo's. I excuse myself to find a bathroom. I lock the door and dial Nat's number before slipping out the front door. Mateo finds me a few minutes later, sitting on his front porch swing.

"You alright? I'm sorry. I know it's a little overwhelming. And this doesn't even include my dad's family. We'll have to rent a banquet hall with a separate inquisition room for that," he says, holding out his hand. "I'm kidding!"

"I can't do this."

"Do what?" Mateo asks, sitting down beside me. He rocks the swing a little bit with his feet.

"I can't do this. I can't. I can't."

I don't have to say it anymore because I can hear Dolores miss a gear as Nat drives down the street.

"I have to go."

I jump up and walk fast without looking back. When I get in the car, I half expect Mateo to clamp his hand down on the door. Except he's still sitting on the swing, watching me go.

Letting me go.

DAILY VERSE:
I am human.

37

It takes me three days to call him. Sitting on the fluffy beanbag in Nat's room, my best friend glaring to make sure I don't hang up, I punch the numbers and hold my breath. Pray he doesn't answer.

Prayer never works.

"Anna. Hey."

"Hi."

Long pause.

"So, um, I owe you an apology."

"Yup."

"Well, look, it's not like I meant to—"

"Meant to what? Run off without an explanation or a goodbye? Accept an invitation to meet my family and then not even take the time to get to know them before judging?"

"Judging? Are you kidding? Your family is great. Don't you get it? That's the problem. I used to have a family like that too. I just...I can't be part of someone else's story."

Another long pause.

"It's cool. We can be friends, right?" Mateo asks.

"Yeah. Of course," I say, probably too fast. "Friends."

"So the other day, Nat invited me to go with you guys on the Fourth of July and I offered to drive. Is that all right with you, or would you rather I bail?"

Nat must have been waiting for this to come up, because as soon as I flick my head toward her, her eyes get big and she starts to whistle and walks out of the room.

"Oh. Um, sure. I'll see you in a few days then, I guess."

"Yeah. Pick you up around nine, okay?"

"Uh-huh."

I stare at the phone a long time after he hangs up. When Nat comes back she shakes her head "no" before I can open my mouth.

"Don't start. I like Mateo. He's my friend now too, and Alex doesn't feel like doing a three-person party on the Fourth. You know we love this holiday. But I'm not leaving you to sit home or at the hospital sulking either. It doesn't have to mean anything. Just a night out, okay?"

Just a night out. A normal experience. But it's another reason to not call Sarah, not have her finish the story she started at the coffee shop. My stomach turns at her name. I close my eyes and sink to the floor. I wish for one single second "just a night out" could be true for me.

DAILY VERSE:

I can still taste what it feels like to be sixteen and totally f#$ked up.

38

My sister is a sponge who reads very well. I had to change the last word of my daily verse because I don't want her dropping the f-bomb while watching the fireworks with her friend Josie's family, or at the hospital tomorrow in front of Gramps, even if he can't hear her say it.

I changed the verse twice today. It started out more innocent. Something about hung-up girls only making mediocre art, and then something about Paul Revere, in honor of Independence Day and all. I was feeling okay about seeing Mateo after an afternoon coffin yoga sesh, but the closer it got to five, the more jittery I got, so I changed my clothes. And my black T-shirt with the neck cut out and my super-short jean cut-offs with the pockets showing required words to match. I finished writing them just as the doorbell rang.

Now we're in the car driving to Nat's, and Mateo keeps glancing at the inside of my arm, then back at me, then at the road. He's nervous. He keeps fidgeting with the radio, not waiting to really see what song is playing before skipping to the next station.

Alex and Nat are waiting outside. Mateo lets out a low whistle when he first catches sight of them. There are showboats, and then there are folks who take that word to a whole new level. Alex's red-and-white striped pants and blue bow tie, combined with Nat's flag dress and blue glitter eyes, makes it looks like they raided the God Bless America superstore in Hell. (Yes, Michigan. Of course I surfed the web to see what "great shopping" Hell boasts. BrightLight's brochure totally broke the "thou shall not lie" commandment.)

"Aren't you glad you get to be seen with us?" I ask. I hug my knees to my chest and stare out the passenger window. Mateo doesn't answer me, but he does tell Nat and Alex they look "totally boss."

The whole way to the West Side River Park, Nat is singing "Saltpeter, John!" and Alex is laughing and asking where her cloister is.

"Translation," I say to Mateo, more out of habit than anything else. "She's singing a song from the ever-so-appropriate musical *1776*, which she and Alex starred in last fall at the Community Playhouse, because that theatre troupe can never seem to get their shows to match the appropriate seasons."

Nat leans forward to say something, but then snatches my arm, pulls it to look at my wrist. She frowns and narrows her eyes a little. She doesn't care about the f-bomb. She cares about the small vertical line going up from the middle of my wrist. In tiny letters: *I never thought I was going to live until thirty.* Her high ponytail swings like a wagging finger behind her.

I lift up my shoulders and turn back around. I don't like the insinuation.

It doesn't mean I'm looking for trouble. It doesn't mean anything. I start to mutter how I was only walking (just walking, with stardust beneath my feet), but think better of it.

By the time we get to the same small square edge of the park where teenagers have gathered on the Fourth of July probably since my parents were kids, everyone is already loosey-goosey hugging and stumbling, falling, breaking into hysterical laughter. Red Solo cups are scattered across the ground. A nameless junior slams the hood of Mateo's Jeep and slurs, "Theredtruckhasakegintheback."

"This won't get busted?" Mateo asks. "I mean, it's a city park."

"It'll get busted," Alex says, "but there are so many MIPs to give out, it's like trying to catch every ant busting out of an anthill. The more-sober survive. Besides, there's, you know, worse stuff for cops to deal with. They don't seem to worry about breaking up this party till after the fireworks."

Somebody's car stereo is pumping bad '80s music. Nat pulls me over to a group of drama and student council girls who are jumping around and singing.

Alex and Mateo stand aside, chatting like BFFs.

This circle is full of shiny smiles, as if every girl dancing truly believes there will never be a moment as fun as the one they're in right now. As if they are invincible. Unlike the kickball field at Satopia all those years ago, I can't feel it with them.

It's like being stuck inside a glass box, watching the way I'm supposed to be, and the loneliness hits like a sucker punch.

There was a short time at the beginning of junior year when I got wasted. A lot. Every time Nat got invited to a party, we'd show up late and I'd go straight to the stolen booze bottles, cheap beer, or trash can full of jungle juice and not stop until Alex was dragging me out over his shoulder, rag-doll style. This stopped when Nat threatened to go to my parents. To tell them every secret I'd ever spilled. Every secret. I didn't get mad, just stopped going to parties.

Yet here I am. So I channel Patti. Do what needs to be done. I take the 72-ounce Slurpee cup that Betsy, one of Nat's favorite student directors, is offering. Her red lipstick is on the straw. I pull the top off, swig, gag, and swig some more. Coke and something—rum, maybe—set my throat and stomach on fire. I slam the rest of it. Betsy takes the cup back just long enough to fill it up. This time the booze slides down with ease. We repeat this ritual once or maybe twice more.

Mateo is watching. I let the ground sway me in the opposite direction.

Then I just keep letting earth and sky and everything in between move me until I'm like the rest of them, dancing and singing the chorus all wild and free. Nat slows down and snatches the empty-again cup away from me. One whiff and her suspicions are confirmed. She pushes it back into Betsy's hand.

"C'mon, before you end up puking and crying in a Port-a-Potty," she yells into my ear, dragging me from the dirt dance floor, and adding, "This is why Patti doesn't drink."

I have no idea what she means.

Mateo is with Alex and a group of guys from soccer. In the last year, I've barely said five words to half these dudes, but Mateo's joking and laughing like a part of their team.

I stop with plenty of space between us.

"Hey," he says. "You okay?"

The words sit in my mouth, sour and thick. I want to say it. I want to scream NO. I want to curl up on the dirt and rock back and forth and wail, because I am so, so, so sad. There's no other way to put it. I know there are more beautiful, expressive adjectives available—melancholy, lugubrious, dejected—and I know sad is simple, overused. But sometimes, big words hide the truth under layers of phonemic fluff.

I'm sad.

I'm here, but I'm a ghost.

I'm here and you're here and I want to…

Instead of saying anything, I walk over and shove my tongue down his throat.

Mateo tries to pull away but I lock my arms around the back of his neck and kiss him so hard it hurts. After two or twenty minutes and a whole lot of "whoas" and laughter, I let go and stare at the ground.

"What the hell was that about?" he says into my ear.

"You don't like kissing me, friend?"

"I don't like getting mauled. I don't understand you—" He pauses like he's tasting my tongue again. "Are you wasted?"

The first whistle-crack-boom echoes into the night, a shower of red falling stars. Mateo tenses against me. His heart thumps.

Between explosions of light, he starts backing up.

"What'syourproblemdude?"

The Slurpee cup might have contained a very uneven ratio of rum to coke.

"Hey, Alex, can you guys get a lift if I get outta here?" Mateo asks over my head. Alex and Nat both snap their heads toward us, frown at me, and nod.

"No prob," Alex answers. "Fun hanging with you."

They do a little bro-shake.

"Where are you going?"

An extra-loud firework echoes into my words. White

sparks float down, an umbrella of a thousand crackling sparklers.

"I'm done, Anna," he says, shoving his hands deep in his pockets. The ground is kind of spinning and my stomach feels like lit gasoline, so I shut my eyes tight. When I open them, he's gone.

*Moments of sorrow or darkness
belonged to me.*

39

For the last week, I haven't talked to anyone but my mom and Bea. And Gramps, if he counts.

I spend my time in the worn brown chair with wooden arms in room 508, watching Gramps go from bad to worse.

Coffin yoga happens everywhere now: in my car, on the kitchen table, in the hospital hallway. I don't care.

I find Bea only three times: under the bathroom sink, locked in Mom's trunk, and lying flat in the backyard garden.

Mom is worse than me. She barely takes a shower or eats more than five bites, and she keeps saying things like "I'm so tired."

Lori is eight months along and was admitted overnight for observation after a round of bad contractions. I caught my dad in with Gramps today. He was crying.

I sleep in Joe's room at night. No one stops me.

DAILY VERSE:
Until the day he died.

40

My yoga practice is starting to fail me. Every time I stretch my eyes wide open and hold my breath, a poem floats to the surface.

~~you took a bus to heaven.~~
~~she says, face lighting up.~~
~~My words are gone, but hers~~
~~match the blue of your eyes.~~
~~Dad believed that faded blue~~
~~was still tied to whatever's above.~~
~~You laughed every time, remember?~~
~~Saying~~
~~there's nothing, nothing but sky.~~

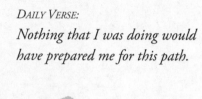

DAILY VERSE:

Nothing that I was doing would have prepared me for this path.

41

Looking at Mom's face as she listens to whoever is on the other end of our phone line, I'm pretty sure Gramps decided to go ahead and die despite the machine's best efforts to keep his body from wilting like eight-day-old spinach.

Her mouth cranks into an upside down U. She mumbles a few things like "I see" and "Okay, okay." Then she is crying and trying not to cry. She's not breathing, which makes it impossible to talk, so she clicks the phone off. Throws it across the kitchen. The battery cover breaks and bounces across the floor. There is a dent in the drywall, which is maybe good. It gives us both something to stare at, since I can't look at her while she's whimpering in that panicked, trying-to-gasp-in-air kind of way.

"That was your father."

Oh.

"Lori is in labor. She's at the hospital. He'd like you and Bea to go up now."

I think, *No. No. No. No. No.*

I think, *This is bad. This baby's birth equates to a whole different sort of death for us.*

I think, *At least this one isn't my fault. Or maybe it is.*

But I say: "Dang it. I haven't even bedazzled 'taking applications for a sugar daddy: eighteen-year waitlist' onto a onesie for it yet."

"I'm heading up there anyway, to meet with Gramps's doctors. Go get Bea. You can ride with me."

Just like that, Mom's mask returns. Back straight and strong. Voice not wavering for even a second. But she keeps pulling her curly ponytail out and putting it back in, tighter and tighter each time.

Bea doesn't have time to hide, though she makes a valiant attempt to become one with the back of the toilet when I bound up the stairs to grab her. My sister's eavesdropping skills are almost as impressive as her Houdini apprenticeship.

"I'm calling it Frog Face. Or Ugly Pants. Or Pukerella," she mutters in the back seat over and over again.

"Bea, be kind. She'll be a little baby. A harmless baby who didn't ask for any of this," Mom says. She is staring ahead, like a corpse, eyes open.

I want to say, "Do any of us ask for any of this? Isn't that the point?"

But instead I fog up my window and write a line from one of my old poems with my fingertip: "Leaving only traces of our traces."

We walk into the hospital. Take the routine deep inhale of sickness and grief. To get acclimated. To prepare. There is no smell of new baby in the lobby because the babies pop into the world on floor four. Which, by the way, is still tinged with illness and last breaths.

My dad is sitting on the floor of the Labor and Delivery hallway. My mom is in the elevator. She starts to step out, going to him on instinct. Instead, she shoves Bea and me forward, hits the door close button a thousand times until the metal shuts, and she beams up, to a place with a different kind of pain.

When he hears our flip-flops shuffle toward him, my father glances up. His face is blotchy, his eyes bloodshot. Crying. He's been crying in the bad way. He's still crying in the bad way.

My brain goes to blank radio station static.

"They just took her. A few seconds ago. She's having an emergency C-section."

Three feet away from the slumped figure on the hospital's linoleum floor, I stop and stand my ground. Like a hunchbacked old man, my dad's shoulders are rounded, his hands plowing through his thick black hair, head between his knees.

"I…I couldn't go in. I couldn't. She begged me and I stood here like my feet were cement bricks. I told the nurse I'd pass out and be a liability. I can't be there if something—I—"

Bea slinks to his side. She takes his hands. With a puff of air, she blows her long ringlet bangs out of her eyes.

"It will be okay, Dad," she soothes in a voice no seven-year-old kid ought to be able to muster.

I know I should be sympathetic. I know a good person, a good daughter, puts the past to rest in moments of crisis.

But I'm running in the other direction. My flip-flops echo out, "I can't. I can't. I can't."

A click and lullaby come on over the loudspeaker, the building-wide signal for a baby being born. When Joe was here, I held my breath for each tiny serenade, the way Nat and I used to do every time we passed a cemetery. Nurses explained the little songs were to keep people smiling, because babies are symbols of happiness and hope. All those lullabies ever did was make me cry, because what if the universe is made of equal and opposite reactions?

There's a mother and baby crying together in the room on my left. A nurse bustles past me. She's got her big bubblegum lips parted in a full-on grin.

"Shove it," I say and duck into the stairwell.

My mother is packing the origami crane into a black duffle bag when I get to Gramps's room. Eyebrows rise, but she doesn't ask.

"Lori's in surgery," I say with intentional indifference.

"Probably one of those alien babies and they have to rip her stomach open to get it out."

"Anna!"

Dust settles between us.

"What's going on?" I ask, a little more gentle than a moment ago. Cards from Gramps's old customers, fishing buddies, fellow origami club members, aren't filling the wall anymore. Only two are left. One says, "You're a Last Word Kind of Guy," which was written on the back of a hospital menu, by me, in red ink. The other one isn't a get-well note. Mom brought it in and taped it up, like there might be magic in it somehow. It has a stick figure computer-drawing on the front with a big, bold type. *"There's always hope when you know where you want to go."*

I open it, even though I remember what it says on the inside because I was sitting next to Joe the day he wrote it.

"G, thanks for helping to get me there. Love you. Joe."

Mom sighs behind me. It sounds like the word "tired."

"So, you are pulling the plug."

A ladybug crawls outside on the window. Every few seconds it stops to open its wings. They remind me of red little-kid scissors. The left wing keeps sticking. I flick the glass.

"No."

Looking at her confirms my fears. Gramps is brain-dead. She wants to tuck him away in some residential home that reeks of antiseptic and is always bathed in yellow light. In this moment, I know it's true: the watching, holding out hope, waiting for someone to die, it's worse than death itself.

"Mom, no. Please. You can't be serious. Didn't the doctors say—"

She looks at Gramps and back to me. Her eyes are wide, like she can't believe I'd have this conversation here. Once upon a time, Mom held a lot of faith in last-ditch recoveries and people deciding if they want to wake up or not. Still does, apparently.

I follow her into the hallway. We're three rooms away from the central RN station, and a nurse with a narrow, kind face is watching us from behind the Diet Coke she's sipping. Our eyes connect and she quick-drops the can back to her desk. She flips open a chart and pretends to not be listening.

"What if there's the slightest chance? A flicker. A one percent possibility, Anna. How could I let him go? I've already signed the forms. We're moving him to a long-term care facility tomorrow."

How could she let him go? How could I let him go? Joe. Gramps. Their faces swirl together in my mind. Gone but here. Here but gone.

The long rectangular light above us starts humming. It gets louder and louder, and then, quiet again. Mom rubs her hands like she's washing them. Like she's doing the sixty seconds in scalding hot water it takes for a chef to be germ free in a commercial kitchen.

"Mom—"

"This is not up for discussion, Anna." She has said my name more in the past fifteen seconds than she has in a year.

"I cannot be responsible for his death," she adds in strangled whispers.

I look at her. The skin under her eyes puffs like dough starting to rise. She leans against a bulletin board, one with emergency procedures and hospital safety standards tacked in with bright, colored pushpins. I don't think she notices how her words stab me.

The word "responsible" wraps around my neck, constricting.

I nod. Because I understand in ways she can't imagine.

The plan forms before I realize it is a plan and I hear myself saying, "Yes, Mom. Of course not. This is the right thing. Why don't you go to Gramps's house and pack some stuff to move to the care facility. Go home and take a shower. Take Bea to Mrs. G. I will sit here with him."

When her gaze meets mine I have to look away. Those eyes are grateful. They are Bea's eyes, staring up at me, pleading.

For a moment I want to open my arms and let her fall in, let her go limp and sweaty with the weight of not choosing.

Gramps wouldn't want to live this way. But Mom can't be the one. If Joe was still here, my dad would be too, standing beside Mom. The O'Mally boys. They'd be strong for all of us.

But he's gone. And I know what I have to do. I killed once. I'm already stained and lost and here but gone. If

I can do anything for them—for Mom, Bea, Gramps, even Dad—it's this. I can set Gramps free. I can take their hope. Hope is not a thing with feathers. It's an anchor. And it will drown them.

42

Excuse me?" I half-whisper, half-mouse squeak to the soda pop nurse who is now actually working on charts and doesn't notice when I first walk up.

I rubbed my eyes for a full three minutes before leaving the room. Irritated eyes cry easier, and also are red and puffy, which people associate with being emotional. That's a Nat trick I picked up along the way. I bite my thumbnail, look up at the ceiling.

"Oh, I'm sorry! What can I do for you, dear?" asks the nurse, who looks too young to call me dear. Her eyelids droop with black liquid liner. I can't help feeling a little bit guilty for the part—I can't read her scrubs—Angel? No...Angela is about to play in this plan.

"I'm, um, I'm just having a really hard—"

Cue choked sobs.

"A really hard—"

Bite lip, sniffle.

"…A really hard time sitting with my Gramps when all those awful beeps keep going off. I jump out of my skin every single time one of the machines makes a noise, and I promised my mom I would stay with him but I'm really getting—I don't know—I, I can't sit there and listen much longer. It's making me crazy…"

I wait, head in my hands, leaning against the desk. Ignore the desire to check if she's seeing through me.

"Oh, honey." She rushes to my side of the desk and gives me a not-even-awkward stranger hug. "I understand completely. Those noises are unnerving, even for me, and your mom mentioned the loss your family already suffered, so I can only imagine how difficult this is for you. How brave."

I feel sick. But I nod.

She places her hand on my back as we walk to Gramps's room. I break away and sit beside his bed as the nurse fiddles around with the five machines surrounding us.

Once, when we were on vacation up north and Bea was fussy and Mom was stressed because she couldn't reach Dad on his cell, she made Joe and me go walk to the nature preserve near our cabin. It wound through a hemlock forest and swamp. It was springtime, too early for beach visits and lake swims. All of a sudden, this crazy symphony of high-pitched alarms echoed out from the swamp. It rattled our ears and bounced off the trees and I couldn't stop laughing even though it scared me.

"Spring peepers!" Joe exclaimed. "Can you believe frogs are making that noise?"

I could not believe it a bit until one hopped right up on the boardwalk and blew his throat up bubblegum style. He did this just once, and then, died on the spot. We watched him deflate. No joke. Like all that time being a blowhard got reversed in death. Slick skin crumpled in on itself, as if breath and bone were one and the same.

I wanted to kick the empty frog off the wood planks, onto the mud and moss below us, but Joe just took my hand and led me back up the path.

My Gramps's skin, it reminds me of a deflated spring peeper.

The nurse squeezes my shoulder and glides out of the room.

I look around at the wires, screens, rolling tan boxes on sterile, cold poles. All the scripts of every pull-the-plug movie I've seen are lining up to run a marathon inside my brain, waiting for the shotgun start.

"Once we flip the switch to off, the machines will stop breathing for him."

"His respiration will begin to slow."

"All the forms need to be signed, and then, whenever you are ready…"

"He will not be able to stay breathing on his own."

"We have no way of knowing how long it will take."

"Eventually, he'll simply slip away."

"It's not easy. Letting go never is."

I'm committing murder. Again.

I can't stay.

He'll die.

He'll die alone.

Outside, the sky is gray and heavy. I get up and pace to the window, back to the bed. It's now or never. Mom won't be gone long. It might not even work. She might get back before it is over. And no matter what, she'll know. They'll all know.

"Gramps. Please wake up."

The clock above us ticks, ticks, ticks. His face is peaceful. His faded gray eyes will not open.

When Joe stopped breathing, I watched Gramps crumple on a bench with splinters and grass climbing up its legs. Five days later, when they released me from the psych ward, I walked out of the hospital and found Gramps sitting on the same bench. I crawled up on his lap, and he held me while his whole body sobbed. "In the end," he said, "we all die alone. But we shouldn't have to live that way too."

I walk over.

Flip the switch.

I half-expect an alarm loud enough to shatter glass, or a car crash, metal twisting, skidding across pavement. Some noise—any noise—to acknowledge death is coming.

But nothing happens. A switch gets flipped. Not a single thing distinguishes the before and the after.

In the doorway, the nurses' station is empty. The hallway is empty. Turning, I begin to walk toward the stairs. The ceiling intercom clicks. A lullaby begins to play. Every soft note sweeps through me with the yellow chill of a ghost.

I break into a run.

43

Between short gasps for breath I take quick peeks back at the hospital. Blaring noises. Ambulances I'm sure are actually police cars. My head fuzzes and statics and blips and all I can think about is when Bea was little and Gramps would babysit. He'd watch *Masterpiece Theatre* on mute because reading lips was better than waking a tiny tornado. I wish life had a mute button.

Pulling out of the parking lot, I hit the gas. Run three stop signs. Weave through the back roads. My purse is in the passenger seat. I fumble around to grab my phone. Open my contacts and scroll through for Nat. I hear my heart. It's strong, alive, not giving up.

"Well, if it isn't my long lost best fried Anna O'Mally. I wondered when you'd finally call me back."

The phone falls between the gas pedal and the brake.

I can't talk to her.

I can't talk to anyone.

I squeeze and squeeze and squeeze the steering wheel, my foot pressing harder and harder toward the floor.

Rows of houses like mine rush by in a giant streak of tan siding and brick. I don't slow down until I find a horizon of fields, giant checkerboards of corn/beans/corn/beans.

I flipped the switch.

When I finally pull over, I get out and stand in a cloud of dirt-road dust. Cough and choke some. Slump against the gravel and sit long enough for pebbles and rocks to stick to my skin.

My phone scoots across the floor of my car, vibrates its way under the brake. I pick it up and hold it away from me, as if it might explode.

Twenty-seven missed calls from my mother. Twenty from my father. Forty-nine from Nat. Only one from Mateo. I give thanks for my ringer being off, and flop back into the driver's seat.

It must be over already.

Everything around me contracts. Gray sky pushes down, junkyard-press style. The weight crushes my chest, pressures me back into the dirt.

I can't ignore who I need right now. I can't pretend it isn't his voice, his hush, all of him. I dial Mateo's number.

"Hello? Hello? Hell-o?!?"

A girl's voice on his line. I pause and double-check

that Mateo's face, the contact picture he put on my phone a few weeks ago, is smiling back at me.

"Anna, it's America."

I can't.

"Um, ah, hey, America, it's Anna." I hear myself talking. It sounds like someone else. Like I'm watching a movie where I know the star is about to train wreck but still can't tear away from the screen.

"Obviously."

"Is Mateo right there?"

Silence. Followed by a light little laugh.

"Ah, no," she says. I can tell she's smiling. "He's indisposed at the moment. It's like a Gomez tribunal going on downstairs. Or a celebration. I don't know, the tone changes every few minutes—"

"I'm sorry…I'm…I don't understand. What are you talking about?"

My other line beeps, beeps, beeps. A merry-go-round of Dad, Mom, Nat.

"He didn't tell you. Well. Tía will be glad to know she isn't the only one he lied to."

"Lied to?" I hear myself ask.

"Pick up tomorrow's paper," America laughs. "Because that's how we all found out. A reporter called here after the school guidance counselor alerted the press. Mateo got into this super schmancy art school in New York City, all expenses paid. For his entire senior year. And he never even told any of us he was applying. I thought his folks were going to stroke out, but then Tía just started sobbing about how Mateo hadn't felt he could be honest with them and his dad started stuttering about his incredible talent, and Val decided he'd better start crying and Mateo sat on the couch staring into space like none of this is happening to him."

"I…I—"

"Listen," America cuts in. "From what I've pieced together, you're kind of a hot mess. You didn't score points wearing his St. Dismas necklace to the table. Tía bought that for him when he got fired because she thought it might keep him out of trouble.

"And getting up and leaving in the middle of dinner? Without saying goodbye or thank you or anything? Yeah. Tía went crazy on Mat about how rude you are and then he let the truth slip—that he only started dating you to piss her off and to maybe get in trouble 'cause he wanted to get fired and stop having so much pressure put on him. It was an epic family dinner, let me tell you. And look, apparently, they are gonna send him to New York, which means he's leaving in a week. He didn't really like you, and he's busy, so maybe just let him go."

The phone is a bomb. I can't hold it any longer. I throw it in the passenger seat. Get in the car. Drive. Just drive.

I drive until I reach the end of our side of the river. There's a parking lot here, a half-empty strip mall.

He's leaving. He never even told me he might be going. All those conversations. All those secrets. I trusted him.

The sky is heavier than ever and it's like my windshield is buckling, and I have to get out but I don't know where to go. Not to Mateo. Not to Nat. Not back home. Not before. Only after. Clouds shift, rays of light hit the river. It sparkles like a thousand pieces of shattered mirrors. I walk that way.

The concrete underside of the bridge slants to the river bank. A mural of a giant carp, mouth open and looking like it might swallow me whole, stretches across it.

My phone will not. stop. ringing. The Mom-Dad-Nat triangle has become a square with the added insult of Mateo, as if America didn't get enough vindication the first time around. I stand with my toes on the edge of the bank, peering over at the swirly, flat brown river.

Joe used to spit over the faded wood deck railing of this riverside restaurant my dad loved. We kids lined up to watch real muddy-colored carp come up and eat it.

I start hacking to see if I can catch a carp too. Because this is what I have left. Not my grandfather. Not my parents. Probably not my freedom, when all is said and done. I have spit. I have the river.

My pocket starts buzzing again. The screen flashes "Mateo."

And suddenly, I'm watching the iPhone I begged my father to get me for no less than twelve months arc through the air before vanishing under the water.

The ripples caused by my sinking phone start to reach the bank. I take off my flip-flops. The ground is cool, mucky.

I stick one toe in the water. It disappears inside the silt. I yank my foot out, slowly sink the whole of it back in the river.

Images line up behind me, nudging me forward. I see me leaning against the glass in the backseat of my dad's old Ford Mustang, watching slits of brown water and sunlight and empty space between slats on the bridge.

I see Joe and me standing on the side of the boat launch, stifling laughs as Dad tries unsuccessfully to dock the old wooden Chris-Craft he bought on a whim, my super pregnant mom waddling and waving her arms like a frantic duck.

I see Gramps, floating face down, his mildewed life-jacket making kissy sounds each time a little wave hits.

I see Mateo tossing pale stones into the water.

I'm thirsty. And sweating. And feeling like filth.

The water sparkles. It calls to me. Invites me to vanish, just for a moment.

My calves get lost. Then my knees. Thighs. Fingers. Wrists. Hips. Waist.

I go under and open my eyes. The water doesn't sting. No body parts float by. Zero three-eyed fish. There's only sunlight, yellow and full of dust or ashes or a mix of both, dancing deeper and deeper.

Toward the riverbed.

Toward the darker spaces below.

I

    start

        down.

There isn't time to be scared when an enormous shadow turns the river into a washing machine and I'm tumbling and getting yanked and then…

Gulping air.

44.

"Are you outta your goddamn mind?"

The man yelling this two inches from my face is panting and dripping. His words smell sour, like maybe a mouse is decomposing under his tongue. His patchy beard reminds me of a mangy dog. His camouflage T-shirt is dark with river water. Ripped jeans cling against his legs.

Huddled up in a puddle on the bank, I shiver like a not-drowned rat.

"I...I...I..."

"You what?" the man screams, shaking my shoulders with two hands. I'm sure there are red imprints of his fingers now glowing hot on my skin. "You what? You think life is so awful you can't even throw yourself off the bridge? You just gotta walk in and sink?"

I try to focus on him. Scrub my face with my hands,

drop my forehead to my knees, and wrap tight around myself. I rock a little, hoping this nutbag will leave me alone.

"I'm calling the police," he says, gruff and impatient.

"No!" I shout this so loud it echoes off the giant carp before being swallowed by the river.

"No? No? So what? I sit here with you and then turn my back for two seconds and your lungs end up full of that sludge?" He gestures hard toward the river. "Or you leave and figure out some other way to off yourself because your boyfriend dumped you or you flunked calculus or your mommy and daddy won't take you to Paris this summer or whatever shit it is you think's so bad."

His every word spews shrapnel into my skin. Instead of making me curl up tighter, though, it gets me mad. Really, really stark-raving-lunatic mad.

"I killed someone," I say, trying to sound how a hardened criminal should.

"Actually," I add with a semi-hysterical laugh, "I've killed two someones. That's what the shit it is. I. Am. A. Murderer. Or murderess. Or whatever."

The guy with river water dripping out of his shaggy brown hair wipes his nose and rocks back on his heels. He stares at me like shrinks one and six did. I start feeling twitchy and nervous and naked even though my black leggings and black T-shirt are plastered to me.

"Me too," he whispers. Even that comes out with a growling fury. "Me too," he repeats.

I stare back at him.

This is the part in any movie script or thriller book where the heroine needs to get up and start screaming and running for her life. Except I don't, because I'm not a heroine. A big army-green duffle bag sits a few feet away.

"So…you were in Vietnam or something?" I ask, letting him know I'm capable of deductive reasoning.

The guy gut-laughs so hard he falls from squatting on his heels straight to his butt. A dirt cloud fireworks around him.

"Try Afghanistan," he says. "I'm probably only five or six years older than you, kid."

I'm not sure why this shocks me right down my spine, but it does. It isn't like the guy looks old. I mean, when I really take him in, he could have been one of Joe's older soccer buddies.

"Oh. Um, oh. Is that why you're—" I stop at the heavy wool blanket he's draping over me.

"Something like that."

There's nothing else to say. Sorry or thanks for volunteering for our military, and I've read the vet hospitals are good with post-traumatic stress, or I'm sure someday the pain will fade…Yeah. It doesn't cut it.

"Look, I wasn't trying to kill myself. I just…I just wanted to be underwater for a second, that's all."

"Don't think so," he says. "And don't ask because you aren't going anywhere alone."

"Can you please not call the police?" I beg. "I've had

way too much go down in the last three hours and I'm not really operating at maximum reasoning at the moment, obviously, and I don't know if I can handle—"

"Do you have someone else I can call? Your mom? Your dad? A friend?"

"How are you homeless with a cell phone?"

"How are you potentially crazier than me?"

"I'm on a first-name basis with the Truth," I say with a shrug.

"Aren't we all."

We eye each other up. There will be no budging, so I fold my arms and grunt what-ev-er and stare at the river until everything is blurry.

"Who do you want me to call?" He's softer this time.

I lie back against uneven, anthill-clumped ground. A long line of clouds charges east and it reminds me of the Death Star, and also, of Joe. Every time we played the guess-the-cloud game his answer was always the same: the Death Star. Even when the cloud was clearly a white elephant.

I cluck my tongue against my teeth. Tap my heel against the ground. I think about making some smart-mouth comment about being a prisoner of war, but can't bring myself to do it.

"You can give me a name and number or I call 911. You have sixty seconds."

He's calling my silence bluff.

"50, 49, 48, 47, 46, 45, 44—"

"Stop it!" I scream, hoarse and high-pitched as I run away from him and toward the stupid enormous carp. I punch it in the mouth over and over and over again until my knuckles bleed and my whole body aches.

He watches from a respectable distance, waiting until I'm hurt and bloody and all cried out before trusting it's safe to get close.

"Nat," I choke out, staring at the red jelly that is my right knuckle. "Can you...can you please call my friend Nat?"

Once he dials and she picks up I can only make out his half of the conversation and the faint sounds of her frantic inflections. It goes something like, throat clearing, "Hello, Nat? My name is Adam, and I just fished your friend..." Pause, placing his hand over his phone to whisper, "What's your name?" before clearing his throat again and continuing, "Ah, I just fished your friend Anna out of the Grey Iron River—no, no, miss, please! Calm down, she is just fine! Yes, she's right here—okay—okay." To me: "Say something!"

To Nat, I yell, "I'm fine. Just wanted to take an afternoon swim."

He says, "We're below Independence Bridge by the empty strip mall...I'll wait with her. Okay then. Thanks. I will. I promise."

I'm beyond annoyed they are in cahoots, so I stomp to the water's edge. Adam barrels down, pile drives me into the ground. When I get the wind he knocked out of me back, I open my mouth to protest.

He holds up one hand to stop me. "Sorry." I can tell he means it. "You can't...you don't get to die in front of me. I can't be responsible."

Man. Everybody loves that line.

He puts his hand on the side of my arm again, but the grip is loose enough to let me break free if I want. My arm is streaked black, words dripping into words. I don't pull away.

"Did you grow up here?"

He shakes his head.

"Down the river," he says. "Bay City."

"Why aren't you there now? I mean, don't you have family or friends or someone you could stay with?"

"I haven't gone back."

"What do you mean? Since you came back from..." I blank on what to say—war? combat? "Your call of duty?"

"Fan of the video game?" he asks.

"Fake killing really isn't my thing," I answer.

Adam ignores the comment.

"I have been close, but I can't," he says. "I meant to go back. Got home a month early and was all set to surprise everyone. Then I got as far as Grey Iron. And I stopped. Just...stopped."

"Did you ever know a guy named Joe O'Mally?" I ask out of nowhere. Joe's name stings my tongue a little.

Adam's brow furrows.

"No, sorry," he says. "Was he a Marine?"

"Oh. No. He was in the Students for a Peaceful Future," I say with a real smile.

Adam gives me a real smile back.

"Smart guy."

"You have no idea."

My eyes fog over, and when they clear I see Nat walking toward us. She isn't running. She isn't coming to bulldoze me over in a giant wave of relief either. She's walking like the grass leading to the riverbank is a minefield. And she's looking at me like I'm a hologram.

"Thanks for coming," is all I can say.

She doesn't respond, but she does go up to Adam and give him a careful hug.

"Hey, Anna," Adam says as I walk behind Nat toward the parking lot. I turn around, cup my hand over my eyes so I can see him without squinting. "Go home, okay?"

I want to nod and say "you too," but for some reason, I just can't.

45

"Give me your keys," Nat snaps without looking at me. It takes a minute to dig them out of my still-soaked pocket. She taps her foot and snatches them away. They disappear inside her purse.

"You are coming with me."

These are not requests. I'm too wet and miserable to argue. Nat slams her door hard. She slams a pair of sweatpants and her *Oklahoma!* cast T-shirt into my lap. She slams her seat belt buckle into its holder. She's basically one giant SLAM! right now.

I frown and sink low in the seat.

Nat starts the car, turns down the radio, checks her rearview mirror. What she isn't saying drums a furious beat in my ears.

"I killed my Gramps this morning."

"No, you didn't," Nat seethes back.

I swivel around to stare at her.

"What are you talking about?"

"Seriously, Anna? I mean, seriously? Do you really think just because you got a nurse to shut off the alarms in his room it meant no alarms would go off at the nurses' station? Your mom called my mom right away."

Nat stops and shoots me an I've-already-been-down-this-road-once-with-you stare. It isn't full of pity or understanding, either.

"By the time she got back to the hospital, they already had him breathing by machine again. The nurse told your mom what she thought happened, and that you had disappeared, and my mom made me talk to your mom to swear I hadn't seen any change in you or any new 'suicidal tendencies.' Those were the exact words they used. By the time our moms hung up, mine was crying and I kept calling but you didn't answer because you were too busy trying to finish what you started a year ago."

A ripping pain stabs into my chest, black spots dot up my eyes. I keep gasping.

"Breathe," Nat commands.

I hang my head between my knees like airline stewardesses suggest in case of an emergency landing. It takes a few minutes, but the throbbing cry for air begins to subside.

"I was not trying to kill myself."

Nat gives me an exasperated look.

"I just needed everything to stop for two seconds," I

whimper. "My dad, and the baby, and Gramps, and then I found out Mateo is a total—"

"Stop right there. I also know all about what happened with him."

Puke rises and falls in my throat. My nose starts running. I'm gagging too much to tell Nat she has no freaking clue.

"I talked to Mateo."

"You what?"

"I know about art school, and how you found out, and about what he said to his family after you ditched out on dinner, I know all of it."

Nat clenches her jaw tight enough to show off every muscle.

"I can't go home," I start to say.

"Shut up."

"Nat, I'm serious. I can't—"

"Where, exactly, would you like me to take you then?"

"Did you already call my mom?"

"No."

Relief spills out in a long, exhausted sigh.

"Can we just…drive for a few minutes?"

She doesn't answer. I turn off the radio. Turn it back on. Hug my knees to my chest.

When Nat pulls into Leibniz's Bakery, she takes a deep breath before talking.

"Can I trust you to stay put if I run inside?"

The front of the bakery is all glass. A long counter runs

along the windows. It has '50s barstools, and there are two people sitting two seats apart, sipping drinks and staring outside. One, I decide, looks like an over tired young mom. Maybe she needs a break from her kids. Maybe she just left her husband. Maybe she left them all. The other guy is old. He has wrinkles in his wrinkles. I bet his eyes are milky. He looks over at the young mom and smiles.

Gramps is alive.

Nat waits behind four people, and she's gesturing as she talks on her phone. My stomach lurches. She glances back and I drop my eyes to my lap.

Gramps is alive.

An enormous sense of relief washes over me, same as light dancing deeper into the river. Even though it means Gramps is stuck between here and gone. Even though Mom might have to let him go. Even though I failed them all, again.

"Who was that?" I ask as soon as Nat gets back in the car. She shoves a white paper bag and cup of black coffee my way. "On the phone. Who were you talking to?"

"It wasn't your mother. Or your father, if that's what you're wondering. Eat, okay?"

My knuckles throb too much to dig into the bag. Nat notices. She pulls out a croissant and a napkin.

"You can take me back to my car. I'm not a fugitive, I guess."

"Right. Like I'm going to leave you alone again?"

"I was only going for a swi—"

"Yeah. And only walking with stardust beneath your

feet. Enough! I'm not doing this. So just shut up and let me figure out what to do with you."

Nat's voice shakes in fury. Her cheeks burn. Her eyes are dry, but her mascara is smeared. I do what she says. I eat. I sip hot coffee. I stare out the window. I wait.

We drive the same blocks over and over and over again. I clear my throat.

"Can we, can I…can you drive me to Gramps? To his house, I mean?"

She doesn't acknowledge what I've asked, but she makes two left turns and one right. We pull into his driveway, and Nat clamps her hand onto my arm. Her fingernails dig into my skin.

"I'm going in with you, and you don't get to do anything alone. No going to the bathroom with the door closed, no disappearing into another part of the house, no messing around with kitchen knives."

"I'm not a one-act play you get to direct, you know."

"Oh believe me, I know. And you want to know why I know?" she says, barking every word. "Because any play you're ever in is written by, directed by, produced by, and starring *you*. We're all just in the audience. We're all just here to watch your performances and applaud and sigh and cry and scream at all the right places."

I'm aware my mouth is wide open but I can't quite make it shut. Nat's never spoken to me like this.

"Listen," she says. "We'll go in for a little while. Then I'm calling your mom and dad. Do you have any idea how scared they are? And how awful your timing is? Twenty minutes. That's all you get."

It's my turn to refuse an answer. I dig the spare key from underneath a half-painted garden gnome. Late sun plays through the wood blinds; slants of light fall across the floor. Mom cleaned up the dishes I'm sure were piled in the sink, but she missed a full coffee cup on the kitchen table. It still smells fresh and I shiver before remembering Mom was here today. I sit where she might have sat. I cup my hands around the mug.

Nat stands near the door, biting her thumbnail.

"I don't know why I'm here," I say, not looking at her.

"Maybe you wanted to be where you can really, I don't know, feel his presence?"

"That's not what I mean," I say, pausing to choose each word with care.

Nat waits.

"I mean…" I suck air in. "I mean, I don't know why I'm here. I don't know why any of us are here."

I lean my head back against the kitchen chair. These words have been pounding inside my head for a year. They've slipped under my skin. They've slithered like tentacles around every part of me. Now I've set them into the world. A single thought, multiplied a million times in my mind. It all whooshes out, leaving only empty space. A hush.

And that's when I remember. Gramps was making me a present. He was going to tell me a story.

I need to find those paper cranes.

46

I hop up and start opening drawers. Nat is at my side within seconds.

"What are you doing?"

"Looking for something."

"What are you looking for?"

She grabs the drawer I'm about to slam shut and blocks my path.

"Paper cranes."

"Paper cranes?"

"Wow. Good echo. Now could you move? Or help?"

"What am I looking for?"

"Oh my God. Forget it. I just have to find them. Please. Move."

Nat steps aside, bewildered. I continue ransacking every space in the kitchen and living room. I'm about to tear apart his office when I see it. The bag. Its leather marked with wear and age. My mind flashes back to Joe's one-year deadaversary. To Mom being gone. To Gramps sitting at my kitchen table. Folding paper.

I almost don't want to look. I almost don't want to find them now. The last time I discovered words inside a crane, they were Joe's. They tasted like betrayal.

Still, I move closer. Sink to my knees. Shift, uncomfortable, until I can't stand it. I open the bag. Inside it sit four large paper cranes. Each one is numbered. 1. 2. 3. 4.

I hold number one in cupped hands and lift its beak to my nose before starting to unfold it. A dried flower petal falls out. It floats into my lap. It is pale pink.

Dear Anna,

He wrote to me. I study the slanted cursive before reading. His angles and lines fit, each letter connecting, cogs in a machine.

I'm not the wordsmith of the family, so bear with me. I've been thinking about doing this for some time now. It isn't an explanation or a big life lesson, though I hope from it you will, indeed, have some new perspectives. Positive perspectives, even if I think you won't see it that way at first. What is it you call your friend? Your Keeper of Secrets? Well, I suppose that's what I'm doing here. I'm entrusting you as our family's Keeper of Secrets. As for why I'm doing it in a series of paper cranes—well, indulge an old man, will you?

Inside this crane, you found a flower petal. I know it doesn't look like much now, but when it was still attached to the plant—my! It was glorious. Lots of things work this way. It's like a tiny screw that went missing once on a big stereo repair job. I put everything back together, but it wouldn't work without that single piece of metal. And I never would have figured out why, if I hadn't known to look for it. I digress. The flower petal is from a Japanese orchid. I gave it to your Gran the day your mother was born.

Your mother was tiny. I held her in my palm. Like a squirming fish, but much more lovely. Or not, in the beginning. (Have you ever seen a seconds-old baby, Anna? They aren't the most beautiful of creatures.) But oh, how I loved her. The very second I laid eyes on her. I knew the world had shifted. Powerful love does this to us. It shifts our gears and makes us understand words like "sacrifice" and "presence" and "hope" in ways you can't yet know.

It's no secret I adore my daughter. But this is a secret: Gran was pregnant when we got married. It's best to just put that out there now. Your mother doesn't know. She believes she was a wedding-night blessing, because this is what I've always told her. She believes the math because we said she was early. Your Gran was a wild, free spirit. We had some fun, and then she showed up at my doorstep sobbing. Her dream was to move to Paris. She was already 37, never going to be a mother. Never going to be a wife. We got married two weeks later, in front of a judge. Those first years were terrible. She left once, for a month. Took off God knows where and left your mother here, with me—with a note saying my literality suffocated her. My inability to understand symbolism made her artistic soul wilt. Her ridiculous notions did the same to me. I am not sure we loved each other back then. I am sure we knew the score.

Things aren't always as they seem. But sometimes, when we wade through long enough, they become more than we could ever imagine. I still don't understand what the hell any of your Gran's paintings mean. But I understood her. And I loved her. I love her still.

"Anna?"

I nearly hit my head on the corner of the old metal filing cabinet that serves as one end of Gramps's desk.

"Are you okay?"

I nod, staring at the page. I glance to the second crane.

"Could you get me some water?" My voice is hoarse and shaky. Nat pauses like she's not sure it's safe to leave me alone. I reach for the second crane and she walks out the door.

Your Gran would be quite proud of me, I have to say! The crane is a symbol of long life and immortality. Did you know that? I didn't either. Sameera told me once. Smart kid. I want you to know I am writing this down because I believe you can handle it. More than that, I believe you will make connections. You will forgive. You will understand. I'm an old man. Not that old—no making dinosaur jokes at my expense—but old enough to have been to my fair share of funerals. And every single funeral is the same at its core. People stand around telling wistful stories and making the dead guy or gal seem like they ought to be on the right hand of God. There are times when I've thought about retelling a dirty joke

the deceased loved or discussing their drink-by-noon habits and such.
But I never do. I tell the good stories, like all the rest.

I flip the paper over, to see if he'd written any more on the other side. He hadn't. What the hell is all this about? I crumple crane two up in my fist and chuck it into the trash. I get up and almost run into Nat.

"It took me a second to find the cups," she says, holding out a glass of ice water. In the corner, Morte, the dead stuffed German shepherd, stands guard. I tip him over.

"So what's up with the cranes?" Nat asks.

I just shake my head.

"You want me to wait in the hallway?"

I nod.

She goes.

I sit back down.

Pick up crane number three.

47

Have you rolled your eyes enough, young lady? I'd like to tell you a story about your parents. I'm still mad as hell at your father. Don't mistake this as an explanation for his behavior. It isn't. There is no excuse for what he did. But we are human. We are fragile creatures made of fragile parts. It's miraculous, when you think about it: like magnets, we bump together and push apart, trying to find connection. We all want to feel slices of joy.

Your dad has been through a great deal in his life. He lost his parents when he was only 21. The accident was gruesome. He had to switch gears from grieving to responsibility within minutes. He became a father for his brother. He married your mom. Out of love. Don't get any ideas from that first crane. Your parents were very much in love. She cared for her boys with everything she had, Tess did (does). Your Gran thought it was a statement against her—the way your mom took to domesticity with such a fervor. I told your

Gran not everything in life was symbolic. Boy! I slept on the couch for two weeks for that remark.

I'm writing small now because I'll run out of paper and I haven't even started yet. Your mom took on a lot of sadness for your dad and Joe. She sponged it up best she could, but it was never enough. When you were a year old, on the day before the anniversary of his parents' deaths, your dad left the house to go for a drive very early in the morning. The details of what happened during the next ten or so hours are sketchy, but the evening ended with your father in the county drunk tank. Something about him getting caught on top of the roof of a bar that was once a firehouse, waving what appeared to be his boxer shorts and yelling to anyone and everyone who'd listen that life is short and to make every second count. That's why your mom got your family out of town every year after that, maybe figuring if he wanted to get half-naked and pontificate about the brevity of existence, remote cabins were better podiums than downtown bar rooftops. The truth is, she tried to put Band-Aids on wounds too deep to heal. When Joe died, your dad broke. That's the best way to describe it. I think he did what he did (though I think the baby part was an accident) to put walls between himself and his family. He's told me as much. He's lost his anchors, his parents. He's lost his brother, whom he raised like a son. There is no denying the fact that one day, you and Bea and your mom will die too. Most people can keep this knowledge buried. But your dad has seen too much. He knows there's no guarantee he'll go first. I think he believed he could lessen the blow. That he could detach.

It was wrong. But human.

48

I don't wait before grabbing the last crane. I can't stop even though there isn't enough room in my head for all these secrets. All these truths. Gramps's words crash into each other. I crawl over to the corner, as if putting my back against the wall will steady me. Will make all of this slow down.

The writing is shorter in this last crane. I picture Gramps bent over the page, scribbling away at my kitchen table, looking up when I walked into the room.

There's no easy way to say this, except to remind you to go back and read crane number two a whole bunch of times. Brace yourself, kiddo. This crane will mean the most to you. And it will hurt. I know how much you loved Joe. How much you looked up to him and thought he could do no wrong. And he loved you too. Sometimes, we think we know what's best for the people we love. Sometimes, we're wrong.

I'll just come out with it: Joe botched your finalist packet for the summer residency you wanted to go to so badly. Remember how you asked him to read the story over to make sure it was perfect? Remember how he said not to change a thing? You never read the document again before sending it, did you? I know you didn't, because he changed it. He took out a few bits, rearranged paragraphs, made it so your words were less focused. He thought success was coming too easy for you. He worried you were in over your head and you needed to grow up some more before having that kind of pressure. He said if you'd really wanted to get in, you would have checked that story again, line by line, before emailing it.

But then the rejection came. And you were so broken up about it. Joe came to me, told me everything. He still thought he did the right thing. I told him the fact that you didn't review the story, may have been more a sign of trust in him than a lack of motivation. This got him thinking. He said he was going to fess up as soon as he figured out a way to explain. But then, he got sick. A summer residency didn't seem important anymore. I'm not telling you this to get you writing again. I'm telling you so you can grieve for Joe knowing the whole truth. In the long run, you need to understand that people—even the best people—are always more and less than we imagine. It's okay to be mad at him, Anna. It doesn't mean you love him less. We all

It stops mid-sentence. I'd walked in the room. He never finished the letter. I'm screaming and screaming and screaming and screaming, but Nat's not rushing in to see what's wrong. Maybe I'm not screaming out loud. Maybe I'm shriveled in the corner, staring straight ahead, understanding coffin yoga on a whole new level. I'm trapped. Trapped inside truth inside of truth inside of truth.

All of a sudden Nat's in front of me, shaking me, saying my name over and over and over. I can't answer. I've screamed myself hoarse inside.

When Nat reaches for the crane in my hand, however, I spring.

"Don't you touch that!"

She stumbles backward.

"Anna!"

"NO!" I cry. I know I look like a caged animal. I can't help it. "You can't read these. They're mine!"

Nat grabs me. She yanks me up and drags me to the car. The lights stay on in Gramps's office.

"Stop it!" I cry, struggling to break free.

"I swear to God I will stick you in the trunk if you try to run." She's seething and choking back tears.

She pushes my stomach against the seat and slams the passenger door. I start to open it, but holding the handle makes me think of the metal on Gramps's machines, which makes me think of Gran and Mom and Dad and Joe and I can't do this anymore.

Nat gets in and stares at me.

"What the hell was that about?"

I can't find words to answer. I can't find words at all.

"You think this isn't mine to grieve too. Fine. I get that. But you can't lock it all up. Do you have any idea how lucky you—"

"Lucky? Lucky? Are you kidding me?"

"Yes, lucky. You get to grieve. Don't you see? You get to show the whole world your pain and we're all here to hold you up and..." her whole face trembles.

"I feel like I have nothing left," I say to myself more than Nat. "Joe. Gramps. My dad and his baby. All those words in the cranes, what they mean, what—never mind. And when I opened myself up for one second...Mateo..."

"Mateo is going to New York! He's not dead! The only reason you don't have him is because you pushed him away!"

She revs Dolores's engine and slams into reverse.

"I can't face them right now, Nat. I can't."

"Well, you have to, because I'm done. I'm done. I'm done. I'm done."

So we're back to where she's slamming everything again, including words.

All the new stories in my head are swerving around each other, trying to connect. When we turn the corner onto one of the four-lane roads spanning the length of the township and city, I beg Nat to keep going, straight across the bridge.

I need to see him, I tell her. She doesn't need to ask who I mean. She bites her lip hard and shakes her head no again and again, but she keeps driving into city limits. I watch the water pass beneath us and remember how much I want to forget.

49

I expect the gothic gates of Forest Grove Cemetery to be rusted and tired. I expect the grass to be overgrown and weedy, the road to be split and uneven. In reality, it looks better than St. Patrick's, only four blocks from my house. Dark green ivy sprawls along the stone walls, huge pots of red geraniums dot the drive. The lawn is shorn short, making each headstone stand even taller. These graves have not been forgotten.

We take several wrong turns as I try to remember the directions to our family plot.

"Maybe left here," I say, pointing to an obelisk.

Instead, Nat turns right.

"I said left—" I start to argue, except suddenly the large birch tree, the one we've always used to locate my grandparents' graves, is in front of us. "Oh. Okay. We're here. You can stay in the car. I'll only be a few minutes."

Nat's whole face is ticking. She opens her mouth. Shuts it with a snap. The seat belt makes a little zippy noise as she leans her head against the gray leather steering wheel and then back against her headrest. Outside, a squirrel runs in circles.

"Go ahead," I say. "Say your piece."

There are forty-three seconds of silence.

"Have you ever asked Mateo about the scar on his face?"

I blink.

"What?"

"The scar. Do you know why it's there?"

I try to pull an answer from thin air, but the truth is, I don't have a clue.

"I'll take that as a no."

"What does this have to do with anything?"

She glares, as if I am the most idiotic person on the planet.

"When Mateo was eight, a group of kids in his neighborhood were playing with a box of firecrackers they found in someone's garage. They took a big glass container—the kind you'd store like five pounds of rice or popcorn kernels inside—and stuffed it with firecrackers, then lit it and ran away. Except the thing didn't explode, and Mateo and some kid named Arnie went to take a look. When they got up to it, it blew up. Mateo got a shard in his chin. The other kid lost one of his eyes. He's never gone to watch fireworks since. Until he went for you."

I told myself I maybe loved Mateo, but I didn't even know this story. And she did.

"How did you find out?"

"I asked him."

We stare at the rows of headstones. My head hurts. My knuckles hurt.

"Well, good for you. You like knowing everybody's secrets, right?" I can't hide my annoyance.

"This is the worst part of being your friend."

The word "friend" hangs between us, cold and alone. For the first time, I wonder if Nat and I will ever share a lunch table again. If we'll make it through this.

"You don't get it," she continues. "You never will. You get to wear your grief however you want. You get to be Patti Smith. You get to ditch your words. You get to write verses on your arm for the whole world to know exactly how you feel. And you don't appreciate how alive it makes you. Sometimes I wish for one second—just one tiny second— you and I could switch places."

I won't give her the benefit of my tears. I yank the door open and jump out, falling over my own feet as I make my way to his grave. Switch places. I've never heard such a selfish thing. Drama whore. That's what she is.

I'm glad my back is to Nat as I walk toward Joe. I don't want her to see my face twist in pain and fear and an ache so black and deep and endless I possibly have an entire universe lost in the pit of my stomach. I've never been a big fan of graveyards. Rows of coffins with rotting corpses doesn't seem that comforting. Yet the minute I see the curved granite slab with Joseph Daniel O'Mally on it, a warmth rises within me. I kneel down, trace the letters of his name, the words "Beloved Son, Brother, Uncle" and the dates. His beginning. His ending.

"Why?" I ask him, quiet at first, then louder and more shrill, until I'm wailing. "Why? Why? Why did you do it? How could you? Why didn't you just tell me? Why didn't you say it before I gave you those germs?"

I pound one fist against the granite and yelp with a pain so sharp I'm knocked onto my butt. Wiping my eyes with my palm, I take in the whole plot. There are daisies and sprigs of mint in a ball jar. Mom. A laminated drawing of what could be a pig, a pink person, or a cloud is pushed into the ground with a stick. Bea. Beside the grave is a piece of paper, held down with a rock. I groan when I read it.

> There's not a day that goes by without thoughts of you. I miss you. And I believe in heaven now, because it's nice to think we'll meet again. Opiate of the masses, indeed. ~L.E.D.

L.E.D.
Laura Elizabeth Donnaly.
Sameera's best friend.

I hold the paper carefully in my hand, like it might explode. Could Nat have been right all along?

I get up and move toward my grandparents' graves, behind Joe's. I need a minute. The sheer amount of horrific information I've swallowed today is enough to open a sinkhole. In the shadow, leaning against the back of Joe's headstone, I see it.

A plant. A prehistoric-looking plant. With purple and orange wings for petals. A plant called Bird of Paradise. It has a paper crane-like flower.

A paper crane flower.

A paper crane. There's a card sticking out of it, but I think I know who it's from before I even read the words. I've only seen a plant like this one other place. And I only know one person in the world sappy enough to quote the most lovelorn line from *Les Misérables* on a handmade card meant to sit beside a grave.

How she cried for him. How she could barely say his name for months after he was gone. How she kept that plant on her dresser. How she looked shocked when I pulled the bracelet from under his bed. It was hers. It was her.

I turn. Nat stands with a few headstones between us crying. Hard.

Nat.

Joe.

No.

No.

No.

"Anna," she says. Everything is there, in the way she says my name. "Anna…"

I hold up my hand to silence her. He never told me. She never told me. The lies. The betrayal. They shared this. They kept each other's secret.

They were together.

"Please, please let me explain—"

"No!" I scream the word loud enough to scare a crow out of the birch tree. He caws his disapproval. "You don't get to say anything! All this time. All this time I was searching for the person he wrote that letter to—"

"Letter? You said it was a receipt." She hiccups after the word "receipt."

"That's what I meant!" I stomp the ground. "All this time you let me go on and on like a fool. Did you just want to laugh? Enjoy the last hoorah on your inside joke?"

Nat's slumped against the ground. She clutches her stomach. Sobs. "That receipt. It couldn't have been me. We never went to a…he had someone else."

"How?" I ask. She doesn't answer, so I ask again. And again.

"How did it happen?"

Nat shrugs. She won't meet my eyes.

"One day, I came to pick you up," she says finally, staring at the tree behind me. "It was his spring break, so he was home. You were still out, I don't remember where. Joe was sitting on the front porch. I sat next to him. We talked like always. But then our knees bumped and we sort of left them there, touching."

The two people I thought I knew best in this world.

"I'm going to be sick."

"I'm sorry," she cries. "I'm sorry, Anna. He called me the next day, pretending to be looking for you, but then we stayed on the phone for hours, and it was late, and he asked if I'd ever ridden a bike down the middle of the street in the dead of night in the early springtime, and I said no, and before I knew it he was shining a headlamp up into my window, all bundled up and waving on that funny cruiser bike of his. And then—"

"Stop. Stop. I don't want to hear any more."

I'm about to turn away when I remember Alex.

"In all of this sneaking around and secret little affair of yours, was this one of the times you broke up with Alex? Does he know? Do you care that you betrayed him? That you betrayed us both?"

"Please," Nat sobs over and over again. She holds one hand up in front of her face, waves it frantically, as if she can make it all disappear. As if she can erase the truth.

"Why shouldn't I call him right now? Huh? Why?"

"Anna, no, please."

"Give me a reason."

"Anna, I never meant to…we never meant to…it just happened. And I do care about Alex. Deeply. That's why I couldn't tell him, when Joe and I—when we started to fall—and then we weren't together and he died and Alex is so good and loving and kind and why would I hurt him for something that can't ever exist?" She's pleading now.

"Stop it," I snap, shaking my head. "You could cry

a new Great Lake and it wouldn't make up for what you did. For what you kept doing by lying to us. Just stop. Save your drama."

"What do you think I've been doing for the last year?" All of a sudden Nat's come alive again. She pulls herself up and marches within inches of my face. Thrusting her finger against my chest, she draws in a ragged breath. Her face is pinched with fury.

"You own all your grief. You get to feel it and mourn it and express it. What did I get to do? Bury mine. I'm an actress, a person who only knows how to do emotion big and bold and raw. But I can't. I've had to stuff it all inside and be there for you. I've held your secrets. I've taken your hurts. But who has been there for mine? The only person I could have ever told is there!"

She throws her hand toward Joe's grave. And then she spins away from me and screams at him.

"And you! You tell me all the things I want to hear. You make me understand what it means to love somebody. And then we—and you—you break it off like it meant nothing to you. Nothing! And I never get to ask you why. I never get closure. I walk around with a you-shaped hole that will never, ever mend. I hate you for that! I hate you for going to some motel with some other girl—for making me think we were real. How could you?"

She picks the plant up and hurls it against the stone. The pot breaks, dirt falling on both sides of the grave. I'm frozen. She's frozen. We aren't facing each other, but I can see her gasping for more, more, more air. Just like me.

She coughs, catching her breath.

Just like Joe.

Oh my God.

Just. Like. Joe.

"Nat. You were sick too. When I got the flu—you and I had it at the same time, didn't we? Did you...it could have been—" I can't finish. The thought knocks the wind right out of me.

Without turning around, she begins again, voice broken.

"I wanted to tell you. I wanted to tell you when we first...I wanted to tell you when he got sick, when you told me it was your fault, but how could that have been the right time, with so much bad happening so fast, and I was heartbroken and couldn't tell my best friend. I couldn't cry about this guy who tore me into pieces because it was Joe and he'd insisted we keep it a secret from you until he could make up his mind and then he was gone and you almost died and then you were home and not all right and I was so scared I'd lose you too. The days turned into weeks and weeks turned into months and months turned into a year, and by then all the things I didn't say stacked so high I was afraid—I just...and then you found that receipt and I broke into a million little pieces all over again. Every delusional thing I told myself about how Joe felt—it crumbled and I couldn't say a word.

"Everyone got pieces of him. Sameera. Your family. Even the Sarahs. I don't even get his memory, Anna. I don't even get to hold on to a sliver of his love. All I have, all I've ever had, is loss. So don't you see? I couldn't let Alex go too. I do love him. In a different way, but I do, and I couldn't see hurting him and losing him and having absolutely nothing left. I don't think I could have held it together, and I couldn't leave you alone."

There's nothing left to say. We both know it. She starts to walk away.

"I'll wait in the car," she says, sniffling and wiping black streaks from her eyes across her cheeks.

I move into the birch's thin shadow. It covers half of Joe's grave, vintage light bathing the rest of the grass, green tips reaching toward the sun. The cemetery closes at dusk. I lay my head against the earth.

I want to hate her. I want to hate Joe. It all rises in me, the stain of lies and loss and hidden truths. But then I think about Gramps and how he folded paper the same way people fold into themselves. I think about how we are fragile. How we are all made of secrets and secret keepers. Every connection shapes us, and we then shape others, and it makes our stories rich and jagged and full of pain and full of love. And it matters. All of it.

50

J oe used to recite this one poem to me a lot when I first
started writing. His high school English class was in
the thick of a poetry unit and he became obsessed with
the sound of William Stafford's works, especially this
one about grass and sky and a heart that stops beating. I
thought it was morbid.

"That last line is so great, how it wraps up all the gone
and here and past and future and right now, like it's right
around us in the clouds," he'd say.

I never forgot Joe's words. Or the poem.

I don't know why I'm thinking about it right now.
Maybe because I'm all of a sudden not mad anymore. I'm
hurt. But it's the kind of hurt that comes with loss and
letting go. It's just another layer in what the word "sad"
means to me.

I'm sad. And missing the way things were. And grieving the way things will never be. And maybe accepting, a little bit, the way things are, right now.

I repeat the lines, shush them into the soil, hope the sounds carry below or above or all around.

I will the words to reach him. Then I feel it. A pulse in the ground. Vibrating sounds, the beat of a heart. I push my ear against the grass. A steady rhythm, getting closer. Opening my eyes, I see Mateo jogging my way.

51

I sit up too late. Nat's BMW's taillights are already disappearing around a bend. A green Jeep is parked on the roadside. Mateo is close enough that I can't run. My eyes dart in every direction, searching for an escape route or place to hide.

"Anna, please." Mateo stops jogging. He's seven headstones away. He holds his hands up where I can see them, and approaches slow. Like I'm a wild animal. Like he's afraid to scare me.

"Just stay right there and let me talk to you. Please. Just listen."

"I can't believe she left me," is all I can eek out as I stare at the place where Nat's car had been sitting.

"She's upset. She felt like you needed space. She called me."

"Of course she did."

Mateo looks hurt.

"Come on, don't be like that. I'll drive you home. I want the chance to explain."

"Explain what? Why does everyone think they get the chance to explain after ripping me into shreds? How do you think you can explain away all the stuff I told you, when everything you were telling me was a lie?"

I rake my hands through my hair. Lean against the tree.

"I know what it looks like," he says, stepping closer. "And I'm not going to act like you're wrong."

"It doesn't matter now. Whatever we were was fake anyway, right? Just a way for you to get back at your parents, or lose your spot in the culinary program so you could go off to New York without even saying goodbye? Don't you think I've had enough of that in my lifetime?"

Mateo doesn't take his eyes off me. Not even for a second.

"I know what I said. When we first saw each other, you know you felt that connection too," he says, searching my face. "But I also knew you looked like trouble and maybe that made me want you more. That's not the truth of what we were, though, or how I feel about you now. I never thought New York was even possible. I didn't believe it would happen—so many things had to fall into place. The scholarship had to be a full ride. My parents had to agree. I wasn't even sure I wanted to go—I mean, the culinary program could be a meal ticket. What's art school? Maybe nothing. I never should have let myself fall—"

"Give me a break."

"Look, when we met it's not like I was thinking, 'Aw, man, where has this girl been all my life?' You're beautiful. But actually, you just looked like—like red paint."

"Red paint? You fake-liked me because I looked like red paint?" I halt between words because the sentences sound so crazy.

"Basically. To everybody else, I think you looked like the color gray, like something dull and empty and strange. I could tell, though. I could see it. And the night I took you home, when we started talking, I felt sure—"

"Sure that I was red paint?"

"Yes."

"Do you know how insane that sounds?"

Mateo laughs a little. He drops his head and nods.

"I gotta believe you know what I mean," he says, looking up at me from heavy-lidded eyes. "You're an artist. I can't explain it except to say you are vivid color. And I wanted to be around you."

"Okay, enough with the bullshit. You've already admitted you used me. I'm done. I'd rather be home."

"No. No, we aren't done. Because I'm trying to explain. My very first thought, after that night we shared a smoke? Yes. It was that you looked like the kind of trouble I needed. But honest to God, Anna, that was the last time I thought it. And when I first kissed you, everything exploded—my feelings, my job, my future—I wanted to stay away from you and figure out my own mess and yet I showed up at your house within a few days. I started believing this was real and then you walked out in the middle of dinner and I was so pissed I just said a bunch of stupid, stupid things. But we just keep bumping back together."

"Fragile magnets," I whisper.

"What?"

I shake my head, picture bad-ass girls dancing like they don't care, swinging microphones, getting carried away by a crowd. I'm channeling. I'm staying in character.

"Never mind. I'm done with people who can't tell the truth."

Mateo has the nerve to look pained, his eyes as vulnerable as the night we met. Maybe more.

"You don't get to call me out on not being truthful when you're dressed like some punk rock poet whose words you steal like penny candy—"

"Did you just say 'words you steal like penny candy'?"

Mateo breaks into a sheepish grin. I've felt like Atlas all day, carrying the world on my shoulders. For whatever reason, "words you steal like penny candy" is the funniest phrase I've ever heard. I can't stop laughing. Between this and a constant flow of tears, my whole face is a giant bee sting, swollen and heavy and zonked.

"Can I get you out of here?" Mateo is cautious as he motions toward his Jeep. "You don't have to say a word to me on the ride home."

It's getting late, and everything is shadowed in orange

light, like an old photograph. It carries the softness of the past, of remembering.

"Fine." I'm too exhausted to argue.

As soon as we get in the Jeep, Mateo opens his mouth again.

"I really like you. I mean, I have never felt like this about—"

"I thought you said we didn't have to talk?"

He shrugs and turns on his radio.

"Are you listening to Patti Smith?"

Mateo shrugs again.

"I like her stuff," he says, staring at the road. "But I will say, for someone you want to be just like, you're a little short on optimism."

"What are you talking about? I wouldn't call Patti an optimist. She's a realist."

"Are you joking me? I mean, her memoir—*Just Kids*— the whole thing is one giant ode to hopefulness."

I blink at him.

"No way," Mateo says, ping-ponging his glance between the road and me. "You're obsessed with being like this woman, but you haven't even read her memoir? Nat bought it for you, right? I mean, I've read her copy—she lent it to me as what she called an 'Anna Study Guide.' What have you been doing for the last year? Using bits and pieces of her world? I gotta tell you, a lot of the book felt like you—I mean, not like the same situations or anything, but the emotion. Patti Smith was kinda a lost soul too, I figured you clicked with the idea. But she found herself. I mean, that's the whole point."

I stuff my hands into my borrowed sweatpants. I can't have my fingers wandering free. I'll reach for him.

52

As soon as we get within two miles of my house, I start panicking. It's not a cute panic either. It's a full-blown attack. I can't breathe. I can't move. Mateo pulls over and leans back in his seat.

"Can you, can you take me to the Roethke House?" I ask as soon as I can gasp enough air to form words.

"I'm not taking you to some dead poet's house to leave you sitting alone, outside, in the dark. I want to take you home, Anna, but I'll wait until you are ready to go."

"I won't be outside." My mind reels. I know I can't see my mom or Bea yet. The aftermath of what I did—what I tried to do—I can't stomach it right now. I can't. I can't go. I need a place to sort out my thoughts. To figure out what I'm going to say. To grieve everything that is and isn't.

I've never used the key around my neck. When Mrs.

Risson realized I was serious about never writing again, she gave it to me and said if I ever needed to find my words, the museum she helps care for might serve as inspiration. I took the key to be nice. I've never taken it off, but it's been hung around my neck for all this time only to remind me what I need to keep locked away. But I don't have to stay outside tonight, and when I tell Mateo this, he turns his Jeep around.

53

We step into the dark house. Mateo bumps a metal coat rack. It tips against me. Startled laughter. We fumble for the light switch. The bulbs are dim at first. We wait in silence until the entryway is a mix of light and shadows. Ah, the metaphor.

"What have you eaten today?" Mateo asks as we tiptoe into the kitchen. He clears his throat and asks again, remembering we are the only two people here. I watch him survey the buttercream walls, the dark wood window trim dividing the top of the glass into three small square panes. He looks at the stove and fridge, both new but made to look old. I follow his eyes: small wooden table, four dining chairs, dishes stacked on shelves above the sink.

"Um…" I pause and walk out of the room. I don't

need to be taken care of, but admitting I haven't had anything but river water and a croissant in my system might not be the best proof.

"Nothing, right?"

When I don't answer, Mateo frowns.

"Okay, we need to remedy that," he says, glancing toward the front door and back to me. "If I leave you here and run to the store, can I trust you'll stay put?"

"What is it with you people? Where am I going to go?" I ask. He glares at me. I pout.

"Yes, fine. I promise. But you don't need to go to the grocery store for me. Let's just go get some fast food or something. Taco Bell's open."

I can't help a tiny grin when Mateo waves off my idea as "ridiculous." He checks his wallet, nods, and walks out the door. I listen to him jog down the steps. There are seven of them, painted gray. An engine rumbles. Tires crunch in the gravel drive. I settle onto a green couch and wait.

I must have fallen asleep, because I wake to the rhythm of Mateo in the kitchen. I can see him through the door, his body moving in and out of the frame. He glances my way, feeling my stare. He flashes a dimpled half-smile.

It occurs to me I've never actually eaten anything Mateo has prepared. The plate of food he brought to my house got devoured by Mom and Bea, but I opted to make a peanut butter and grape jelly sandwich instead. The smells coming from the kitchen are rich and warm. My stomach responds with a growl.

"Come on in here," Mateo says.

The plate set down in front of me is simple. I never understood, until this moment, what it means to have someone make art for you. It doesn't matter the medium is a plate of wilted spinach with a balsamic-drizzled crepe in the middle, stuffed to the point of bursting with rice and mushrooms and kale.

I can't explain how this food tastes like more than food, but it does. Maybe it's because this is the first real meal I've had since yesterday. Maybe it's the late hour. Maybe it's eating at the table of a poet who spoke in waltzes and phrases of flowers. Maybe it is the way Mateo watches me chew and swallow, every muscle in his face defined by worry, compassion, and something like love.

"You are really, really good at this," I say, nodding toward my plate.

"Thanks."

"How did you choose? I mean, I know you can draw amazingly well and all, but how did that kind of art win out over this? Cause I have to say, this is to die for."

"Not the best word choices for today, hmm?"

"Don't change the subject," I warn, dragging my fork across my plate.

"Cooking is personal for me. I love to cook. I love to make food for my family, friends. But cooking for strangers kind of sucks. It's not my thing. I don't want to do it for the rest of my life just because I'm good at it. It's hard because there's a lot of pressure on me to go to culinary school. My parents aren't going to be around forever. Val's gonna need help, which means I need to make money. But I don't know. Art degrees can lead to jobs too, despite what high school counselors claim." He leans into me.

I lean back, sharing his joke.

"Stay with me tonight," I say when the last bite is settling into my stomach.

I leave the plate on the table. Dishes are scattered across the counter. Cooking as art is a messy business. I lead him to the bedroom upstairs. My hands might be sweating too much. My experience is limited to some tongue action and a single boob feel-up at the park during a game of spin-the-water-bottle one afternoon. It doesn't inspire confidence. I need to stop thinking. Walk. Hold his hand. Breathe. Stop blushing. Stop sweating into his palm. Stop thinking about what to stop doing.

The four-poster bed is short, the dark wood matching the windows and stairs. It has a red-and-white quilt of entwined circles, like a mandala.

Mateo stops at the door. He holds me by the small of my back and my neck, kisses me like I'm fragile. Like he's a warm breeze just passing through.

"I'll stay," he whispers. "But not like this."

He steps into the room and folds back the quilt. There are no sheets underneath, but I crawl in anyway, trying not to cry as he pulls the cover back over me. Tucks me in like a child.

"Don't," he murmurs, catching a tear with the side of

his finger. "It's not that I don't want to. I just don't want it to be like this. I'm gonna call Nat and have her somehow let your parents know you're safe. And then I'll stay on the couch. But I won't go downstairs until you're sleeping."

I only feel two more tears slide down my nose.

Fate is like a secret friend that helps push you back into life.

54

When I open my eyes again, the pale rays of morning dance along the walls and floor like the long legs of a ballerina.

I stretch out, get still and coffin stiff. My eyes find a single spider thread swaying from the ceiling. I start to count seconds in my head. It takes until minute three to realize I've been pulling inhales deep, cleansing out yesterday's haze.

By minute nine, my fingers lock and reach up above my head.

By minute eleven, I'm humming Patti's song, "This is the Girl."

By minute fifteen, I give up and sit cross-legged on the bed. There is a note beside me. I don't have to read it to know he's gone.

55

Dear Anna,
Sleeping on the couch sucked. It was uncomfortable,
plus required me to take a cold shower and smoke an
entire pack to keep from wandering back upstairs. I just
want to tell you there will always be us, okay? Read the
Patti Smith book, and you'll know what I mean.
Love,
Mateo
P.S. If you aren't home by 11 a.m....well...just go home.

I fold a crooked crane. I'd never been patient enough
to learn how to make my corners crisp, my lines symmet-
rical. Still, it doesn't fall over when I set it on the nightstand. Or when the front door slams shut, shaking the
floor from the first step all the way to the four-poster bed.

56

Anna O'Mally, I know you're here. Best answer me on the first go-round," Mrs. Risson calls as she walks up the steps. Her voice is soft. Even though she's yelling, it only sort of trickles to the second floor.

I hop out of bed and quickly pull the quilt up. I must have slept like the dead. There's barely a wrinkle, as if I'd been a stray sock.

"Mrs. Risson?" I answer like this is totally normal, me breaking into the museum and spending the night. I hope Mateo did the dishes before leaving.

We meet at the top of the stairs. Through her fierce hug, I touch the notches of her bony spine. Without a word she turns and walks back down and into the living room. I follow.

"How?" I ask.

"Natalie called me. My, that child has a flare for the drama. Said for reasons she could not speak of, she would not be able to come pick you up today. Made me swear on all great poets living and dead I would not call your mother, but would instead just come fetch you. A pact I did not keep, mind you," she says, tilting her head down so she can look me in the eyes without her glasses between us. "I'm a mother too, you know. That wasn't an option. Instead I told your mom exactly where you are. I offered to deliver you home, suggesting it might keep you from trying to run again. After speaking to your dad, she agreed, although with great hesitation."

Mrs. Risson stands in a puddle of sunshine on scuffed wood floors. Her long black skirt, purple shirt, and multi-colored glasses take me back to my second row seat in her classroom. I am still her student, whether I want to be or not, and I plop on the couch and wait for her lecture.

But instead she sits down beside me and takes my hand. Like a friend.

"You know, when I first read your work in my class three years ago, I knew you were one of the brightest students I've ever had, probably will ever have, considering how close to retirement I am," she says with a soft chuckle.

"There is a musicality of language that cannot be taught, Anna. And there is a perspective creative minds comprehend the world through, a lens in which all art is divined. You have such a mind. I pushed you because I believe in you."

She pauses. I'm not dreaming, but it feels like a dream all the same.

"I flunked you last year because I still believe in you. Everyone thinks you stopped writing as a sign of your mourning. But I'm not so sure."

I pop my head up in surprise.

"I think you were getting a lot of accolades. Also, a lot of pressure. Wanting to please people can be a terrible burden, especially when the pleasing is in direct correlation with what you produce from your mind. What I hope for you, Anna, what I've hoped for you all year, is for you to find your words. But not because you need to win awards or make people proud. Because you loved to write. It's the loving, more than the talent, that's the rarest gift."

I finger the key re-tied around my neck. I hold tight to St. Dismas. The circle medallion warms in the center of my palm.

"Thank you for coming," I say. My head rests on her shoulder. Her head rests back on my own.

A little while later, she goes through the house, room by room, making sure the museum feels as untouched and holy as it did before my arrival last night. When she returns, we walk together out the front door. Her key clicks the lock. I squint, feeling disoriented as cars whiz past and birds and squirrels chatter in the trees.

Everything is the same and different all at once, and I am going home.

57

We moved to this house when I'd just turned thirteen and Joe was fifteen. He drove my mom's car, with me bouncing around—no seat belt—in the backseat and Mom fretting over every "rolling stop" as we traversed the three miles from our old home to our brand-spanking-new one. Joe was being such a teenager. I remember Mom complaining to Dad about this as we sat on cardboard boxes, eating pizza. He didn't like the new house because it lacked soul. Our old house was old, like built in the 1970s, she mimicked, her fingers making air quotations. Dad pulled her ponytail. He said Joe has more than enough soul for this house, that he'd fill it to the brim in no time.

It's true, because I feel it—I feel him—as I step through the front door. Mom rushes to me, grabs my face and smells my head, and with halting whispers says she loves me over and over and over again, turning me in circles to make sure I'm in one piece.

There are things I know I need to say.

But all I can do is walk up the stairs and slink into my bedroom, pushing the door shut behind me. The Bea-shaped lump at the bottom of my bed wiggles up and out from under the covers. She throws herself into my arms with the velocity of a penny thrown from the Empire State Building and wraps her spindly legs monkey-style around me.

"Don't ever go away like that again," she sobs into my neck. "I won't hide anymore. I won't try to make time stop for us. I'll be good, and if you want me to hate Josephine Arabelle, I will. Even though she is really, really cute, Anna, with bright-red hair and big blue eyes and a kinda pointy head but our same ears. But I'll still call her Puker-ella and Frog Face. I promise. Just stay."

I cradle my sister, soothe her with shushes. Josephine with strawberry hair and blue eyes. Josephine with our elvish ears. My sister. My sisters. Bea nuzzles against me without question or expectation of a response. Buzzy's understanding of what people need is always crystal clear.

Through the door, I hear my mother's light frame leaning, then sliding, down the wall. I hear muffled whimpers. I hear all the things we don't say to each other.

And then I fall asleep again, caught in a web of sister and home and mother and loss and not knowing what will come next.

58

Mom sits on my bed, watches Bea sleep. Watches me watch her.

"It's time to let Gramps go," she says.

Her voice shakes and I reach out my hand. She squeezes it.

"I'm glad you're here," she whispers. I move closer to Bea so the three of us can share my double bed. Mom curls up next to me, but she doesn't start to cry. Instead she repeats, "I'm glad you're here," like when her old turntable needle sticks and Mick Jagger croons the same line over and over and over again because Mom's favorite record, *Black and Blue* is scratched.

I lift the needle by telling her about yesterday. I tell her how I wanted Gramps to be free from pain, how I wanted to protect them from having to hope or choose.

How I whispered William Stafford to Joe. I tell her about the croissant bag stinging my bloodied knuckles. About Mateo's cooking. I don't tell her about Nat and Joe, because I'm not sure it is my secret to share. So I talk about Adam under the bridge and how I ran away from Dad while he sat on the hospital floor, and how I slept in a real poet's room, and I just keep talking and talking until my throat is dry and Bea is stirring and my stomach is rumbling again. Mom listens to every word. I can tell because her whole body leans into the stories, the way she used to lean into my imaginary tales of tree-house villages and secret universes inside flower petals.

When I finish, I straighten into my coffin pose. I close my eyes and I tell her what I've locked underneath dyed hair and stolen words. I tell her I gave Joe my germs. It's my fault our family fell apart, and now I'll never be able to make it right again.

Only after she knows I have no words left does she sit up.

"Oh my love," she says, stroking my hair. "I'm so sorry. I wish you told me a year ago. I can't believe I let you suffer like this...I can't believe I didn't see...Anna, please, listen to me. It wasn't you. He could have caught that bug anywhere."

"Yeah." I cringe. "Anywhere."

"And even if it was the same flu you had, honey, even if you tried to share your germs, it wasn't your fault his body failed him. And everything—everything that happened in the aftermath, your dad and I own that. Those were choices we made. Not you. Please, baby, believe me when I say life is too short and too uncertain to let shame or guilt guide you."

She's crying and I put my head in her lap.

"I'm glad you're here," she says once more.

"Me too," I say. I think I mean it.

59

My father lifts me off the ground in a hug to rival any straightjacket. Mom told me he drove around the city all night looking for me. Tabs of skin under his eyes fold over and over again. His thick black hair stands up in every direction. He bears the mark of new dad, and old dad, exhaustion.

"Anna Banana," he says, squeezing me until I can't breathe. He lets go at the same speed as a blood pressure cuff. He's afraid I'll slip away.

"Congratulations, Dad."

"Where were you? Do you have any idea how worried we were? What it was like for your mother—"

"Jack." Mom steps in gently. She rests a hand on his arm. He looks at her a long moment, and backs off.

"I'm so glad you're okay, honey." The tears aren't sad

or scared. They're filled with joy. I can't remember the last time, or any time for that matter, my dad cried this way.

"How's the baby?" I ask.

He grins, then covers his mouth, like he did something wrong.

"It's okay, Dad," I say, tucking short hairs behind my ear. "Um, Bea told me her name. It's beautiful."

"I'd love you to come downstairs and meet her," he croaks, afraid to meet my eyes.

"Now or later?"

"Later." His tone has shifted into familiar space, like when he used to tell me I couldn't go hang at the coffee shop without getting my homework done, or that family dinner—no friends invited—was a non-negotiable.

The four of us walk down the hallway. No one says it, but the memory of one year ago shocks our bodies with varying degrees of pain and missing. I clear my throat.

"Mom," Bea pipes up beside me as we reach the room. "Where will Gramps go when he dies?"

My parents exchange glances. My dad clears his throat. We make the same coughed-out "ahem" when we're nervous.

"Well, Bea," Dad begins. "He'll go to heaven with God and Gran and Joe, and my parents, and—"

"No, Dad," Bea says, wrinkling her nose. "I know he'll be with Joe and they'll watch over us, of course, because Joe is right now. I meant his body. Where will it go?"

We stop and stare at Bea. The matter-of-fact way she spoke of Joe makes the hair on my neck stand up. Leave it to Bea to know the language of stars and souls and a world not quite here.

"Uh, his body will go to the funeral home, and the funeral director will, um…" Mom pauses and looks to Dad for help.

"He'll turn Gramps into ashes, sweetheart. So we can scatter his love in all the places he held most dear."

Bea screws up one side of her face for a minute, working out what she's just heard. Then she nods once, curiosity satisfied.

"I'm really going to miss our dates to the County Fair," she says, turning sharp to face Mom. "He'd want you to still take me, and to ride the teacups with me, even if I do throw up every time."

A nurse comes in wearing purple scrubs. She has a clipboard of papers and says the doctor will be by in just a moment to go over everything. She holds her hand on the clipboard longer than necessary, so it touches my mom's, gently.

The doctor sounds a lot like the movie scripts. The information is dry. It's delivered as kindly as possible, but the words are the same, big and technical and resulting in death. We listen. Bea flies Gramps's favorite paper crane, long wings catching an invisible airstream above her head. Dad holds his father-in-law's hand. He keeps his eyes on Mom. In this moment, I love him again.

The nurse comes back with an envelope, the kind for

bills or business letters. It has my name written across it, in a familiar, carefully slanted script.

"This was left for Anna?" She raises her voice into a question as she says my name.

It's rounded at the crease from something inside. Scooting to the corner of the room, I face the windows and pull out a string of wooden beads, perfectly smooth, some dark, some light. A small cross hangs in the middle. Also, a piece of paper, torn small and folded in half.

This is my grandmother's rosary. A prayer with each bead. M

The envelope floats to the floor. I hold the rosary tight.

"Maybe Bea and I should…I mean, maybe Bea and I will go to the chapel for a while," I say.

My parents turn to each other first, without shyness or anger or uneven sadness. Mom speaks for both of them.

"Okay. But it might not be long now."

I move to Gramps. Dad backs up, giving me room. I hear an alarm go off down the hall. Someone is being saved. Someone not named George.

Leaning my forehead against his forehead, I think of all the things I can't say, hoping he'll hear me. It feels like he does. Against the windowsill, next to the fern my father sent, Bea is shrinking. She's trying to hide and trying to be here all at once.

I grab her hand and lead her through the heavy automatic doors to the room with dark blue carpet, pale blue walls, oak benches, and a yellow cross with Jesus pinned to it. He's painted tan with white tattered clothes and bright-red blood running from his palms and feet. This Catholic hospital has a very strange version of the word "comforting."

We sit side by side and hold hands. Bea rests against me. I move my fingers back and forth against each bead. Fifty-nine prayers. That hardly seems like enough.

"Knock, knock."

Nat.

She's standing in the doorway of the chapel, dressed in her white button-down shirt with black button covers and matching black skirt.

"Hey." I move over to meet her, my legs already stiff from sitting.

"Are you okay?" she asks, head lowered. "I had to come and—"

"I'm okay. It might take some time, for both of us, you know? But it will be okay. I mean that."

Joe's paper crane is tucked in my back pocket.

"I'm so sorry." It comes out as a whisper. Her chin trembles. She doesn't move any closer.

"I lied to you too," I say.

She meets my eyes.

"I lied to you," I repeat. "About the receipt."

"I—I don't understand."

"I found a letter Joe wrote. Not a motel receipt. I don't know why I told that story. I guess I wanted to have part of his secret for myself. But it isn't mine. So…here."

I hold out the crumpled crane. Nat stares at the paper like it's dynamite.

"Trust me," I say. This time, my voice falters. "You want to read this. You want to know."

I glance away. When she takes the origami from my hand, I shed the weight of a boulder, not a folded page of Joe's story.

"Thank you," we say at the same time.

"Do you have time to sit with us for a few minutes?" I ask, turning back toward Bea.

Nat, being Nat, knows I need to lighten the mood. She steps in and pulls my sister onto her lap and sings some Mary Poppins tunes. Bea twirls a piece of Nat's hair as she listens. I sit beside them, my fingers gliding along the rosary. The minutes tick by. Bea hops on and off our laps. She makes snow angels on the carpet.

"I have to go," Nat announces, putting on a brave face and rolling her eyes. "There's a private party at the Bay City Yacht Club tonight. Verrrrrrryyyy fannnnccccy."

"Hey, Nat," I hesitate. "I'm really sorry you lost him too."

I go back to my rosary. Bead one. A prayer for my parents.

They walk in a bit later holding hands, and for a single wild second, I think we're whole again.

But then my dad lets go and Mom rushes to us and scoops Bea up and motions for me to crawl into her embrace and she cries without noise while Dad sticks his hands in the pockets of his dark jeans, unsure of where he belongs.

"It's all right, Mom. It's all right."

Sometimes roles reverse in families. Sometimes a daughter soothes her mother. Sometimes she meets her father's eyes and communicates without words, the way grown-ups do, that she understands.

60

The tree outside my window is full of starlings. They cry out to one another, hundreds and hundreds of high-pitched chattering calls in a closed loop. Even with the window closed, it echoes around me.

This is my favorite part of fall. Each year, when limbs and branches go skeletal, the starlings return for a week or so, fluttering in and out of our tree, soaring together in breathing black clouds. Sameera told me once this is called murmuration. I love that word. It feels like a feather, floating slow to the ground.

I watch the window a while, until Bea runs outside and tosses an orange ball, scattering the birds. She twirls around and around, looking up, laughing, as they swoop and dive and sway skywards.

Reaching up to touch the glass, I wince. The soft spot

on my left inner arm itches like mad, and I don't dare scratch it. Under the Post-it-size white bandage there, the skin is still red and puffy.

Art is an accurate statement
of the time in which it is made.

These words have become my permanent daily verse. Two lines of small typeface quoting Robert Mapplethorpe, Patti Smith's first love and eternal best friend. Her keeper of secrets.

Nat went with me on my eighteenth birthday, held my hand, all the while claiming that not throwing a hissy about my decision to get a real tattoo was a present in itself. Mom cried a little when I pulled up the green sleeve on my Sarah Lawrence hoodie and showed her what I'd done. But she didn't lecture, or get mad or even roll her eyes. Instead, she took a deep breath, said she liked the quote choice, and reminded me to take the dishes out of the dishwasher.

"Anna-mana-bo-fana-fee-fi-mo-manna—"

Bea skips into my room, still twirling.

"We have an hour," she says between pirouettes. "Will you rake leaves into a giant pile for me? We can jump in them, and then, when Dad gets here to pick us up, I'm gonna hide inside the pile and jump out and scare him! Oh, and do you think Josie is gonna wail when she sits on Santa's lap, like I did when I was little?"

"You've cried every year. It's our day-after-Thanksgiving tradition," I interrupt, jabbing her playfully in the ribs.

"What? The mall Santa is gross and smells like boogers," she says with a shrug. "I'm a big sister now, though, so I'll be cool. But you'll be there, right?"

"Of course." Dad's almost as clumsy with a four-month-old as Lori, who dumped my dad in a postpartum haze. She claimed he had way too much baggage. Bea thinks Lori gave him the boot because Dad let his black curls turn salt and pepper, and ditched the Corvette for a shiny blue minivan. I think it's all the time he's been spending over here.

"So can you help me make a leaf pile now?"

"I would, Buzz, but I'm short on time. I have a couple errands I need to run."

She crosses her arms and sticks out her bottom lip.

"Go ask Mom. She wanted the yard raked."

She stomps out the door, but a second later I hear "Mom!" followed by "Yipee!" and then the slam of our front door.

Pictures of the last three months are scattered across my desk. Seniors, I'm learning, document every second of life. I brush aside pics of Nat and me dancing at Homecoming; of the day I pixie-cut my hair, which is more mousey brown than black these days; of Mom and me visiting Bronxville, New York, where I'll be a freshman at Sarah Lawrence next fall. This picture is my favorite, taken minutes after I rocked the interview so hard they bumped my application to the top of the early decision Y-E-S pile. My arms are spread open wide, my head is tilting up to the sun, and Mom's clapping beside me, hints of laugh lines creasing her eyes.

The Patti grid above my desk is gone. The only thing hanging there now is a small pencil drawing. It arrived a month ago in a manila envelope. It's a girl's face, wild hair falling down over one eye. I recognized the expression. It's me, looking at Mateo. A replica of the photo he took with my camera. On the back, in his slanted handwriting, it says, "Still needs a title. Let me know when you decide what it should be."

Two letters sit unsealed on the corner of my desk. The first is addressed to Mrs. Risson, just two miles from here. The second is addressed to New York. The New York-bound letter is thick, page upon page of little details and big stories. (How my dad and Lori broke up, how my mom is going back to work, how Bea got a standing ovation at the school talent show. Her magic act included pulling a live bunny from a hat. The bunny's name is Houdini and now lives, mostly cage-free, in her bedroom.) It also contains a few careful truths: turns out Don't-Call-Me-Doctor Liza isn't so bad. Your picture is still up in the alley. It's still my favorite.

We haven't spoken in months. But he'll be home soon for holiday break. So I end the letter by telling him I've finally titled the drawing he sent. I kept changing my mind on what to call it. "Fragile Magnets." "Mirrors." "It was a moment." But all those words could mean different things to him. So I opted for simple. Clear. "I miss you. Come see me."

Mrs. Risson's envelope doesn't have any pages inside. Instead, it has a cheap jump drive. If she plugs it into her computer, she'll find every assignment I blew off my junior year. Not because I want her to change my old grade or anything. I just want her to know I did them.

I seal both and set them on a large cardboard box on the floor next to Patti's book, *Just Kids*. I've read it several times now, because I love how she tells her truth, and because her words still sit warm and heavy in the depths of my chest.

Walking outside, I see Bea diving into a growing leaf pile, throwing up handfuls of red and orange and brown. Mom's leaning on the rake, laughing.

"Hey," she calls to me. "What's in the box?"

I stop in front of my car and glance down at the box in my arms. It's big, but weighs almost nothing. The envelopes still sit on top.

"Just some papers. I have to go to the post office and then run a quick errand. I'll be back before Dad gets here."

Mom nods and turns her attention back to Bea, who swims through a sea of crunching leaves.

Driving downtown, I keep the windows down. Air rushes against my hands and cheeks. When I get to the post office, there are only three people in front of me. I sort of wish the line could be longer. My palms sweat against the envelopes. The clerk weighs them, stamps them and before I can think twice, drops them into a slot in the counter. She doesn't even pause to see my reaction as she calls, "Next!"

I step aside. One errand down. One to go.

The river is a steely gray today. It matches the sky. Yellow knit beret yanked down over my ears, I get out, open the back door of my car, and pull the box from the seat.

A few days after Gramps died, Dad and I were at his house, going through some of his things. I found the box of five hundred paper cranes he finished just before Joe died. I asked Dad if I could have it. Later, when Mom and Bea were sleeping, I snuck down to the basement and retrieved a similar box of Joe's. It had three hundred and ninety-two cranes. At night, when I can't sleep, I've been slowly adding to his collection, and yesterday, I hit five hundred.

One thousand paper cranes. Some stories say they grant one thousand years of prosperity. Some claim eternal good luck. Others promise a wish, or good health to those who fall ill.

Reaching the middle of the bridge feels like reaching the climax in a story arc. I'm at the top of the mountain. Nowhere to go but down.

In this case, down is okay.

It means I'm free.

The breeze picks up just as I reach the center. Cars whiz east and west, drivers mostly staring straight ahead. I wonder where they're going, who they are going to see. One slows down to make sure I'm not dumping a body or something. I lean over the edge. The waters of the Grey Iron move fast, swirl in strange currents, as if waiting for something. Above me, a steady stream of charcoal clouds moves like a sky river in the opposite direction.

For a second I'm frozen here, holding a box of memories, watching water and sky. And then, without fanfare or a big shift of psyche, I turn the box upside down. I watch cranes dive and swing and catch in the air. I watch as it rains a thousand different colors. I watch as a flock of stories lands in the river. Just as I turn to leave, I see one last paper bird laying at my feet. I hold it in the palm of my hand.

One paper bird means something different than a thousand birds together, just like one piece of a life, one memory, is never the whole story. We are made of secrets and contradictions, stardust and possibilities.

My instinct is to tuck this red crane in my jacket and go home, put it on a shelf, and remember. But I lift my hand high and wait. A gust answers. The bird flies from my fingers. It darts in the wind. When I can no longer see it sailing downriver, I take a purple marker from my coat pocket and pull up my sleeve as far as it will go. I need room to write, as I start to scribble against my skin:

Everyone gets one last line. But first lines, stories of love and loss and hope floating on backs of paper cranes? We choose how many of those we get to tell.

All we have to do is breathe deep. Breathe life in.

My eyes slip closed, and I do. I breathe. I breathe. I breathe.

Acknowledgments

This book exists because of the people in my life who never let me stop rewriting my story.

To my agent, Sarah Davies, thank you for believing in me and in the heart of this book. Sarah cares for those who grow in her Greenhouse with a fierce passion and I am lucky to be a part of her community. To Brian Farrey-Latz, who loves Anna's story as much as I do and passed that love to the entire Flux team. This book could not have a better home.

Alison DeCamp is the kind of friend a writer dreams of having. Thank you for pushing me, saving my sanity, and having a great teenager to be my first official reader (thanks, Anna!). My critiquers, who are also dear friends— Caroline Starr Rose, Valerie Geary, Taryn Albright, Emily Meier, Molly Baker, and bookseller extraordinaire Katie Capaldi—all had such valuable insights. Also, fellow Greenhouser Tess Sharpe, whose sharp eyes and wise thoughts kept me accountable and brave.

I'm forever indebted to the educators and co-workers who made me a writer. Louise Harrison, my high school creative writing teacher, is the reason (still, almost two decades later) I believe in words. Through countless books of poems and short stories, thousands of Hershey Kisses, and more patience than a patron saint, she served as the guide I needed to find my true voice. Skip Renker is the best college professor anyone could ever ask for, and quite literally saved my life by helping me find my words again. For fourteen years now, my Harbor Light Newspaper family has proved writing can be such a joy-filled career. What a gift it is to work with folks who love words, and each other, so much.

Even at my angst-filled teenage worst, my parents, Max and Pat Spaulding, and my brother Zach, still turned up for every poetry reading. Their support has never wavered and I am beyond grateful. This book is yours as much as mine. As an adult, I can still be oh-so-difficult, especially when drafting a novel.

There will never be an adjective strong enough to describe the wonder of my husband, Justin. And finally, Noah, Max, and Elizabeth—you have shown me time and time again the gift of new first lines. Being your mom will always be my greatest joy.

© Charles O'Neill

About the Author

Kate Bassett (Harbor Springs, MI) is the Michigan Press Association award-winning editor of her small town's paper, *Harbor Light News*, and a contributing writer for the magazine *Traverse*. She has covered Mount Everest climbers, *New York Times* bestselling authors, and pet pig obituaries with the same philosophy for eleven years: voice matters.

"He can hear you, you know," Mateo says, walking away. "Come on, we're going to the alley over here."

I hear them leaving together, chatting like old friends. Nat laughs three times. I don't turn around and follow, though. I'm staring at statue dude. Not because I think he's cool. Truth be told, he looks ridiculous. I stare because I want to see him blink. I wait to see his chest rise or fall. I stiffen too, open my eyes wide.

But then Mateo is beside me again, and his fingers are warm when they lace through mine.

"Come with me. I want to show you something," he says, lips against my ear.

I hesitate, searching the statue's face. The blank stare I've been trying to master is there, effortless. Instead of staying and trying for nineteen minutes at least, to find the same emptiness, I let Mateo pull me away. And that's when it hits me: no matter how much I want it to be true, I can't be dead and alive all at once.

"Wow. Wow. Wow. Wow. Wow." Nat's a tape recorder stuck on one word as she walks up and down the alley.

Both sides are covered with graffiti, from ground to rooftop. It isn't gang tags or boobs on a window. It's blended color and portraits of people. It's the dirty brown river cutting through town. Giant, empty auto factories cast shadows against painted waters. Cars once made here are reborn on brick. There are full moons and silhouettes. Street dances. This is a story, mapped across walls, created by many different hands.

A row of real picture frames, sprayed white and drilled into the bricks, runs along at eye level. Inside, art is stacked on top of art: paper drawings and charcoal smudges and acrylic canvases and dimpled watercolors. Each frame has something in it—a sunset; a girl standing by a tree; an abstract piece my Gran would love; a couple, eyes cast down and toward each other. The frames run the length of the wall.

"What is this place?" I ask when I find my breath.

"Ha. Told you."

"Yeah, yeah."

"Admit it."

"I don't have a clue what you mean."

"Is 'wrong' not a word that exists in your vocabulary?"

I roll my eyes. Mateo grabs my hand and holds it to his chest. My skin glows, matches a painting of sun on the river. I try to pull away, but he holds tight.

"Fine. Okay. I've never been here."

"It's the best spot in town," Mateo says with obvious appreciation. He stops and catches my eye. "And right now, it's more beautiful than ever."

As I walk, Mateo stays a few steps behind. He's telling us how the alley got transformed from some garbage-strewn, no-nothing place. A bunch of street artists got together and did a blitz paint one night. More and more people started coming and adding all their best and most detailed works, and then the frames got added and now all these non-spray-paint artists come down and tack up their work.

"It's this totally organic, anonymous art show. Every so often someone else comes and covers up what was there before," he says.

There are pages upon pages of art tacked into the glass-less frames. The one I'm standing next to has a watercolor farm on top, with a tall tree and a tire swing and tiny specks of wind visible in the sky. When I go to pull it off, Mateo pulls my hand away.

"Unwritten rule." He smiles. "No peeking. The past is the past, you know what I mean?"

"She might not know what you mean," Nat calls from a little way away. She reaches up and traces some of the spray-painted sky above her. "But she could sure use a lesson."

"You could spend a lifetime here and not see everything," Mateo says, not pressing the point. "Or you could come back tomorrow and it might look totally different."

"What makes you such an expert in the underground art world?" I ask. I walk to the next frame. Inside it is a pencil drawing of a guy a few years older than us. He's got this unfiltered mischief in his face, the kind that disappears after age ten or so in real life. I can't help matching his smile.

"Wow," I murmur, stealing Nat's phrase. "This one is so...real. I almost feel like this guy is going to open his mouth and crack a joke."

I motion for Mateo to come look, but he stays rooted where he is.

"You don't think I know art, huh?"

"What do you mean? You cook. You're a chef." I stare at him.